All Your
Perfects

All Your
Perfects

Colleen Hoover

**SIMON &
SCHUSTER**

London · New York · Sydney · Toronto · New Delhi

First published by Atria, an imprint of Simon and Schuster, 2018

This version published by Simon and Schuster UK, 2022

7 9 10 8 6

Simon & Schuster UK Ltd
1st Floor
222 Gray's Inn Road
London WC1X 8HB

Simon & Schuster Australia, Sydney
Simon & Schuster India, New Delhi

www.simonandschuster.co.uk
www.simonandschuster.com.au
www.simonandschuster.co.in

A CIP catalogue record for this book
is available from the British Library

Paperback ISBN: 978-1-3985-1973-2
eBook ISBN: 978-1-3985-1974-9

Printed and bound in Great Britain by
CPI Group (UK) Ltd, Croydon, CR0 4YY

MIX
Paper from
responsible sources
FSC® C171272

To Heath.
I love you more today than any day that has come before it.
Thank you for being legit.

All Your
Perfects

Chapter One

Then

The doorman didn't smile at me.

That thought plagues me during the entire ride up the elevator to Ethan's floor. Vincent has been my favorite doorman since Ethan moved into this apartment building. He always smiles and chats with me. But today, he simply held the door open with a stoic expression. Not even a, *"Hello, Quinn. How was your trip?"*

We all have bad days, I guess.

I look down at my phone and see that it's already after seven. Ethan should be home at eight, so I'll have plenty of time to surprise him with dinner. *And myself.* I came back a day early but decided not to tell him. We've been doing so much planning for our wedding; it's been weeks since we had an actual home-cooked meal together. Or even sex.

When I reach Ethan's floor, I pause as soon as I step out

of the elevator. There's a guy pacing the hallway directly in front of Ethan's apartment. He takes three steps, then pauses and looks at the door. He takes another three steps in the other direction and pauses again. I watch him, hoping he'll leave, but he never does. He just keeps pacing back and forth, looking at Ethan's door. I don't think he's a friend of Ethan's. I would recognize him if he were.

I walk toward Ethan's apartment and clear my throat. The guy faces me and I motion toward Ethan's door to let him know I need to get past him. The guy steps aside and makes room for me but I'm careful not to make further eye contact with him. I fish around in my purse for the key. When I find it, he moves beside me, pressing a hand against the door. "Are you about to go in there?"

I glance up at him and then back at Ethan's door. *Why is he asking me that?* My heart begins to race at the thought of being alone in a hallway with a strange guy who's wondering if I'm about to open a door to an empty apartment. *Does he know Ethan isn't home? Does he know I'm alone?*

I clear my throat and try to hide my fear, even though the guy looks harmless. But I guess evil doesn't have a telling exterior, so it's hard to judge. "My fiancé lives here. He's inside," I lie.

The guy nods vigorously. "Yeah. He's inside all right." He clenches his fist and taps the wall next to the door. "Inside my fucking girlfriend."

I took a self-defense class once. The instructor taught us to slide a key between our fingers, poking outward, so if you're attacked you can stab the attacker in the eye. I do this, prepared for the psycho in front of me to lunge any second now.

He blows out a breath and I can't help but notice the air between us fills with the smell of cinnamon. What a strange thought to have in the moment before I'm attacked. What an odd lineup that would be at the police station. *"Oh, I can't really tell you what my attacker was wearing, but his breath smelled good. Like Big Red."*

"You have the wrong apartment," I tell him, hoping he'll walk away without an argument.

He shakes his head. Tiny little fast shakes that indicate I couldn't be more wrong and he couldn't be more right. "I have the right apartment. I'm positive. Does your fiancé drive a blue Volvo?"

Okay, so he's stalking Ethan? My mouth is dry. Water would be nice.

"Is he about six foot tall? Black hair, wears a North Face jacket that's too big for him?"

I press a hand against my stomach. *Vodka would be nice.*

"Does your fiancé work for Dr. Van Kemp?"

Now *I'm* the one shaking my head. Not only does Ethan work for Dr. Van Kemp . . . his father *is* Dr. Van Kemp. *How does this guy know so much about Ethan?*

"My girlfriend works with him," he says, glancing at the apartment door with disgust. "*More* than works with him, apparently."

"Ethan wouldn't . . ."

I'm interrupted by it. *The fucking.*

I hear Ethan's name being called out in a faint voice. At least it's faint from this side of the door. Ethan's bedroom is against the far side of his apartment, which indicates that whoever she is, she isn't being quiet about it. She's screaming his name.

While he fucks her.

I immediately back away from the door. The reality of what is happening inside Ethan's apartment makes me dizzy. It makes my whole world unstable. My past, my present, my future—all of it is spinning out of control. The guy grips my arm and stabilizes me. "You okay?" He steadies me against the wall. "I'm sorry. I shouldn't have blurted it out like that."

I open my mouth, but uncertainty is all that comes out. "Are you . . . are you sure? Maybe those sounds aren't coming from Ethan's apartment. Maybe it's the couple in the apartment next door."

"That's convenient. Ethan's neighbor is named Ethan, too?"

It's a sarcastic question, but I immediately see the regret in his eyes after he says it. That's nice of him—finding it in himself to feel compassion for me when he's obviously experiencing the same thing. "I followed them," he says. "They're in there together. My girlfriend and your . . . boyfriend."

"Fiancé," I correct.

I walk across the hallway and lean against the wall, then eventually slide down to the floor. I probably shouldn't plop myself on the floor because I'm wearing a skirt. Ethan likes skirts, so I thought I'd be nice and wear one for him, but now I want to take my skirt off and tie it around his neck and choke him with it. I stare at my shoes for so long, I don't even notice that the guy is sitting on the floor next to me until he says, "Is he expecting you?"

I shake my head. "I was here to surprise him. I've been out of town with my sister."

Another muffled scream makes its way through the door. The guy next to me cringes and covers his ears. I cover mine, too. We sit like this for a while. Both of us refusing to allow the noises to penetrate our ears until it's over. It won't last long. Ethan can't last more than a few minutes.

Two minutes later I say, "I think they're finished." The guy pulls his hands from his ears and rests his arms on his knees. I wrap my arms around mine, resting my chin on top of them. "Should we use my key to open the door? Confront them?"

"I can't," he says. "I need to calm down first."

He seems pretty calm. Most men I know would be breaking down the door right now.

I'm not even sure I want to confront Ethan. Part of me wants to walk away and pretend the last few minutes didn't happen. I could text him and tell him I came home early and he could tell me he's working late and I could remain blissfully ignorant.

Or I could just go home, burn all his things, sell my wedding dress, and block his number.

No, my mother would never allow that.

Oh, God. My mother.

I groan and the guy immediately sits up straight. "Are you about to be sick?"

I shake my head. "No. I don't know." I pull my head from my arms and lean back against the wall. "It just hit me how pissed my mother is going to be."

He relaxes when he sees I'm not groaning from physical illness, but rather from the dread of my mother's reaction when she finds out the wedding is off. Because it's definitely off. I lost count of how many times she's mentioned how much the deposit was in order to get on the waiting list at the venue. "Do you realize how many people wish they could get married at Douglas Whimberly Plaza? Evelyn Bradbury was married there, Quinn. *Evelyn Bradbury*!"

My mother loves to compare me to Evelyn Bradbury. Her family is one of the few in Greenwich who is more prominent than my stepfather's. So of course my mother uses Evelyn Bradbury as an example of high-class perfection at every opportunity. I don't care about Evelyn Bradbury. I have half a mind to text my mother right now and simply say, The wedding is off and I don't give a fuck about Evelyn Bradbury.

"What's your name?" the guy asks.

I look at him and realize it's the first time I've really taken him in. This might be one of the worst moments of his life, but even taking that into consideration, he's extremely handsome. Expressive dark brown eyes that match his unruly hair. A strong jaw that's been constantly twitching with silent rage since I walked out of the elevator. Two full lips that keep being pressed together and thinned out every time he glances at the door. It makes me wonder if his features would appear softer if his girlfriend weren't in there with Ethan right now.

There's a sadness about him. Not one related to our current situation. Something deeper . . . like it's embedded in him. I've met people who smile with their eyes, but he frowns with his.

"You're better looking than Ethan." My comment takes him off guard. His expression is swallowed up in confusion because he thinks I'm hitting on him. That's the last thing I'm doing right now. "That wasn't a compliment. It was just a realization."

He shrugs like he wouldn't care either way.

"It's just that if you're better looking than Ethan, that

makes me think your girlfriend is better looking than me. Not that I care. Maybe I do care. I *shouldn't* care, but I can't help but wonder if Ethan is more attracted to her than he is to me. I wonder if that's why he's cheating. Probably. I'm sorry. I'm usually not this self-deprecating but I'm so angry and for some reason I just can't stop talking."

He stares at me a moment, contemplating my odd train of thought. "Sasha is ugly. You have nothing to worry about."

"Sasha?" I say her name incredulously, then I repeat her name, putting emphasis on the *sha*. "Sa*sha*. That explains a lot."

He laughs and then *I* laugh and it's the strangest thing. Laughing when I should be crying. Why am I not crying?

"I'm Graham," he says, reaching out his hand.

"Quinn."

Even his smile is sad. It makes me wonder if his smile would be different under different circumstances.

"I would say it's good to meet you, Quinn, but this is the worst moment of my life."

That is a very miserable truth. "Same," I say, disappointed. "Although, I'm relieved I'm meeting you now rather than next month, after the wedding. At least I won't be wasting marriage vows on him now."

"You're supposed to get married next month?" Graham looks away. "What an asshole," he says quietly.

"He really is." I've known this about Ethan all along. He's an asshole. Pretentious. But he's good to me. *Or so I thought.* I lean forward again and run my hands through my hair. "God, this sucks."

As always, my mother has perfect timing with her incoming text. I retrieve my phone and look down at it.

Your cake tasting has been moved to two o'clock on Saturday. Don't eat lunch beforehand. Will Ethan be joining us?

I sigh with my whole body. I've been looking forward to the cake tasting more than any other part of the wedding planning. I wonder if I can avoid telling anyone the wedding is off until Sunday.

The elevator dings and my attention is swept away from my phone and to the doors. When they open, I feel a knot form in my throat. My hand clenches in a fist around my phone when I see the containers of food. The delivery guy begins to walk toward us and my heart takes a beating with every step. *Way to pour salt on my wounds, Ethan.*

"Chinese food? Are you kidding me?" I stand up and look down at Graham who is still on the floor, looking up at me. I wave my hand toward the Chinese food. "That's *my* thing! Not his! *I'm* the one who likes Chinese food after sex!" I turn back toward the delivery guy and he's frozen, staring at me, wondering if he should proceed to the door or not. "Give me that!" I take the bags from him. He doesn't even question me. I plop back down on the floor with the two bags of Chinese food and I rifle through them. I'm pissed to see that Ethan simply duplicated what I always order. "He even ordered the same thing! He's feeding Sasha my Chinese food!"

Graham jumps up and pulls his wallet out of his pocket. He pays for the food and the poor delivery guy pushes open the door to the stairwell just to get out of the hallway faster than if he were to walk back to the elevator.

"Smells good," Graham says. He sits back down and grabs the container of chicken and broccoli. I hand him a fork and let him eat it, even though the chicken is my favorite. This isn't a time to be selfish, though. I open the Mongolian beef and start eating, even though I'm not hungry. But I'll be damned if Sasha or Ethan will eat any of this. "Whores," I mutter.

"Whores with no food," Graham says. "Maybe they'll both starve to death."

I smile.

Then I eat and wonder how long I'm going to sit out here in the hallway with this guy. I don't want to be here when the door opens because I don't want to see what Sasha looks like. But I also don't want to miss the moment when she opens the door and finds Graham sitting out here, eating her Chinese food.

So I wait. And eat. With Graham.

After several minutes, he sets down his container and reaches into the takeout bag, pulling out two fortune cookies. He hands one to me and proceeds to open his. He breaks open the cookie and unfolds the strip of paper, then reads his fortune out loud. "You will succeed in a great business endeavor today." He folds the fortune in half after reading it. "Figures. I took off work today."

"Stupid fortune," I mutter.

Graham wads his fortune into a tiny ball and flicks it at Ethan's door. I crack open my cookie and slip the fortune out of it. "If you only shine light on your flaws, all your perfects will dim."

"I like it," he says.

I wad up the fortune and flick it at the door like he did. "I'm a grammar snob. It should be your *perfections*."

"That's what makes me like it. The one word they misuse is *perfects*. Kind of ironic." He crawls forward and grabs the fortune, then scoots back against the wall. He hands it to me. "I think you should keep it."

I immediately brush his hand and the fortune away. "I don't want a reminder of this moment."

He stares at me in thought. "Yeah. Me neither."

I think we're both growing more nervous at the prospect of the door opening any minute, so we just listen for their voices and don't speak. Graham pulls at the threads of his blue jeans over his right knee until there's a small pile of threads on the floor and barely anything covering his knee. I pick up one of the threads and twist it between my fingers.

"We used to play this word game on our laptops at night," he says. "I was really good at it. I'm the one who introduced Sasha to the game, but she would always beat my score. Every damn night." He stretches his legs out. They're a lot longer than mine. "It used to impress me until I saw an eight-hundred-dollar charge for the game on her bank statement. She was buying extra letters at five dollars a pop just so she could beat me."

I try to picture this guy playing games on his laptop at night, but it's hard. He looks like the kind of guy who reads novels and cleans his apartment twice a day and folds his socks and then tops off all that perfection with a morning run.

"Ethan doesn't know how to change a tire. We've had two flats since we've been together and he had to call a tow truck both times."

Graham shakes his head a little and says, "I'm not looking for reasons to excuse the bastard, but that's not so bad. A lot of guys don't know how to change a tire."

"I know. That's not the bad part. The bad part is that I *do* know how to change a tire. He just refused to let me because it would have embarrassed him to have to stand aside while a girl changed his tire."

There's something more in Graham's expression. Something I haven't noticed before. Concern, maybe? He pegs me with a serious stare. "Do *not* forgive him for this, Quinn."

His words make my chest tighten. "I won't," I say with complete confidence. "I don't want him back after this. I keep wondering why I'm not crying. Maybe that's a sign."

He has a knowing look in his eye, but then the lines around his eyes fall a little. "You'll cry tonight. In bed. That's when it'll hurt the most. When you're alone."

Everything suddenly feels heavier with that comment. I don't want to cry but I know this is all going to hit me any minute now. I met Ethan right after I started college and we've been together four years now. That's a lot to lose in one moment. And even though I know it's over, I don't want to confront him. I just want to walk away and be done with him. I don't want to need closure or even an explanation, but I'm scared I'll need both of those things when I'm alone tonight.

"We should probably get tested."

Graham's words and the fear that consumes me after he says them are cut off by the sound of Ethan's muffled voice.

He's walking toward the door. I turn to look at his apartment door but Graham touches my face and pulls my attention back to him.

"The worst thing we could do right now is show emotion, Quinn. Don't get angry. Don't cry."

I bite my lip and nod, trying to hold back all the things I know I'm about to need to scream. "Okay," I whisper, right as Ethan's apartment door begins to open.

I try to hold my resolve like Graham is doing, but Ethan's

looming presence makes me nauseous. Neither of us looks at the door. Graham's stare is hard and he's breathing steadily as he keeps his gaze locked on mine. I can't even imagine what Ethan will think in two seconds when he opens the door fully. He won't recognize me at first. He'll think we're two random people sitting on the hallway floor of his apartment building.

"Quinn?"

I close my eyes when I hear Ethan say my name. I don't turn toward his voice. I hear Ethan take a step out of his apartment. I can feel my heart in so many places right now, but mostly I feel it in Graham's hands on my cheeks. Ethan says my name again, but it's more of a command to look at him. I open my eyes, but I keep them focused on Graham.

Ethan's door opens even wider and a girl gasps in shock. *Sasha*. Graham blinks, holding his eyes closed for a second longer as he inhales a calming breath. When he opens them, Sasha speaks.

"Graham?"

"Shit," Ethan mutters.

Graham doesn't look at them. He continues to face me. As if both of our lives aren't falling apart around us, Graham calmly says to me, "Would you like me to walk with you downstairs?"

I nod.

"Graham!" Sasha says his name like she has a right to be angry at him for being here.

Graham and I both stand up. Neither of us look toward Ethan's apartment. Graham has a tight grip on my hand as he leads me to the elevator.

She's right behind us, then next to us as we wait for the

elevator. She's on the other side of Graham, pulling on his shirtsleeve. He squeezes my hand a little harder, so I squeeze his back, letting him know we can do this without a scene. Just walk onto the elevator and leave.

When the doors open, Graham ushers me on first and then he steps on. He doesn't leave room for Sasha to step on with us. He blocks the doorway and we're forced to face the direction of the doors. The direction of Sasha. He hits the button for the lobby and when the doors begin to close, I finally look up.

I notice two things.

1) Ethan is no longer in the hallway and his apartment door is closed.
2) Sasha is so much prettier than me. Even when she's crying.

The doors close and it's a long, quiet ride to the bottom. Graham doesn't let go of my hand and we don't speak, but we also don't cry. We walk quietly out of the elevator and across the lobby. When we reach the door, Vincent holds it open for us, looking at us both with apology in his eyes. Graham pulls out his wallet and gives Vincent a handful of bills. "Thanks for the apartment number," Graham says.

Vincent nods and takes the cash. When his eyes meet mine, they're swimming in apology. I give Vincent a hug since I'll likely never see him again.

Once Graham and I are outside, we just stand on the sidewalk, dumbfounded. I wonder if the world looks different to him now because it certainly looks different to me. The sky, the trees, the people who pass us on the sidewalk. Everything seems slightly more disappointing than it did before I walked into Ethan's building.

"You want me to hail you a cab?" he finally says.

"I drove. That's my car," I say, pointing across the street.

He glances back up at the apartment building. "I want to get out of here before she makes it down." He looks genuinely worried, like he can't face her at all right now.

At least Sasha is trying. She followed Graham all the way to the elevator while Ethan just walked back inside his apartment and closed his door.

Graham looks back at me, his hands shoved in his jacket pockets. I wrap my coat tightly around myself. There's not much left to say other than goodbye.

"Goodbye, Graham."

His stare is flat, like he's not even in this moment. He backs up a step. Two steps. Then he spins and starts walking in the other direction.

I look back at the apartment building, just as Sasha bursts through the doors. Vincent is behind her, staring at me. He waves at me, so I lift a hand and wave back to him. We both know it's a goodbye wave, because I'm never stepping foot inside Ethan's apartment building again. Not even for whatever stuff of mine litters his apartment. I'd rather him just throw it all away than face him again.

Sasha looks left and then right, hoping to find Graham. She doesn't. She just finds me and it makes me wonder if she even knows who I am. Did Ethan tell her he's supposed to get married next month? Did he tell her we just spoke on the phone this morning and he told me he's counting down the seconds until he gets to call me his wife? Does she know when I sleep over at Ethan's apartment that he refuses to shower without me? Did he tell her the sheets he just fucked her on were an engagement gift from my sister?

Does she know when Ethan proposed to me, he cried when I said yes?

She must not realize this or she wouldn't have thrown away her relationship with a guy who impressed me more in one hour than Ethan did in four years.

Chapter Two

Now

Our marriage didn't collapse. It didn't suddenly fall apart.

It's been a much slower process.

It's been *dwindling*, if you will.

I'm not even sure who is most at fault. We started out strong. Stronger than most; I'm convinced of that. But over the course of the last several years, we've weakened. The most disturbing thing about it is how skilled we are at pretending nothing has changed. We don't talk about it. We're alike in a lot of ways, one of them being our ability to avoid the things that need the most attention.

In our defense, it's hard to admit that a marriage might be over when the love is still there. People are led to believe that a marriage ends only when the love has been lost. When anger replaces happiness. When contempt replaces bliss. But

Graham and I aren't angry at each other. We're just not the same people we used to be.

Sometimes when people change, it's not always noticeable in a marriage, because the couple changes together, in the same direction. But sometimes people change in opposite directions.

I've been facing the opposite direction from Graham for so long, I can't even remember what his eyes look like when he's inside me. But I'm sure he has every strand of hair on the back of my head memorized from all the times I roll away from him at night.

People can't always control who their circumstances turn them into.

I look down at my wedding ring and roll it with my thumb, spinning it in a continuous circle around my finger. When Graham bought it, he said the jeweler told him the wedding ring is a symbol for eternal love. An endless loop. The beginning becomes the middle and there's never supposed to be an end.

But nowhere in that jeweler's explanation did he say the ring symbolizes eternal *happiness*. Just eternal love. The problem is, love and happiness are not concordant. One can exist without the other.

I'm staring at my ring, my hand, the wooden box I'm holding, when out of nowhere, Graham says, "What are you doing?"

I lift my head slowly, completely opposite of the surprise I'm feeling at his sudden appearance in the doorway. He's already taken off his tie and the top three buttons of his shirt are undone. He's leaning against the doorway, his curiosity pulling his eyebrows together as he stares at me. He fills the room with his presence.

I only fill it with my absence.

After knowing him for as long as I have, there's still a mysteriousness that surrounds him. It peeks out of his dark eyes and weighs down all the thoughts he never speaks. The quietness is what drew me to him the first day I met him. It made me feel at peace.

Funny how that same quietness makes me uneasy now.

I don't even try to hide the wooden box. It's too late; he's staring straight at it. I look away from him, down at the box in my hands. It's been in the attic, untouched, rarely even thought of. I found it today while I was looking for my wedding dress. I just wanted to see if the dress still fit. It did, but I looked different in it than I did seven years ago.

I looked lonelier.

Graham walks a few steps into the bedroom. I can see the stifled fear in his expression as he looks from the wooden box to me, waiting for me to give him an answer as to why I'm holding it. Why it's in the bedroom. Why I thought to even pull it out of the attic.

I don't know why. But holding this box is certainly a conscious decision, so I can't respond with something innocent like "I don't know."

He steps closer and the crisp smell of beer drifts from him. He's never been much of a drinker, unless it's Thursday, when he goes to dinner with his coworkers. I actually like the smell of him on Thursday nights. I'm sure if he drank every day I'd grow to despise the smell, especially if he couldn't control the drinking. It would become a point of contention between us. But Graham is always in control. He has a routine and he sticks to it. I find this aspect of his personality to be one of his sexiest traits. I used to look forward to his return on Thursday nights. Sometimes I would dress up for him and wait for him right here on the bed, anticipating the sweet flavor of his mouth.

It says something that I forgot to look forward to it tonight.

"Quinn?"

I can hear all his fears, silently smashed between each letter of my name. He walks toward me and I focus on his eyes the whole time. They're uncertain and concerned and it makes me wonder when he started looking at me this way. He used to look at me with amusement and awe. Now his eyes just flood me with pity.

I'm sick of being looked at this way, of not knowing how to answer his questions. I'm no longer on the same wavelength as my husband. I don't know how to communicate with him anymore. Sometimes when I open my mouth, it feels like the wind blows all my words straight back down my throat.

I miss the days when I needed to tell him everything or I would burst. And I miss the days when he would feel like time cheated us during the hours we had to sleep. Some mornings I would wake up and catch him staring at me. He would smile and whisper, *What did I miss while you were sleeping?* I would roll onto my side and tell him all about my dreams and sometimes he would laugh so hard, he would have tears in his eyes. He would analyze the good ones and downplay the bad ones. He always had a way of making me feel like my dreams were better than anyone else's.

He no longer asks what he misses while I sleep. I don't know if it's because he no longer wonders or if it's because I no longer dream anything worth sharing.

I don't realize I'm still spinning my wedding ring until

Graham reaches down and stills it with his finger. He gently threads our fingers together and carefully pulls my hand away from the wooden box. I wonder if his intention is to react like I'm holding an explosive or if that's truly how he feels right now.

He tilts my face upward and he bends forward, pressing a kiss to my forehead.

I close my eyes and subtly pull away, making it appear as though he caught me while I was already mid-movement. His lips brush across my forehead as I push off the bed, forcing him to release me as I watch him take a humbling step back.

I call it the divorce dance. Partner one goes in for the kiss, partner two isn't receptive, partner one pretends he didn't notice. We've been dancing this same dance for a while now.

I clear my throat, my hands gripping the box as I walk it to the bookshelf. "I found it in the attic," I say. I bend down and slide the box between two books on the bottom shelf.

Graham built me this bookshelf as a gift for our first wedding anniversary. I was so impressed that he built it from scratch with his bare hands. I remember he got a splinter in the palm of his hand while moving it into the bedroom for me. I sucked it out of his palm as a thank-you. Then I pushed him against the bookshelf, knelt down in front of him, and thanked him some more.

That was back when touching each other still held hope. Now his touch is just another reminder of all the things I'll never be for him. I hear him walking across the room toward me so I stand up and grip the bookshelf.

"Why did you bring it down from the attic?" he asks.

I don't face him, because I don't know how to answer him.

He's so close to me now; his breath slides through my hair and brushes the back of my neck when he sighs. His hand tops mine and he grips the bookshelf with me, squeezing. He brings his lips down against my shoulder in a quiet kiss.

I'm bothered by the intensity of my desire for him. I want to turn and fill his mouth with my tongue. I miss the taste of him, the smell of him, the sound of him. I miss when he would be on top of me, so consumed by me that it felt like he might tear through my chest just so he could be face-to-face with my heart while we made love. It's strange how I can miss a person who is still here. It's strange that I can miss making love to a person I still have sex with.

No matter how much I mourn the marriage we used to have, I am partly—if not wholly—responsible for the marriage it's turned into. I close my eyes, disappointed in myself. I've perfected the art of avoidance. I'm so graceful in my evasion of him; sometimes I'm not sure if he even notices. I pretend to fall asleep before he even makes it to bed at night. I pretend I don't hear him when my name drips from his lips in the dark. I pretend to be busy when he walks toward me, I pretend to be sick when I feel fine, I pretend to accidentally lock the door when I'm in the shower.

I pretend to be happy when I'm breathing.

It's becoming more difficult to pretend I enjoy his touch. I don't enjoy it—I only *need* it. There's a difference. It makes me wonder if he pretends just as much as I do. Does he want me as much as he professes to? Does he wish I wouldn't pull away? Is he thankful I do?

He wraps an arm around me and his fingers splay out against my stomach. A stomach that still easily fits into my wedding dress. A stomach unmarred by pregnancy.

I have that, at least. A stomach most mothers would envy.

"Do you ever . . ." His voice is low and sweet and completely terrified to ask me whatever he's about to ask me. "Do you ever think about opening it?"

Graham never asks questions he doesn't need answers to. I've always liked that about him. He doesn't fill voids with unnecessary talk. He either has something to say or he doesn't. He either wants to know the answer to something or he doesn't. He would never ask me if I ever think about opening the box if he didn't need to know the answer.

Right now, this is my least favorite thing about him. I don't want this question because I don't know how to give him his answer.

Instead of risking the wind blowing my words back down my throat, I simply shrug. After years of being experts of avoidance, he finally stops the divorce dance long enough to ask a serious question. The one question I've been waiting for him to ask me for a while now. And what do I do?

I shrug.

The moments that follow my shrug are probably why it's taken him so long to ask the question in the first place. It's the moment I feel his heart come to a halt, the moment he presses his lips into my hair and sighs a breath he'll never get back, the moment he realizes he has both arms wrapped around me but he still isn't holding me. He hasn't been able to hold me for a while now. It's hard to hold on to someone who has long since slipped away.

I don't reciprocate. He releases me. I exhale. He leaves the bedroom.

We resume the dance.

Chapter Three

Then

The sky turned upside down.

Just like my life.

An hour ago, I was engaged to the man I've been in love with for four years. Now I'm not. I turn the windshield wipers on and watch out the window as people run for cover. Some of them run inside Ethan's apartment building, including Sasha.

The rain came out of nowhere. No sprinkles to indicate what was coming. The sky just tipped over like a bucket of water and huge drops are falling hard against my window.

I wonder if Graham lives close by or if he's still walking. I flip on my blinker and pull out of my usual parking spot at Ethan's for the very last time. I head in the direction Graham began walking a few minutes ago. As soon as I turn left, I see him duck into a restaurant to take cover from the storm.

Conquistadors. It's a Mexican restaurant. One I'm not too fond of. But it's close to Ethan's apartment and he likes it, so we eat here at least once a month.

A car is pulling out of a space in front of the restaurant, so I patiently wait for them to leave and then I ease my car into their spot. I get out of the car without knowing what I'll say to Graham once I walk inside.

"Need a ride home?"

"Need company?"

"Up for a night of revenge sex?"

Who am I kidding? The last thing I want tonight is revenge sex. That's not why I'm following him, so I hope he doesn't assume that's the case once he sees me. I still don't know why I'm following him. Maybe it's because I don't want to be alone. Because like he said, the tears will come later, in the silence.

When the door closes behind me and my eyes adjust to the dim lighting in the restaurant, I spot Graham standing at the bar. He's removing his wet coat and laying it over the back of the chair when he sees me. He doesn't appear at all shocked to see me. He pulls out the chair next to him with the confident expectation that I'll walk over to him and take it.

I do. I sit right next to him and neither of us says a word. We just commiserate in our silent misery.

"Can I get you two any drinks?" a bartender asks.

"Two shots of whatever will help us forget the last hour of our lives," Graham says.

The bartender laughs, but neither of us laughs with him. He sees how serious Graham is being, so he holds up a finger. "I have just the thing." He walks to the other end of the bar.

I can feel Graham watching me, but I don't look at him.

I don't really want to see how sad his eyes are right now. I almost feel worse for him than I do for myself.

I pull a bowl of pretzels in front of me. They're a mixture of shapes, so I begin to pull out all the sticks and I lay them on the bar in the shape of a grid. Then I pull out all the O-shaped pretzels and scoot the bowl of the traditionally shaped pretzel knots toward Graham.

I lay my pretzel in the center of the grid. I look at Graham and wait quietly. He looks at the pretzels I've strategically placed on the bar and then he looks back at me. A very slow and guarded smile makes its appearance. Then he reaches into the bowl, pulls out a pretzel knot and places it in the square above mine.

I pick the spot to the left of the center square, placing my pretzel carefully in my square.

The bartender lays two shots down in front of us. We pick them up at the same time and swing our chairs so that we're facing each other.

We sit in silence for a good ten seconds, waiting for the other to make the toast. Graham finally says, "I have absolutely nothing to toast to. Fuck today."

"Fuck today," I say in complete agreement. We clink our shot glasses together and tilt our heads back. Graham's goes down a lot smoother than mine. He slams his glass on the counter and then picks up another pretzel. He makes the next move.

I'm picking up the next pretzel when my phone starts buzzing in my jacket pocket. I pull it out. Ethan's name is flashing across the screen.

Graham then pulls his phone out and sets it on the bar. Sasha's name is flashing across his screen. It's comical, really.

What must the two of them think, walking out and seeing both of us sitting on the floor together, eating their Chinese food.

Graham places his phone on the bar, faceup. He puts his finger on his phone, but instead of answering it, he gives his phone a shove. I watch as it slides across the bar and disappears over the edge. I hear his phone crash against the floor on the other side of the bar, but Graham acts as if he isn't at all fazed with the idea of having a broken phone.

"You just broke your phone."

He pops a pretzel into his mouth. "It's full of nothing but pictures and texts from Sasha. I'll get a new one tomorrow."

I lay my phone on the bar and I stare at it. It's silent for a moment, but Ethan calls for a second time. As soon as his name flashes across the screen, I have the urge to do exactly what Graham just did. I'm due for a new phone, anyway.

When the ringing stops and a text from Ethan comes through, I give my phone a shove. We watch as my phone slips over the other side of the bar.

We go back to playing tic-tac-toe. I win the first game. Graham wins the second. Third is a draw.

Graham picks up another one of the pretzels and eats it. I don't know if it was the shot I took or if I'm just confused by the turmoil of today, but every time Graham looks at me, I can feel the look trickle down my skin. And my chest. Everywhere, actually. I can't tell if he makes me nervous or if I just have a buzz. Either way, this feeling is better than the devastation I would be feeling right now if I were at home alone.

I replace the piece of pretzel grid that Graham just ate. "I have a confession," I say.

"Nothing you say can beat the past couple of hours of my life. Confess away."

I lean my elbow against the bar and prop my head on my hand. I give him a sidelong glance. "Sasha came outside. After you walked away."

Graham can see the shame in my expression. His eyebrows raise in curiosity. "What did you do, Quinn?"

"She asked which way you went. I refused to tell her." I sit up straight and swing the chair so that I'm facing him. "But before I got in my car, I turned around and said, 'Eight hundred dollars on a *word* game? *Really*, Sasha?'"

Graham stares at me. Hard. It makes me wonder if I crossed a line. I probably shouldn't have said that to her, but I was bitter. I don't regret it.

"What'd she say?"

I shake my head. "Nothing. Her mouth kind of fell open in shock, but then it started raining and she ran back inside Ethan's apartment building."

Graham is staring at me with so much intensity. I hate it. I wish he'd laugh or get angry that I interfered. *Something*.

He says nothing.

Eventually, his eyes lower until he's staring down between us. We're facing each other, but our legs aren't touching. Graham's hand that's resting on his knee moves forward a little until his fingers graze my knee, just below the hem of my skirt.

It's both subtle and obvious. My entire body tenses at the contact. Not because I don't like it, but because I can't remember the last time Ethan's touch sent this much heat through me.

Graham traces a circle over the top of my knee with his

finger. When he looks up at me again, I'm not confused by the look in his eyes. It's very clear what he's thinking now.

"You want to get out of here?" His voice is both a whisper and a plea.

I nod.

Graham stands and pulls his wallet out of his pocket. He lays some cash on the bar and then slips into his jacket. He reaches down and threads his fingers through mine, leading me through the restaurant, out the door and hopefully toward something that makes this day worth waking up for.

Chapter Four

Now

Graham once asked me why I take such long showers. I don't remember what my excuse was. I'm sure I said they were relaxing, or that the hot water was good for my skin. But I take such long showers because it's the only time I allow myself to grieve.

I feel weak for needing to grieve since no one has died. It doesn't make sense that I grieve so much for those who never even existed.

I've been in the shower for half an hour now. When I woke up this morning, I incorrectly assumed it would be a quick, painless shower day. But that changed when I saw the blood. I shouldn't be shocked. It happens every month. It's happened every month since I was twelve.

I'm standing flat against the shower wall, allowing the spray of the shower to fall over my face. The stream of water dilutes my tears and it makes me feel less pathetic. It's easier to convince myself I'm not crying *that* hard when most of what's falling down my cheeks is water.

I'm doing my makeup now.

Sometimes this happens. One second I'm in the shower, the next second I'm not. I lose myself in the grief. I get so lost that by the time I climb my way out of the dark, I'm in a new place. This new place is me, naked, in front of the bathroom mirror.

I slide the lipstick over my bottom lip and then my top. I set it down and stare at my reflection. My eyes are red from the grief but my makeup is in place, my hair has been pulled back, my clothes are folded neatly on the counter. I look at my body in the mirror, covering both breasts with my hands. From the outside, I look healthy. My hips are wide, my stomach is flat, my breasts are average and perky. When men look at me, sometimes their eyes linger.

But inside, I am not at all attractive. I am not internally appealing by Mother Nature's standards, because I do not have a working reproductive system. Reproduction is why we exist, after all. Reproduction is required to complete the circle of life. We are born, we reproduce, we raise our offspring, we die, our offspring reproduce, they raise *their* offspring, *they* die. Generation after generation of birth, life, and death. A beautiful circle not meant to be broken.

Yet . . . I am the break.

I was born. That's all I'm able to do until I die. I'm standing on the outside of the circle of life, watching the world spin while I am at a standstill.

And because he is married to me . . . Graham is at a standstill.

I pull on my clothes, covering up the body that has repeatedly failed us.

I walk into our kitchen and find Graham standing in front of the coffeepot. He looks up at me and I don't want him to know about the blood or the grief in the shower so I make the mistake of smiling at him. I quickly wipe the smile away but it's too late. He thinks it's a good day. My smiles give him hope. He walks up to me because, like an idiot, I'm not holding any of my usual weapons. I normally make sure I have both hands full with either a purse, a drink, an umbrella, a jacket. Sometimes all those things at once. Today I have nothing to shield myself from his love, so he hugs me good morning. I'm forced to hug him back.

My face fits perfectly between his neck and shoulder. His arms fit perfectly around my waist. I want to press my mouth against his skin and feel the chills that break out against my tongue. But if I do that I know what would follow.

His fingers would be skimming my waist.

His mouth, hot and wet, would find mine.

His hands would be freeing me from my clothes.

He would be inside me.

He would make love to me.

And when he stopped, I would be filled with hope.

And then all that hope would eventually escape with the blood.

I would be left devastated in the shower.

And then Graham would say to me, "Why do you take such long showers?"

And I would respond, "Because they're relaxing. The hot water is good for my skin."

I close my eyes and press my hands against his chest, easing myself away from him. I push away from him so often now, I sometimes wonder if my palms have imprinted against his chest.

"What time is dinner at your sister's house?" My questions ease the rejection. If I push away as I'm asking a question, the distraction makes it seem less personal.

Graham moves back to the coffeemaker and picks up his cup. He blows on it as he shrugs. "She gets off work at five. So probably seven."

I grab my weapons. My purse, a drink, my jacket. "'K. See you then. Love you." I kiss his cheek with my weapons safely separating us.

"I love you, too."

He says the words to the back of my head. I rarely give him the opportunity to say them to my face anymore.

When I get to my car, I send a text to Ava, my sister.

Not this month.

She's the only one I discuss it with anymore. I stopped talking to Graham about my cycle last year. Every month since we started trying for a baby years ago, Graham would console me when I'd find out I wasn't pregnant. I appreciated it in the beginning. Longed for it, even. But month after month, I grew to dread having to tell him how broken I was. And I knew if I was growing to dread him having to console me, that he was more than likely already tired of the disappointing routine. I decided early last year to only bring it up if the outcome were ever different.

So far, the outcome is always the same.

Sorry Babe,

my sister texts back.

You busy? I have news.

I back out of my driveway and set my phone to Bluetooth right before I call her. She answers in the middle of the first ring. Instead of hello, she says, "I know you don't want to talk about it, so let's talk about me."

I love that she gets me. "What's new with you?"

"He got the job."

I grip the steering wheel and force my voice to sound excited. "Did he? Ava, that's great!"

She sighs, and I can tell she's forcing herself to sound sad. "We move in two weeks."

I feel the tears threaten my eyes, but I've cried enough for one day. I really am happy for her. But she's my only sibling and now she's moving halfway across the world. Her husband, Reid, is from a huge family in France, and before they even got married, Ava said they would eventually move to Europe. The thought of it has always excited her so I know she's holding back her giddiness out of respect for my sadness over the distance this will put between us. I knew Reid applied for a few jobs last month, but a small part of me was selfishly hoping he wouldn't receive an offer.

"Will you guys be moving to Monaco?"

"No, Reid's job will be in Imperia. Different country, but it's only an hour drive to Monaco. Europe is so tiny, it's weird. You drive an hour here and you end up in New York. You drive an hour in Europe and you end up in a country that speaks a whole different language."

I don't even know where Imperia is but it already sounds like a better fit for her than Connecticut. "Have you told Mom yet?"

"No," she says. "I know how dramatic she's going to be,

so I figured I'd tell her in person. I'm on my way to her house right now."

"Good luck with that."

"Thanks," she says. "I'll call you and let you know how thick she lays on the guilt. See you at lunch tomorrow?"

"I'll be there. And it'll give her a whole day to calm down."

When we end the call, I find myself stuck at a red light on an empty street.

Literally *and* figuratively.

———

My father died when I was only fourteen. My mother remarried not long after that. It didn't surprise me. It didn't even upset me. My mother and father never had a relationship worth envying. I'm sure it was good in the beginning, but by the time I was old enough to know what love was, I knew they didn't have it.

I'm not sure my mother ever married for love, anyway. Money is her priority when it comes to seeking out a soul mate. My stepfather didn't win her over with his personality. He won her over with his beach house in Cape Cod.

Contrary to her wardrobe and attitude, my mother isn't rich. She grew up in a meager life in Vermont, the second of seven children. She married my father when he was moderately wealthy, and as soon as they had my sister and me, she demanded he buy her a home in Old Greenwich, Connecticut. It didn't matter that he had to work twice as hard to afford her lavish spending. I think he liked being at work more than he liked being home.

When my father passed away, there were assets, but not

enough to afford my mother the same lifestyle she was used to. It didn't take her long to rectify it, though. She married my stepfather in a private ceremony within a year of burying my father. She barely had to go eight months on a budget.

Even though my sister and I grew up in a wealthy lifestyle, we were not, and *are* not wealthy. Our mother has long spent anything my father left all those years ago. And my stepfather has biological children of his own who will receive his wealth when he dies. Because of all these factors, Ava and I have never considered ourselves wealthy, despite growing up and being raised by people who were.

It's why, as soon as we both graduated college, we immediately started working and paying our own bills. I never ask my mother for money. One, because I think it's inappropriate for a grown, married woman to have to ask her parents for help. And two, because she doesn't give freely. Everything comes with stipulations when it's given by my mother.

She will occasionally do things for Ava and me that we're both very grateful for. She paid off our vehicles for Christmas last year. And when I graduated college before meeting Graham, she helped me find an apartment and paid the first month's rent. But mostly, she spends her money on us in ways that benefit her. She'll buy us clothes she thinks we should wear because she doesn't like the ones we buy ourselves. She'll buy us spa days for our birthday and force us to spend it with her. She'll visit our homes and complain about our furniture and two days after she leaves, a delivery person will show up with all new furniture she picked out herself.

Graham absolutely hates it when she does this. He says a gift is a nice gesture, but an entire couch is an insult.

I'm not ungrateful for the things she does for me. I just know that I have to make my own way in life because even though money surrounds me, it doesn't line my pockets.

One of the things I've always been grateful for is our weekly lunches. Without fail, Ava and I join her for lunch at the country club near her house. I absolutely hate the place, but I enjoy time with Ava and we tolerate our mother enough to be able to look forward to our weekly lunches.

However, I have a feeling all that is going to change now that Ava is moving to Europe. She'll be preparing to move for the next week, which makes this our last lunch. The fullness that was just added to her life has made mine feel even emptier.

"Can't you fly home for lunch every week?" I ask Ava. "How am I supposed to entertain your mother all by myself?" We always refer to our mom as *your* mother when we're discussing her. It started as a joke in high school, but now we say it so often, we have to watch ourselves in front of her so that we don't slip up.

"Bring an iPad and Skype me in," she says.

I laugh. "Don't tempt me."

Ava picks up her phone and perks up when she reads a message. "I have an interview!"

"That was fast. What's the job?"

"It's for an English tutor at a local high school there. Doesn't pay shit but if I get the job, I'll learn how to cuss in French and Italian a lot faster."

Reid makes enough money that Ava doesn't have to work, but she's always had a job. She says the housewife role isn't a fit for her and I think that's what drew Reid to her. Neither of them want kids and Ava has always liked staying busy, so it works for them.

There are moments I envy her lack of desire for children. So many issues in my life and marriage would be nonexistent if I didn't feel so incomplete without a child.

"It's going to feel so weird without you, Ava," my mother says, claiming her seat at the table. I ordered her usual, a martini with extra olives. She sets her purse down in the chair next to her and pulls an olive from the toothpick. "I didn't think your move would bother me this much," my mother continues. "When are you coming home to visit?"

"I haven't even left yet," Ava says.

My mother sighs and picks up her menu. "I can't believe you're leaving us. At least you don't have kids. I can't imagine how I'd feel if you whisked grandchildren away from me."

I laugh under my breath. My mother is the most dramatic person I know. She hardly wanted to be a mother when Ava and I were little and I know for a fact she's in no hurry to be a grandmother. That's one aspect of her personality I'm able to find relief in. She doesn't nag me about having a baby. She only prays I never adopt.

Ava brought up adoption at one of our lunches with my mother two years ago. My mother actually scoffed at the idea. *"Quinn, please tell me you aren't pondering the idea of raising some-one else's child,"* she said. *"It could have . . . issues."*

Ava just looked at me and rolled her eyes, then texted me under the table. *Yes, because biological children never have issues. Your mother needs to take a look in the mirror.*

I'm going to miss her so much.

I already miss you so much, I text her.

Still here.

"Honestly, girls, do neither of you know table etiquette by now?"

I look up and my mother is glaring at our phones. I lock mine and shove it in my purse.

"How is Graham?" my mother asks. She only asks out of courtesy. Even though Graham and I have been married for over seven years, she still wishes he were anyone else. He's never been good enough for me in her eyes, but not because she wants the best for me. If it were up to my mother, Graham would be Ethan and I'd be living in a house as big as hers and she'd be able to brag to all her friends about how much richer her daughter is than Evelyn Bradbury.

"He's great," I say, without elaborating. Because honestly, I'm only assuming Graham is great. I can't tell anymore what he's feeling or thinking or if he's great or good or miserable. "Really great."

"Are you feeling okay?"

"I feel fine. Why?"

"I don't know," she says, giving me the once-over. "You just look . . . tired. Are you getting enough sleep?"

"Wow," Ava mutters.

I roll my eyes and pick up my menu. My mother has always had a knack for direct insults. It never bothers me much because she jabs both Ava and me an even amount. Probably because we look so much alike. Ava is only two years older than me. We both have the same straight brown hair that reaches just past our shoulders. We have the same eyes that are identical in color to our hair. And according to our mother, we both look tired a lot.

We order our food and make small talk until it arrives.

Lunch is almost in the bag when someone approaches our table. "Avril?"

Ava and I both look up as Eleanor Watts adjusts her baby blue Hermès bag from one shoulder to the other. She tries to make it appear subtle, but she might as well hit us over the head with it while screaming, "Look at me! I can afford a fifteen-thousand-dollar purse!"

"Eleanor!" my mother exclaims. She stands and they air kiss and I force a smile when Eleanor looks at us.

"Quinn and Ava! Ladies, you are as beautiful as ever!" I have half a mind to ask her if I look tired. She takes an empty seat and cradles her arms around her bag. "How are you, Avril? I haven't seen you since . . ." She pauses.

"Quinn's engagement party to Ethan Van Kemp," my mother finishes.

Eleanor shakes her head. "I can't believe it's been that long. Look at us, we're grandparents now! How did that even happen?"

My mother picks up her martini glass and sips from it. "I'm not a grandmother yet," she says, almost as if she's bragging about it. "Ava is moving to Europe with her husband. Children interfere with their wanderlust," she says, waving her hand flippantly toward Ava.

Eleanor turns to me, her eyes scanning my wedding ring before they move back to my face. "And what about you, Quinn? You've been married a while now." She says this with ignorant laughter.

My cheeks burn, even though I should be used to this conversation by now. I know people don't mean to be insensitive but the intention doesn't make the comments hurt any less.

"When are you and Graham going to have a baby?"

"Do you not want children?"

"Keep trying, it'll happen!"

I clear my throat and pick up my glass of water. "We're working on it," I say, right before taking a sip. I want that to be the end of it, but my mother ensures it isn't. She leans in toward Eleanor like I'm not even here.

"Quinn is struggling with infertility," my mother says, as if it's anyone's business other than mine and Graham's.

Eleanor tilts her head and looks at me with pity. "Oh, honey," she says, placing her hand over mine. "I'm so sorry to hear that. Have the two of you considered IVF? My niece and her husband couldn't conceive naturally, but they're expecting twins any day now."

Have we considered IVF? *Is she serious right now?* I should probably just smile and tell her that's a great idea, but I'm suddenly aware that I have a limit and it was just reached. "Yes, Eleanor," I say, pulling my hand from hers. "We've been through three unsuccessful rounds, actually. It drained our savings account and we had to take out a second mortgage on our home."

Eleanor's face reddens and I'm immediately embarrassed by my reply, which means my mother is probably mortified. I don't look at her to validate my assumption, though. I can see Ava taking a swig of her water, trying to hide her laughter.

"Oh," Eleanor says. "That's . . . I'm sorry."

"Don't be," my mother interjects. "There's a reason for everything we go through, right? Even the struggles."

Eleanor nods. "Oh, I believe that wholeheartedly," she says. "God works in mysterious ways."

I laugh quietly. Her comment is reminiscent of the many

comments my mother has said to me in the past. I know she doesn't mean to be, but Avril Donnelly is the most insensitive of anyone.

Graham and I decided to start trying for a baby after only one year into our marriage. I was so naïve, thinking it would happen right away. After the first few unsuccessful months, I started to worry. I brought it up to Ava . . . and my *mother*, of all people. I told them my concerns before I even brought them up to Graham. My mother actually had the nerve to say that maybe God didn't think I was ready for a child yet.

If God doesn't give babies to people who aren't ready for them, He's got a lot of explaining to do. Because some of the mothers He chose to be fertile are very questionable. My own mother being one of them.

Graham has been supportive throughout the entire ordeal, but sometimes I wonder if he gets as frustrated as I do with all the questions. They get harder to answer over and over. Sometimes when we're together and people ask why we haven't had children yet, Graham blames it on himself. "I'm sterile," he'll say.

He's far from sterile, though. He had his sperm count tested in the beginning and it was fine. Actually, it was *more* than fine. The doctor used the word *lavish*. "You have a lavish amount of sperm, Mr. Wells."

Graham and I joked about that forever. But even though we tried to turn it into a joke, it meant the issue was all me. No matter how *lavish* his sperm count was, they weren't any good to my uterus. We had sex on a strict ovulation schedule. I took my temperature regularly. I ate and drank all the right foods. Still nothing. We pinched every penny we had and tried IUI and then IVF and were met with unsuccessful results.

We've discussed surrogacy, but it's just as expensive as IVF, and according to our doctor, due to the endometriosis I was diagnosed with at twenty-five, my eggs just aren't very reliable.

Nothing has been successful and we can't afford to keep repeating things we've already attempted, or even trying new techniques. I'm starting to realize it might never happen.

This past year has been the absolute hardest of all the years. I'm losing faith. Losing interest. Losing hope.

Losing, losing, losing.

"Are you interested in adoption?" Eleanor asks.

My eyes swing to hers and I do my best to hide my exasperation. I open my mouth to answer her, but my mother leans in. "Her husband isn't interested in adoption," she says.

"*Mother*," Ava hisses.

She dismisses Ava with a flip of her hand. "It's not like I'm telling the whole world. Eleanor and I are practically best friends."

"You haven't seen each other in almost a decade," I say.

My mother squeezes Eleanor's hand. "Well, it certainly doesn't feel like that long. How is Peter?"

Eleanor laughs, welcoming the change of subject as much as I do. She starts telling my mother about his new car and his midlife crisis, which technically can't be a midlife crisis because he's well into his sixties, but I don't correct them. I excuse myself and head to the restroom in an attempt to run away from the constant reminder of my infertility.

I should have corrected her when my mother said Graham isn't interested in adoption. It's not that he's not interested, we just haven't had any luck in getting approved with an agency due to Graham's past. I don't understand how an adoption agency won't take into consideration that outside of that devastating conviction when he was a teenager, he's never so much as had a parking ticket. But, when you're only one of thousands of couples applying to adopt, even one strike against you can rule you out.

My mother is wrong. Neither of us is opposed to the idea, but we just can't get approved and we can no longer afford to keep trying. The treatments drained our bank account and now that we have a second mortgage on our home, we wouldn't even know how to afford the process if we *were* approved.

There are so many factors, and even though people think we haven't considered all of our options, we've considered them many times.

Hell, Ava even bought us a fertility doll when she went to Mexico three years ago. But nothing—not even superstition—has worked in our favor. Graham and I decided early last year to leave it up to chance, hoping it will happen naturally. It hasn't. And to be honest, I'm tired of swimming upstream.

The only thing holding me back from giving up completely is Graham. I know deep down if I let go of the dream of children, I will be letting go of Graham. I don't want to take the possibility of becoming a father away from him.

I'm the infertile one. Not Graham. Should he be punished by my infertility, too? He says kids don't matter to him as much as I matter to him, but I know he says that because he doesn't want to hurt me. And because he still has hope. But ten or twenty years from now, he'll resent me. He's human.

I feel selfish when I have these thoughts. I feel selfish

every time Graham and I have sex because I know I'm clinging to a hope that isn't there, dragging him along in a marriage that will eventually become too dull for either of us.
Which is why I spend hours every day online, searching for
something that might give me an answer. Anything. I'm in
support groups, I read all the message boards, the stories of
"miracle conceptions," the private adoption groups. I'm even
in several parenting groups just in case I do eventually have
a child. I'll be well prepared.

The one thing I don't participate in online is social media. I deleted all my accounts last year. I just couldn't take the
insensitive people on my timeline. April Fools' Day was the
worst. I lost track of how many of my friends think it's funny
to announce a fake pregnancy.

They have absolutely no compassion for people in my
situation. If they knew how many women have spent years
dreaming of a positive result, they'd never even think to
make light of it.

And don't get me started on the number of my friends
who complain about their children on their timeline. *"Evie
was up all night crying! Ugh! When will she sleep through the freaking night?"* or *"I can't wait for school to start back! These boys are
driving me insane!"*

If those mothers only knew.

If I were a mother, I wouldn't take a single moment of
my child's life for granted. I'd be grateful for every second
they whined or cried or got sick or talked back to me. I'd
cherish every second they were home during the summer
and I'd miss them every second they were away at school.

That's why I deleted social media. Because with every
status I saw, I became more and more bitter. I know those

mothers love their children. I know they don't take them for granted. But they don't understand what it's like not to be able to experience the things that bring them stress. And rather than despise every person I'm friends with online, I decided to delete my accounts in hopes it would bring me a small semblance of peace. But it hasn't.

Even without social media, not a single day goes by without being reminded that I might never be a mother. Every time I see a child. Every time I see a pregnant woman. Every time I run into people like Eleanor. Almost every movie I watch, every book I read, every song I hear.

And lately . . . every time my husband touches me.

Chapter Five

Then

I've never brought a guy to my apartment who wasn't Ethan. In fact, Ethan rarely came here, either. His apartment is nicer and much larger, so we always stayed there. But here I am, about to have rebound sex with a complete stranger just hours after I caught my fiancé having an affair.

If Ethan is capable of an affair, I am certainly capable of revenge sex with an extremely attractive guy. This entire day has been one bizarre event after another. *What's one more?*

I open the door and make a quick scan of the apartment in case there's anything I need to hide. In doing so, I realize I'd have to hide *everything* and that's not possible with Graham one step behind me. I step aside and allow him to enter my apartment.

"Come in," I say.

Graham walks in after me, taking in my apartment with

his sad eyes. It's a small one-bedroom, but all the pictures of Ethan and me make it feel even smaller. Suffocating.

Leftover wedding invitations are still spread out over the dining room table.

The wedding dress I bought two weeks ago hangs from the entryway closet door. Seeing it makes me angry. I pull it down, fold the wedding bag over, and shove it in the closet. I don't even bother to hang it. I *hope* it gets wrinkled.

Graham walks over to my bar and picks up a photo of Ethan and me. In the picture, Ethan had just proposed and I said yes. I was flashing my ring at the camera. I stand next to Graham and look at the photo with him. His thumb brushes over the glass. "You look really happy here."

I don't respond, because he's right. I look happy in that photo because I *was* happy. Extremely happy. And oblivious. How many times had Ethan cheated on me? Did it happen before he even proposed to me? I have so many questions but I don't think I want the answers enough to eventually subject myself to an interrogation of Ethan.

Graham sets the photo down on the bar, facedown. And just like we did with our phones, he presses his finger against it and gives it a shove across the bar. It flies over the edge and shatters when it hits my kitchen floor.

Such a careless, rude thing to do in someone else's apartment. But I like that he did it.

There are two more pictures on the bar. I take the other one of Ethan and me and place it facedown. I push it across the bar and when that one shatters, I smile. So does Graham.

We both stare at the last photo. Ethan isn't in this one. It's a picture of me and my father, taken just two weeks before he died. Graham picks it up and brings it in closer for inspection. "Your dad?"

"Yeah."

He sets the photo back on the counter. "This one can stay."

Graham makes his way to the table where the leftover wedding invitations are laid out. I didn't choose the invitations. My mother and Ethan's mother did. They even mailed them out for us. My mother dropped these off two weeks ago and told me to look on Pinterest for crafts to make out of leftover invitations, but I had no desire to do anything with the invitations.

I'll definitely be throwing them away now. I don't want a single keepsake from this disaster of a relationship.

I follow Graham to the table and I take a seat on it, pulling my legs up. I sit cross-legged as Graham picks up one of the invitations and begins reading it aloud.

"The honor of your presence is requested at the nuptials of Quinn Dianne Whitley, daughter of Avril Donnelly and the late Kevin Whitley of Old Greenwich, Connecticut, to Ethan Samson Van Kemp, son of Dr. and Mrs. Samson Van Kemp, also of Old Greenwich. The event will take place at the prestigious Douglas Whimberly Plaza on the evening of . . ."

Graham pauses reading and looks at me. He points at the wedding invitation. "Your wedding invitation has the word *prestigious* in it."

I can feel the embarrassment in my cheeks.

I hate those invitations. When I saw them for the first time, I threw a fit at the pretentiousness of the entire thing, but my mother and pretentious go hand in hand. "My mother's doing. Sometimes it's easier to just let her get her way than put up a fight."

Graham raises an eyebrow and then tosses the invitation back onto the pile. "So, you're from Greenwich, huh?"

I can hear the judgment in his voice, but I don't blame him. Old Greenwich was recently rated one of the wealthiest cities in America. If you're a part of that wealth, it's commonplace to assume you're better than those who aren't. If you *aren't* part of that wealth, you judge those who are. It's a trend I refuse to be a part of.

"You don't come across as a girl who hails from Old Greenwich," he adds.

My mother would find that insulting, but his comment makes me smile. I take it as the compliment he meant it to be. And he's right . . . my microscopic apartment and the furnishings herein in no way resemble the home I grew up in.

"Thank you. I try very hard to separate myself from the dredges of high society."

"You'd have to try even harder if you wanted to convince people you're a *part* of high society. And I mean that in a good way."

Another comment my mother would be insulted by. I'm starting to like this guy more and more.

"Are you hungry?" I glance into the kitchen, wondering if I even have food to offer him. Luckily, he shakes his head.

"Nah. I'm still kind of full from all the Chinese food and infidelity."

I laugh quietly. "Yeah. Me too."

Graham scans my apartment once more, from my kitchen, to the living room, to the hallway that leads to the bedroom. Then his eyes land on me so hard I suck in a breath. He stares at me, then at my legs. I watch him as his eyes take in every part of me. It feels different, being looked at this way by someone who isn't Ethan. I'm surprised I like it.

I wonder what Graham thinks when he looks at me. Is he just as shocked as me that he ended up here, in my apartment, staring at me, rather than in his own apartment, standing by his own table, staring at Sasha?

Graham slips a hand inside his jacket pocket and pulls out a small box. He opens it and hands it to me. There's a ring inside of it. An obvious engagement ring, but it's significantly smaller than the one Ethan bought for me. I actually like this one better than mine. I wanted something a little subtler, but Ethan went with the most expensive one his father could afford.

"I've been carrying it around for two weeks," Graham says. He leans against the table next to me and stares down at the ring in my hand. "I haven't had the chance to propose because she kept blowing me off. I've been suspicious for a while now. She's such a good liar."

He says the last part of that sentence like he's impressed.

"I like it." I take the ring out of the box and slide it onto my right hand.

"You can keep it. I don't need it anymore."

"You should return it. It was probably expensive."

"I got it off eBay. It's nonrefundable."

I hold both hands out in front of me and compare the two rings. I look at my engagement ring and wonder why I never thought to tell Ethan beforehand that I didn't need something ostentatious. It's like I was so desperate to marry him, I lost my voice. My opinions. *Me.*

I slide my engagement ring off my left hand and put it in

the box, replacing the one that Graham bought Sasha. I hand the box to Graham, but he won't take it.

"Take it," I say, shoving it at him in an attempt to trade rings.

He leans back on his hands so that I can't offer it to him. "That ring could buy you a new car, Quinn."

"My car is paid for."

"Then give the ring back to Ethan. He can give it to Sasha. She'd probably like it better than the one I bought for her."

He won't take the ring, so I place it on the table. I'll mail it to Ethan's mother. She can decide what to do with it.

Graham stands up and shoves his hands in his jacket pockets. He really is better looking than Ethan. I wasn't saying that to flatter him earlier. Ethan's good looks derive mostly from confidence and money. He's always been well groomed, well dressed and a little bit cocky. If a person believes they're good-looking enough, the rest of the world eventually believes it, too.

But Graham's attractiveness is more sincere. He doesn't have any spectacular features that stand out individually. His hair isn't a unique shade of brown. His eyes are dark, but they don't verge on black or unusual. If anything, the flat chestnut makes his eyes look even more sad than they would if his eyes were blue or green. His lips are smooth and full, but not in a way that would make me think about their distinctiveness if they weren't right in front of me. He's not extremely tall to where his height would be something one would point out. He's probably right at six feet tall.

His attractiveness comes from the combination of all the many pieces of him. His unspectacular features somehow come together to create this pull in my chest. I love the way he looks at the world through a pair of calm eyes when his life is in complete turmoil. I'm completely drawn in by the way he smiles with only half of his mouth. When he speaks sometimes, he pauses and runs a thumb over his bottom lip. It's unintentionally sexy. I'm not sure I've ever been so physically attracted to someone I know so little.

Graham looks at the front door and I wonder if he changed his mind. Did I do something to turn him off? Is he still thinking about Sasha? He looks like he's about to call it a night. He pushes off the table and I remain seated, waiting on him to give me all the reasons why this isn't a good idea. He moves his body so that he's standing directly in front of me. It's like he doesn't know what to do with his hands before he tells me goodbye, so he just shoves them in the pockets of his jeans. His gaze falls to my neck before traveling back up to my face. It's the first time his eyes have looked more intense than anything else. "Where's your bedroom?"

I'm shocked by his forwardness.

I try to hide my internal conflict because I would love more than anything to get back at Ethan by fucking his lover's hot boyfriend. But knowing that's also why Graham is here makes me wonder if I want to be someone else's revenge sex.

It beats being alone right now.

I slide off the table and stand up. Graham doesn't step back, so our bodies touch briefly before I move past him. I feel it everywhere, but mostly in my lungs. "Follow me."

I'm still nervous, but not nearly as nervous as when I was putting the key into the front door. Graham's voice calms me. His entire presence calms me. It's hard to be intimidated by someone so sad.

"I never make my bed," I admit as I open the door to my

messy bedroom. I turn on a lamp and Graham's frame fills the doorway.

"Why not?" He takes a couple steps into my bedroom and it's the strangest sight. This guy I don't know at all, standing in my bedroom. The same bedroom where I should be wallowing on my bed in brokenhearted anguish right now.

And what about Graham? Does this feel just as strange to him? I know he's had doubts about Sasha or he wouldn't have been following her to Ethan's apartment building with an engagement ring burning a hole in his pocket.

Has Graham been looking for an out? Have I? Am I just now realizing it? Because right now, I'm nervous and anxious and everything I shouldn't be just hours after my life took a turn for the worse.

I'm staring wordlessly at Graham when I realize I haven't answered his question about why I don't make my bed. I clear my throat. "It takes approximately two minutes to properly make a bed. That means the average person wastes an entire thirty-eight days of their life making a bed they're just going to mess up."

Graham looks amused. He gives me one of his half smiles and then glances at my bed. Watching him take in my bed makes me feel unprepared for this. I was prepared for a reunion with Ethan tonight. Not for sex with a stranger. I don't know that I want the lights on. I don't even know that I want to be wearing what I'm wearing. I don't want Graham to have to take clothes off my body that were intended for another man. I need a moment to collect myself. I haven't had a moment yet and I think I need one.

"I need to . . ." I point toward the bathroom door. "I need a minute."

Graham's lips curl up into a slightly bigger smile and I realize in this moment that those incredible lips are about to be touching mine and I suddenly don't feel worthy. It's a weird feeling because I am a confident woman. But Graham sets a standard for confidence that I'm not used to. His confidence makes mine feel like uncertainty.

I shut myself in the bathroom and stare at the closed door. For a moment, I forget what I'm even doing in here, but then I remember I'm about to have sex with a guy who isn't Ethan for the first time in four years. I kick it into high gear. I open my closet door and sift through it to find the most unassuming thing I can find. It's a blush-colored nightgown with spaghetti straps. It isn't see-through, but he'll be able to tell I'm not wearing the bra I'm currently ripping off. I pull the gown on and walk over to the bathroom sink. I pull my hair up into a loose bun to get it out of my face and then I brush my teeth and my tongue until I'm convinced my mouth won't remind him of the Chinese food we stole earlier.

I check myself in the mirror and stare for a little too long. I just can't seem to wrap my mind around the fact that today is ending this way. Me . . . anticipating sex with a man who isn't my fiancé.

I blow out a calming breath and then open my bathroom door.

I'm not sure what I expected, but Graham looks the same. He's still standing in front of the bathroom door, still wearing his jeans and his T-shirt. And his jacket. *And* his shoes. I'm looking at his shoes when he whispers, "Wow."

I look back up at him. He's closer. His face is so close to mine and I really want to reach up and touch his jaw. I don't usually pay attention to a person's jaw, but his is strong and covered in stubble, leading all the way up to his mouth that looks as sad as his eyes.

I think he notices our proximity because he immediately takes a step back and waves his hand toward my bed.

My pillows are all lined up and my duvet is tucked under the mattress and completely wrinkle-free. The corner of it is neatly folded over, revealing the sheet beneath it.

"You made my bed?" I walk toward the bed and take a seat on it. This isn't how I envisioned this starting, but it's only because I've been stuck in an Ethan routine for the last four years.

Graham lifts my duvet and I pull my legs up and climb into my bed. I scoot over far enough for him to join me, but he doesn't. He just pulls the covers over me and sits down on the bed, facing me. "It's nice, huh?"

I adjust my pillow and roll over onto my side. He tucked the end of my blanket beneath the mattress, so it doesn't give way. It feels snug and tight around my feet and legs. I actually kind of like it. And somehow even the top of the blanket seems to be snuggling me.

"I'm impressed."

He reaches a hand to a loose strand of hair and tucks it behind my ear. The gesture is sweet. I don't know Graham very well at all, but I can tell he's good. I could tell he was good the second Ethan opened the door and Graham didn't physically attack him. It takes someone with a healthy amount of confidence and self-control to walk away quietly from a situation like that.

Graham's hand comes to rest on my shoulder. I'm not sure what changed in him since we walked out of the bar, or even since walking into my bedroom. But I can tell his thoughts are no longer where they were earlier. He slides his hand down the blanket, coming to rest on my hip. His entire expression seems rife with indecision. I try to ease the conflict a little.

"It's okay," I whisper. "You can go."

He sighs heavily with relief. "I thought I could do this. Me and you. Tonight."

"I thought I could, too, but . . . it's way too soon for a rebound."

I can feel the heat of his hand through the duvet. He moves it up a little and grips my waist as he leans forward. He kisses me softly on the cheek. I close my eyes and swallow hard, feeling his lips move to my ear. "Even if it wasn't too soon, I still wouldn't want to be your rebound." I feel him pull away. "Goodnight, Quinn."

I keep my eyes closed as he lifts off the bed. I don't open them until he turns off my lamp and closes my bedroom door.

He wouldn't want to be my rebound?

Was that a compliment? Or was that him saying he's not interested?

I mull over his parting words for a moment, but I soon shove them to the back of my mind. I'll think about Graham's words tomorrow. All I feel like thinking about in this moment is everything I've lost in the past few hours.

My entire life changed today. Ethan was supposed to be my other half for the rest of my life. Everything I thought I knew about my future has been derailed. Everything I thought I knew about Ethan has been a lie.

I hate him. I hate him because no matter what happens from this point forward, I will never be able to trust someone like I trusted him.

I roll onto my back and stare up at my ceiling. "Fuck you, Ethan Van Kemp."

What kind of last name is that, anyway? I say my name out loud and add his last name to it. "Quinn Dianne Van Kemp."

It's never sounded as stupid as it sounds right now. I'm relieved it will never be my name.

I'm relieved I caught him cheating.

I'm relieved I had Graham to walk me through it.

I'm relieved Graham decided to leave just now.

In that heated moment with Graham in the restaurant, I felt revengeful. I felt like sleeping with him would somehow ease the pain Ethan caused me today. But now that Graham has left, I realize nothing will cushion this feeling. It's just one huge, inconvenient, painful wound. I want to lock my front door and never leave my apartment. Except for ice cream. Tomorrow I'll leave for ice cream but after that, I'm never leaving my apartment again.

Until I run out of ice cream.

I toss the covers away and walk to the living room to lock the front door. When I reach up to the chain lock, I notice a yellow Post-it stuck to the wall next to the door. There's a phone number on it. Beneath the phone number is a short message.

Call me someday. After *your rebound guy.*

Graham

I have a mixed reaction to his note. Graham seems nice and I've already established my attraction to him, but at this point, I'm not sure I can stomach the thought of dating again.

It's only been a couple of hours since my last relationship. And even if I got to a point where I felt like dating again, the last person I would want to date would be the ex-boyfriend of the girl who had a hand in ruining everything good in my life.

I want as far from Ethan and Sasha as I can get. And sadly, Graham would only remind me of them.

Even still, his note makes me smile. But only for a second.

I go back to my room and crawl under my covers. I pull them over my head, and the tears begin to fall. Graham was right when he said, *"You'll cry tonight. In bed. That's when it'll hurt the most. When you're alone."*

Chapter Six

Now

The day Ava left for Europe, she left me a gift. It was a bag of exotic tea that's supposed to help with infertility. The problem was, it tasted like I had ripped open a bag of tea and poured it straight on my tongue, then washed it down with coffee beans.

So . . . the miracle fertility tea is out of the question. I'm leaving it up to chance again. I've decided I'll try for one more month. Maybe two, before I tell Graham I'm finished trying.

Two more months before I tell him I really am ready to open that wooden box on my bookshelf.

I'm sitting on our kitchen counter in one of Graham's T-shirts when he walks through the door. My bare legs are dangling, feet pointing toward the floor. He doesn't immediately notice me, but once he does, I become his entire focus. I grip the counter between my legs, opening them just enough to let him in on my plans for the night. His eyes are locked on my hands as he pulls at his tie, sliding it from his collar, dropping it to the floor.

That's one of my favorite things about him working later than me. I get to watch him take his tie off every day.

"Special occasion?" He grins as he takes me in with one fell swoop. He's walking toward me and I give him my best seductive smile. The one that says I want to put all the pretending behind us for the night. Pretending we're okay, pretending we're happy, pretending this is exactly the life we'd choose if the choice were ours.

By the time he reaches me, his jacket is off and the first few buttons of his shirt are undone. He slips off his shoes at the same time his hands slide up my thighs. I wrap my arms around his neck and he presses against me, ready and eager. His lips meet my neck and then my jaw and then he presses them gently against my mouth. "Where would you like me to take you?" He picks me up and secures me against him as I lock my legs around his waist.

I whisper in his ear. "Our bedroom sounds nice."

Even though I've all but given up on the chances of becoming pregnant, I'm obviously still clinging to that small sliver of hope on at least a monthly basis. I don't know if that makes me strong or pathetic. Sometimes I feel I'm both.

Graham drops me on the bed, our clothes covering the distance from the kitchen to our room like scattered breadcrumbs. He settles himself between my legs and then pushes inside me with a groan. I take him in with silence.

Graham is consistent in every possible way outside of the bedroom. But inside the bedroom, I never know what I'm going to get. Sometimes he makes love to me with patience and selflessness, but sometimes he's needy and quick and selfish. Sometimes he's talkative while he's inside me, whispering words that make me fall even more in love with him. But sometimes he's angry and loud and says things that make me blush.

I never know what I'm going to get with him. That used to excite me.

But now I tend to want only one of the many sides of him in the bedroom. The needy, quick, and selfish side of him. I feel less guilt when I get this side of him because lately, the only thing I really want out of sex is the end result.

Sadly, tonight is not the selfish version of Graham in the bedroom. Tonight he's the exact opposite of what I need from him right now. He's savoring every second of it. Pushing into me with controlled thrusts while he tastes all the parts of my neck and upper body. I try to be as involved as he is, occasionally pressing my lips to his shoulders or pulling at his hair. But it's hard to pretend I don't want him to get it over with. I turn my head to the side so he can leave his mark on my neck while I wait.

He eventually begins to pick up the pace and I tense a little, anticipating the end, but he pulls out of me unexpectedly. He's lowering himself down my body, drawing my left nipple into his mouth when I recognize this pattern. He's going to make his way down, slowly tasting every part of me until he eventually slides his tongue between my legs, where he'll waste a precious ten minutes and I'll have to think too much about what day it is, what time it is, what fourteen days from now will be, what I would do or say if the test is finally positive, how long I'll cry in the shower if it's negative again.

I don't want to think tonight. I just want him to hurry.

I pull his shoulders until his mouth is back near mine and I whisper in his ear, "It's okay. You can finish." I try to guide him back inside of me but he pulls back. I make eye contact with him for the first time since we were in the kitchen.

He brushes my hair back gently. "Are you not in the mood anymore?"

I don't know how to tell him I was never in the mood to begin with without hurting his feelings. "It's fine. I'm ovulating."

I try to kiss him, but before my lips meet his, he rolls off me.

I stare at the ceiling, wondering how he can possibly be upset with me for that comment. We've been trying to get pregnant for so long now. This routine is nothing new.

I feel him leave the bed. When I look at him, his back is to me and he's pulling on his pants.

"Are you seriously mad because I'm not in the mood?" I ask, sitting up. "If you don't recall, we were just having sex less than a minute ago, regardless of my mood."

He spins around and faces me, taking a pause to gather his thoughts. He pulls a frustrated hand through his hair and then steps closer to the bed. The clench of his jaw reveals his irritation, but his voice is quiet and calm when he speaks. "I'm tired of fucking for the sake of science, Quinn. It would be nice if just one time I could be inside you because you *want* me there. Not because it's a requirement to getting pregnant."

His words sting. Part of me wants to lash out and say something hurtful in return, but most of me knows he's only saying it because it's true. Sometimes I miss the spontaneous lovemaking, too. But it got to a point where all our failed attempts at getting pregnant began to hurt too much. So much that I realized the less sex we had, the less disappointment I would feel. If we only had sex during the days I was ovulating, I would be disappointed a fewer number of times.

I wish he could understand that. I wish he knew that sometimes the trying is harder for me than the failing. I try to empathize with his feelings, but it's hard because I don't know that he truly empathizes with mine. How could he? He's not the one failing every time.

I can be disappointed in myself later. Right now, I just need him back on this bed. Back inside me. Because he's right. Sex with my husband is definitely a requirement to getting pregnant. And today is our best chance this month.

I kick the covers off me so that I'm sprawled out on the bed. I press one of my hands against my stomach and pull his attention there. "I'm sorry," I whisper, trailing my fingers upward. "Come back to bed, Graham."

His jaw is still clenched, but his eyes are following my hand. I watch his struggle as part of him wants to storm out of the room and part of him wants to storm me. I don't like that he's not convinced I want him yet, so I roll over onto my stomach. If there's one thing about me physically that Graham loves the most, it's the view of me from behind. "I want you inside me, Graham. That's all I want. I promise." *I lie.*

I'm relieved when he groans.

"Dammit, Quinn." And then he's on the bed again, his hands on my thighs, his lips against my ass. He slips one hand beneath me and presses it flat against my stomach, lifting me enough so that he can easily slide into me from behind. I moan and grasp the sheets convincingly.

Graham grips my hips and lifts himself up onto his knees, pulling me back until he's all the way inside me.

I no longer have the patient Graham. He's a mixture of emotions right now, thrusting into me with impatience and anger. He's focused on finishing and not at all focused on me and that's exactly how I want it.

I moan and meet his thrusts, hoping he doesn't recognize that the rest of me is disconnected to this moment. After a while, we somehow move from both being on our knees, to me being pressed stomach first into the mattress as all his weight bears down on me. He grips my hands that are gripping the sheets and I relax as he releases a groan. I wait for him to fill me with hope.

But he doesn't.

Instead, he pulls out of me, pressing himself against the small of my back. Then he groans one final time against my neck. I feel it meet my skin, warm and wet as it slides down my hip and seeps into the mattress.

Did he just . . .

He did.

Tears sting at my eyes when I realize he didn't finish inside me. I want to climb out from under him, but he's too heavy and he's still tense and I can't move.

As soon as I feel him begin to relax, I attempt to lift up. He rolls over onto his back. I roll away from him, using the sheet beneath me to wipe myself clean. Tears are streaming down my cheeks and I swipe at them angrily. I am so angry I can't even speak. Graham just watches me as I try to conceal the anger I'm feeling. And the embarrassment.

Graham is my husband, but tonight he was a means to an end. And even though I tried to convince him otherwise, he just proved that to himself by not giving me the only thing I wanted from him tonight.

I can't stop the tears from falling, but I try anyway. I pull the blanket up to my eyes and Graham rolls off the bed and grabs his pants. My quiet tears begin to turn to sobs and my shoulders begin to shake. It's not like me to do this in front of him. I usually save this for my long showers.

As Graham grabs his pillow off the bed, part of him looks like he wants to console me while the other part looks like he wants to scream at me. The angry part wins out and he begins to walk toward the door.

"Graham," I whisper.

My voice stops him in his tracks and he turns around and faces me. He seems so heartbroken, I don't even know what to say. I wish I could say I'm sorry for wanting a baby more than I want him. But that wouldn't help, because it would be a lie. I'm not sorry. I'm bitter that he doesn't understand what sex has become to me over the last few years. He wants me to continue to want him, but I can't when sex and making love have always given me hope that it might be that one in a million chance I'll get pregnant. And all the sex and love-making that leads to the hope then leads to the moment all that hope is overcome by devastation.

Over the years, the entire routine and the emotions it brings started running together. I couldn't separate the sex from the hope and I couldn't separate the hope from the devastation. Sex became hope became devastation.

SexHopeDevastation. Devastation. Devastation.

Now it *all* feels devastating to me.

He'll never understand that. He'll never understand that it isn't *him* I don't want. It's the devastation.

Graham watches me, waiting for me to follow his name up with something else. But I don't. I can't.

He nods a little, turning away from me. I watch the muscles in his back tense. I watch his fist clench and unclench. I can see him release a heavy sigh even though I can't hear it. And then he opens the bedroom door with ease before slamming it shut with all his strength.

A loud thud hits the door from the other side. I squeeze my eyes shut and my whole body tenses as it happens again. And then again.

I listen as he punches the door five times from the other side. I listen as he releases his hurt and rejection against the wood because he knows there's nowhere else it can go. When everything is silent again . . . I shatter.

Chapter Seven

Then

It's been difficult getting over Ethan. Well, not *Ethan* per se. Losing the relationship was harder than losing Ethan. When you associate yourself with another person for so long, it's difficult becoming your own person again. It took a few months before I finally deleted him from my apartment completely. I got rid of the wedding dress, the pictures, the gifts he'd given me over the years, clothes that reminded me of him. I even got a new bed, but that probably had more to do with just wanting a new bed than being reminded of Ethan.

It's been six months now and the only reason I'm on my second date with this Jason guy is because the first one wasn't a complete disaster. And Ava talked me into it.

As much as my mother loved Ethan and still wishes I'd forgive him, I think she would like Jason even more. That should probably be a positive but it isn't. My mother and I have very different tastes. I'm waiting for Jason to say or do something that my mother would hate so that I can be drawn to him a little more than I am.

He's already repeated several questions he asked me last Friday. He asked how old I was. I told him I was twenty-five, the same age I was last Friday. He asked me when my birthday was and I told him it was still July 26.

I'm trying not to be a bitch, but he makes it difficult when it's clear he didn't pay attention to a single thing I said last week.

"So you're a Leo?" he asks.

I nod.

"I'm a Scorpio."

I have no idea what that says about him. Astrology has never been my thing. Besides, it's hard to pay attention to Jason because there's something much more interesting behind him. Two tables away, smirking in my direction, is Graham. As soon as I recognize him, I immediately look down at my plate.

Jason says something about the compatibility of Scorpios and Leos and I look him in the eyes, hoping he can't see the chaos I'm feeling right now. But my resolve is broken because Graham is standing now. I can't help but look over Jason's shoulder and watch as Graham excuses himself from his table. He locks eyes with me again and begins to head in our direction.

I'm squeezing the napkin in my lap, wondering why I'm suddenly more nervous at the sight of Graham than I've ever been around Jason. I make eye contact with Graham right before he approaches the table. But as soon as I look at him, he looks away. He nods his head once, in the direction he's walking. He passes our table, his hand just barely touching my elbow. A one second graze of his finger across my skin. I suck in air.

"How many siblings do you have?"

I lay my napkin on the table. "Still just the one." I push my chair back. "I'll be right back. I need to use the restroom."

Jason scoots back, half standing as I push my chair in. I smile at him and turn toward the restrooms. Toward Graham.

Why am I so nervous?

The bathrooms are at the rear of the restaurant. You have to make a turn behind a partition to find the hallway. Graham has already disappeared around the corner, so I pause before I make the turn. I put my hand on my chest, hoping it will somehow calm what's happening inside of it. And then I blow out a quick breath and walk into the hallway.

Graham is leaning casually against a wall, his hand in the pocket of his suit. The sight of him both excites me and comforts me, but I'm also nervous because I feel bad for never calling him.

Graham smiles his lazy half smile at me. "Hello, Quinn." His eyes still frown a little with his smile and I'm happy to see that. I don't know why. I like that he always looks to be battling some inner perpetual turmoil.

"Hey." I stand awkwardly a few feet away from him.

"Graham," he says, touching his chest. "In case you forgot."

I shake my head. "I didn't. It's kind of hard to forget every detail of the worst day of your life."

My comment makes him smile. He pushes off the wall and takes a step closer to me. "You never called."

I shrug like I haven't given his phone number much

thought. But in reality, I look at it every day. It's still stuck to the wall where he left it. "You said to call you after my rebound guy. I'm just now getting around to the rebound guy."

"Is that who you're with tonight?"

I nod. He takes a step closer, leaving only two feet between us. But it feels like he's suffocating me.

"What about you?" I ask. "Are you with your rebound girl?"

"My rebound was two girls ago."

I hate that answer. I hate it enough to be done with this conversation. "Well . . . congratulations. She's pretty."

Graham narrows his eyes as if he's trying to read all the things I'm not saying. I take a step toward the women's restroom and put my hand on the door. "It was good to see you, Graham."

His eyes are still narrowed and he tilts his head a little. I'm not sure what else to say. I walk into the women's restroom and allow the door to swing shut behind me. I let out a huge sigh. That was intense.

Why was that so intense?

I walk over to the sink and turn on the water. My hands are shaking, so I wash them in warm water, hoping the lavender soap helps calm my nerves. I dry them and then look at them in the mirror, trying to convince myself I wasn't that affected by Graham. But I was. They're still shaking.

For six months I've wanted to call him, but for six months I've talked myself out of it. And now, knowing he's moved on and he's with someone else, I might have blown my chance. Not that I wanted one. I still hold fast to the belief that he would remind me too much of what happened. If I do decide to start something up with someone, I'd want it to be someone brand-new. Someone completely unrelated to the worst days of my life.

Someone like Jason, maybe?

"Jason," I whisper. *I should get back to my date.*

When I open the door, Graham is still in the same spot. Still looking at me with his head tilted. I stop short and the door hits me in the back when it swings shut, pushing me forward a step.

I glance toward the end of the hallway and then look back at Graham. "Were we not finished?"

He inhales a slow breath as he takes a step toward me. He stops only a foot from me this time, sliding both hands back into his pockets. "How are you?" His voice is quiet, like it's hard for him to get it out. The way his eyes are searching mine makes it obvious he's referring to everything I've been through with the breakup. Calling off the wedding.

I like the sincerity in his question. I'm feeling all the same comfort his presence brought me that night six months ago. "Good," I say, nodding a little. "A few residual trust issues, but other than that I can't complain."

He looks relieved. "Good."

"What about you?"

He stares at me a moment, but I don't see what I'm hoping to see in his eyes. Instead, I see regret. Sadness. Like maybe he still hasn't recovered from losing Sasha. He shrugs, but doesn't answer with words.

I try not to let my pity show, but I think it does. "Maybe this new girl will be better than Sasha. And you'll finally be able to get over her."

Graham laughs a little. "I'm over Sasha," he says with conviction. "Pretty sure I was over Sasha the moment I met you."

He gives me absolutely zero time to absorb his words before he throws more of them at me. "We better get back to our dates, Quinn." He turns and walks out of the hallway.

I stand still, dumbfounded by his words. *"Pretty sure I was over Sasha the moment I met you."*

I can't believe he just said that to me. He can't say something like that and then just walk away! I stalk after him, but he's already halfway to his table. I catch Jason's eye and he smiles when he sees me, standing up. I try to compose myself, but it's hard as I watch Graham lean down and give his date a quick kiss on the side of her head before he takes his seat across from her again.

Is he trying to make me jealous? If he is, it's not working. I don't have time for frustrating men. I barely have time for boring men like Jason.

Jason has walked around the table to pull out my chair for me. Before I take my seat, Graham makes eye contact with me again. I swear I can see him smirk a little. I don't know why I stoop to his level, but I lean over and give Jason a quick kiss on the mouth.

Then I sit.

I have a clear shot of Graham as Jason walks back around to his side of the table. Graham is no longer smirking.

But I am.

"I'm ready to get out of here," I say.

Chapter Eight

Now

Ava and I talked on the phone almost every day when she lived in Connecticut, but now that she's halfway across the world, we seem to talk even more. Sometimes twice a day, even with the time difference.

"I have to tell you something."

There's a trepidation in her voice. I close my front door and walk my things to the kitchen counter. "Are you okay?" I set down my purse, pull the phone from between my shoulder and ear, and grip the phone in my hand.

"Yes," she says. "I'm fine. It's nothing like that."

"Well, what is it? You're scaring me, so it's obviously bad news."

"It's not. It's . . . good news actually."

I sink to the living room sofa. If it's good news, why does she sound so unhappy?

And then it clicks. She doesn't even have to say it. "You're pregnant?" There's a pause. It's so quiet on her end of the phone, I look down at mine to make sure we're still connected. "Ava?"

"I'm pregnant," she confirms.

Now *I'm* the quiet one. I put my hand against my chest, feeling the remnant pounding of my heart. For a moment, I feared the worst. But now that I know she's not dying, I can't help but wonder why she doesn't sound happy. "Are you okay?"

"Yeah," she says. "It's unexpected of course. Especially finding out so soon after moving here. But we've had a couple of days to let it sink in now. We're actually excited."

My eyes well up with tears but I'm not sure why I feel like crying. This is good. She's excited. "Ava," I whisper. "That's . . . wow."

"I know. You're going to be an aunt. I mean, I know you already are because of Graham's sister's children, but I just never thought you'd be an aunt because of me."

I force a smile but realize it isn't enough, so I force a laugh. "Your mother is going to be a grandma."

"That's the craziest part," she says. "She didn't know how to take the news. She's either drowning in martinis today or out shopping for baby clothes."

I swallow down the immediate envy, knowing my mother knew before I did. "You . . . you told her already?"

Ava releases a sigh full of regret. "Yesterday. I would have told you first but . . . I wanted Mom's advice. On how to tell you."

I lean my head back against the couch. She was scared to tell me? Does she think I'm that unstable? "Did you think I'd be jealous of you?"

"No," she says immediately. "I don't know, Quinn. Upset, maybe? Disappointed?"

Another tear falls, but this time it isn't a tear of joy. I quickly wipe it away. "You know me better than that." I stand up in an attempt to compose myself, even though she can't see me. "I have to go. Congratulations."

"Quinn."

I end the call and stare down at my phone. How could my own sister think I wouldn't be happy for her? She's my best friend. I'm happy for her and Reid. I'd never resent her for being able to have children. The only thing I resent is that she conceived so easily by *accident*.

Oh, God. I'm a terrible person.

No matter how much I'm trying to deny it, I do feel resentment. *And* I hung up on her. This should be one of the best moments of her life, but she loves me too much to be fully excited about it. And I'm being too selfish to allow that.

I immediately call her back.

"I'm sorry," I blurt out as soon as she answers.

"It's okay."

"No, it's not. You're right. I'm grateful that you were trying to be sensitive to what Graham and I are going through, but really, Ava. I am so happy for you and Reid. And I'm excited to be an aunt again."

I can hear the relief in her voice when she says, "Thank you, Quinn."

"There is one thing, though."

"What?"

"You told your *mother* first? I will never forgive you for that."

Ava laughs. "I regretted it as soon as I told her. She

actually said, '*But will you raise it in Europe? It'll have an accent!*'"

"Oh, God help us."

We both laugh.

"I have to name a *human,* Quinn. I hope you help me because Reid and I are never going to agree on a name."

We chat a little longer. I ask her the typical questions. How she found out. *Routine doctor's visit.* When she's due. *April.* When they'll find out what they're having. *They want it to be a surprise.*

When the conversation comes to an end, Ava says, "Before you hang up . . ." She pauses. "Have you heard back from the last adoption agency you applied to?"

I stand up to walk toward the kitchen. I'm suddenly thirsty. "I have," I tell her. I grab a water out of the refrigerator, take the cap off, and bring it to my mouth.

"That doesn't sound good."

"It is what it is," I say. "I can't change Graham's past and he can't change my present. No point in dwelling on it."

It's quiet on Ava's end of the line for a moment. "But what if you can find a baby through private adoption?"

"With what money?"

"Ask your mother for the money."

"This isn't a purse, Ava. I'm not letting your mother buy me a human. I'd be indebted to her for eternity." I look at the door just as Graham walks into the living room. "I have to go. I love you. Congratulations."

"Thank you," she says. "Love you, too."

I end the call just as Graham's lips meet my cheek. "Ava?" He reaches for my water and takes a drink.

I nod. "Yep. She's pregnant."

He nearly chokes on the water. He wipes his mouth and laughs a little. "Seriously? I thought they didn't want kids."

I shrug. "Turns out they were wrong."

Graham smiles and I love seeing that he's genuinely happy for them. What I hate, though, is that his smile fades and concern fills his eyes. He doesn't say it, but he doesn't have to. I see the worry. I don't want him to ask me how I feel about it, so I smile even wider and try to convince him I'm perfectly fine.

Because I am. Or I will be. Once it all sinks in.

———

Graham made spaghetti carbonara. He insisted on cooking tonight. I usually like when he cooks, but I have a feeling he only insisted tonight because he's afraid I might be having a negative reaction to the fact that my sister can get pregnant by accident and I can't even get pregnant after six years of trying on purpose.

"Have you heard back from the adoption agency yet?"

I look up from my plate of food and stare at Graham's mouth. The mouth that just produced that question. I grip my fork and look back down at my plate.

We've gone a month without discussing our infertility issues. Or the fact that neither of us has initiated sex since the night he slept in the guest room. I was hoping we could go *another* month.

I nod. "Yeah. They called last week."

I see the roll of his throat as he breaks eye contact with me and scoots his fork aimlessly around his plate. "Why didn't you tell me?"

"I'm telling you now."

"Only because I asked."

I don't respond to him again. He's right. I should have told him when I got the call last week, but it hurts. I don't like talking about things that hurt. And lately everything hurts. Which is why I barely talk anymore.

But I also didn't tell him because I know how much guilt he still holds over that incident. The incident that has been responsible for our third rejection from an adoption agency.

"I'm sorry," he says.

His apology creates an ache in my chest because I know he isn't apologizing for our snippy exchange. He's apologizing because he knows we were turned down because of his past conviction.

It happened when he was only nineteen. He doesn't talk about it a lot. Hardly ever. The wreck wasn't his fault, but because of the alcohol in his system, it didn't matter. The charge still lingers on his record and will forever put us out of the running when couples *without* criminal charges are approved in place of us.

But that was years ago. It's not something he can change and he's been punished enough for what happened when he was just a teenager. The last thing he needs is for his own wife to blame him, too.

"Don't apologize, Graham. If you apologize for not being approved for adoption then I'll have to apologize for not being able to conceive. It is what it is."

His eyes momentarily meet mine and I see a flash of appreciativeness in him.

He runs his finger around the rim of his glass. "The adoption issue we're having is a direct result of a poor decision

I made. You can't control the fact that you can't conceive. There's a difference."

Graham and I aren't a perfect example of a marriage, but we are a perfect example of knowing when and where the blame should be placed. He never makes me feel guilty for not being able to conceive and I've never wanted him to feel guilty for a choice he already holds way too much guilt for.

"There may be a difference, but it isn't much of one. Let's just drop it." I'm tired of this conversation. We've had it so many times and it changes nothing. I take another bite, thinking of a way we can change the subject, but he just continues.

"What if . . ." He leans forward now, pushing his plate toward the center of the table. "What if you applied for adoption on your own? Left me out of the equation?"

I stare at him, thinking of all that question entails. "I can't. We're legally married." He doesn't react. Which means he knew exactly what he was suggesting. I lean back in my chair and eye him cautiously. "You want us to get a divorce so I can apply on my own?"

Graham reaches across the table and covers my hand with his. "It wouldn't mean anything, Quinn. We would still be together. But it might make our chances better if we just . . . you know . . . pretended I wasn't in the picture. Then my past conviction couldn't affect our chances."

I contemplate his idea for a moment, but it's just as preposterous as the fact that we keep trying to conceive. Who would approve a divorced, single woman to adopt a child over a stable, married couple with more income and more opportunity? Becoming approved by an agency isn't an easy process, so actually being selected and the birth mother going through with the adoption are even harder. Not to mention the fees. Graham brings in twice as much money as me and we still might not be able to afford it, even if I were somehow approved for the process.

"We don't have the money." I expect that to be the end of it, but I can tell by his expression that he has another suggestion. I can also tell by the way he's not readily suggesting whatever it is he's thinking that it must include my mother. I immediately shake my head and grab my plate. I stand up. "We aren't asking her. The last time I spoke to her about adoption, she told me God would give me a child when I was ready. And like I told Ava earlier, the last thing we need is for her to feel like she owns a piece of our family." I walk the plate to the sink. Graham scoots back in his chair and stands.

"It was just an idea," he says, following me into the kitchen. "You know, there's a guy at my work who said his sister tried for seven years to get pregnant. She found out three months ago that she's having a baby. Due in January."

Yes, Graham. That's called a miracle. And it's called a miracle because the chances of it happening are slim to none.

I turn on the water and wash my plate. "You talk about it to people at work?"

Graham is next to me now, lowering his plate into the sink. "Sometimes," he says quietly. "People ask why we haven't had kids."

I can feel the pressure building in my chest. I need to be done with the conversation. I want Graham to be done, too, but he leans against the counter and dips his head. "Hey."

I give him a sidelong glance to let him know I'm listening, but then I move my attention back to the dishes.

"We barely talk about it anymore, Quinn. I don't know if that's good or bad."

"It's neither. I'm just tired of talking about it. It's all our marriage has become."

"Does that mean you're accepting it?"

"Accepting what?" I still don't look at him.

"That we'll never be parents."

The plate in my hand slips out of my grasp. It lands against the bottom of the sink with a loud clutter.

But it doesn't break like I do.

I don't even know why it happens. I'm gripping the sink now and my head is hanging between my shoulders and tears just start falling from my eyes. *Fuck.* I really can't stand myself sometimes.

Graham waits several seconds before he moves to console me. He doesn't put his arms around me, though. I think he can tell I don't want to be crying right now and hugging me is something he's learned doesn't help in these situations. I don't cry in front of him near as much as I cry alone, but I've done it enough for him to know that I'd rather do it alone. He runs his hand over my hair and kisses the back of my head. Then he just touches my arm and moves me out of the way of the sink. He picks up the plate and finishes washing the dishes. I do what I do best. I walk away until I'm strong enough to pretend the conversation never happened. And he does what he does best. He leaves me alone in my grief because I've made it so hard for him to console me.

We're getting really good at playing our parts.

Chapter Nine

Then

I'm on my bed. I'm making out with Jason.

I blame Graham for this.

I would have never invited Jason back to my apartment had I not seen Graham. But for some reason, seeing him there filled me with . . . *feelings*. And then watching him kiss his date on the side of her head filled me with jealousy. And then watching him grab her hand across the table as we walked past them filled me with regret.

Why did I never call him?

I should have called him.

"Quinn," Jason says. He's been kissing my neck, but now he's not. He's looking down at me, his expression full of so many things I don't want to be there right now. "Do you have a condom?"

I lie and tell him no. "I'm sorry. I wasn't expecting to bring you back here tonight."

"It's fine," he says, lowering his mouth to my neck again. "I'll come prepared next time."

I feel bad. I'm almost positive I'll never have sex with Jason. I am positive he won't be coming back to my apartment after tonight. I'm even *more* positive I'm about to ask him to leave. I wasn't this positive before dinner. But after running into Graham, I realize how it should feel to be with another person. And the way I feel around Jason pales in comparison to how I feel when I'm around Graham.

Jason whispers something inaudible against my neck. His fingers have made their way up my shirt and over my bra.

Thank God the doorbell rings.

I slide off the bed in a hurry. "It's probably my mother," I say to him, straightening out my clothes. "Wait here. I'll be right back."

Jason rolls onto his back and watches me leave the room. I rush to the door, knowing exactly who I hope it is before I even open it. But even still, I gasp when I look through the peephole.

Graham is standing at my door, looking down at his feet.

I press my forehead to my door and close my eyes.

What is he doing here?

I attempt to straighten out my shirt and my hair before opening the door. When I'm finally face-to-face with him, I grow irritated at the way I feel in his presence. Graham doesn't even touch me and I feel it everywhere. Jason touches me everywhere and I feel it nowhere.

"What . . ." The word that just left my mouth is somehow full of more breath than voice. I clear my throat and try again. "What are you doing here?"

Graham smiles a little, lifting a hand to the doorframe. The smirk on his face and the fact that he's chewing gum are two of the sexiest things I've ever seen at one time. "I thought this was the plan."

I am so confused. "The plan?"

He laughs halfheartedly. But then he tilts his head. He points behind me, into my apartment. "I thought . . ." He points behind him, over his shoulder. "At the restaurant. There was this look . . . right before you left. I thought you were asking me to come over."

His voice is louder than I need it to be right now. I check over my shoulder to make sure Jason hasn't come out of the bedroom. Then I try to shield Graham from my apartment a little better by slipping more on the other side of the door. "What *look*?"

Graham's eyes narrow a bit. "You didn't give me a look?"

I shake my head. "I did not give you a look. I wouldn't even know what look to give you that would say, '*Hey, ditch your date and come over to my place tonight.*'"

Graham's lips form a tight line and he looks down at the floor with a hint of embarrassment. He raises his eyes, but his head is still dipped when he says, "Is he here? Your date?"

Now *I'm* the one who's embarrassed. I nod. Graham releases a sigh as he leans against the doorjamb. "Wow. I read that one wrong."

When he looks at me again, I notice the left side of his face is red. I step closer to him and reach up to his cheek. "What happened?"

He grins and pulls my hand from his cheek. He doesn't let go of it. I don't want him to.

"I got slapped. It's fine. I deserved it."

That's when I see it. The outline of a handprint. "Your date?"

He lifts a shoulder. "After what happened with Sasha, I vowed to be completely honest in every aspect of my relationships from then on. Jess . . . my date tonight . . . didn't see that as a good quality."

"What did you say to her?"

"I broke it off with her. I told her I was into another girl. And that I was going to her apartment to see her."

"Because this other girl supposedly gave you a look?"

He smiles. "I *thought* she did, anyway." He brushes his thumb across the top of my hand and then he releases it. "Well, Quinn. Maybe another time."

Graham takes a step back and it feels like he pulls all my emotions with him as he turns to walk away.

"Graham," I say, stepping out into the hallway. He turns around, and I don't know if I'm going to regret what I'm about to say, but I'll regret it even more if I don't. "Come back in fifteen minutes. I'll get rid of him."

Graham shoots me the perfect thank-you smile, but before he walks away, his eyes move past me. To someone behind me. I turn around and see Jason standing in the doorway. He looks pissed. Rightfully so.

He swings open the door and walks out into the hallway. He walks past Graham, shoving him with his shoulder. Graham just stands silent, staring at the floor.

I feel terrible. But if it hadn't happened this way, I would have shot him down on his way out of my apartment later. Rejection sucks, no matter how it's presented.

The door to the stairwell slams shut and neither of us speak as we listen to Jason's footsteps fade down the stairs.

When all is quiet, Graham finally lifts his head and makes eye contact with me. "You still need that fifteen minutes?"

I shake my head. "Nope."

Graham walks toward me as I step back into my apartment. I hold the door open for him, certain that he won't be leaving here as quickly as he did last time. Once he's inside, I close the door and then turn around. Graham is smiling, looking at the wall beside my head. I follow his line of sight to the Post-it he left six months ago.

"It's still here."

I smile sheepishly. "I would have called you eventually. Maybe."

Graham pulls down the sticky note and folds it in half, sliding it into his pocket. "You won't be needing it after tonight. I'll make sure you have my number memorized before I leave here tomorrow."

"That confident you're staying over?"

Graham takes an assured step closer. He places a hand against the door beside my head, forcing my back against the door. It isn't until he does this that I realize why I find him so attractive.

It's because he makes *me* feel attractive. The way he looks at me. The way he talks to me. I'm not sure anyone has ever made me feel as beautiful as he makes me feel when he looks at me. Like it's taking everything in him to keep his mouth away from mine. His eyes fall to my lips. He leans in so close, I can smell the flavor of gum he's chewing. *Spearmint.*

I want him to kiss me. I want him to kiss me even more than I wanted Jason to *stop* kissing me. And that was a lot. But I feel like whatever is about to start with me and Graham, it needs to start with complete transparency. "I kissed Jason. Earlier. Before you got here."

My comment doesn't seem to dismay him. "I figured as much."

I put my hands on his chest. "I just . . . I want to kiss you, too. But it's weird because I just kissed someone else. I'd like to brush my teeth first."

Graham laughs. *I love his laugh.* He leans in and presses his forehead to the side of my head, causing my knees to lock. His lips are right over my ear when he whispers. "Hurry. Please."

I slip around him and rush to my bathroom. I pull open the drawer and grab my toothbrush and toothpaste like I'm racing against time. My hands are shaking as I squeeze the toothpaste onto my toothbrush. I turn on the water and start brushing my teeth furiously. I'm brushing my tongue when I look in the mirror and see Graham walk into the bathroom behind me. I laugh at how ridiculous this is.

I haven't kissed a guy in six months. Now I'm brushing away the germs of one guy while the next one waits in line.

Graham seems to be enjoying the ridiculousness of this moment just as much as I am. He's now leaning against the sink next to me, watching as I spit toothpaste into the sink. I rinse my toothbrush and then toss it aside, grabbing an empty glass. I fill it with water and take a sip, swishing the water around in my mouth until I'm certain my mouth is as clean as it's going to get. I spit the water out and take another sip. This time I just swallow the water, though, because Graham takes the cup from me and sets it near the sink. He pulls the piece of gum out of his mouth, tossing it in the trash can, then he slides his other hand around my head and doesn't even ask if I'm ready yet. He brings his mouth to mine, assured and eager, like the last sixty seconds of preparation have been pure torture. The moment our lips touch, it's as if an ember that's been slow-burning for six long months finally bursts into flames.

He doesn't even bother with an introductory, slow kiss. His tongue is in my mouth like he's been there many times before and knows exactly what to do. He turns me until my back is against the sink and then he lifts me, setting me down on my bathroom counter. He settles himself between my legs, grabbing my ass with both hands, pulling me against him. I wrap my arms around him, lock my legs around him. I try to convince myself I did not go my whole life never realizing this kind of kiss existed.

The way his lips move against mine makes me question the skills of every guy that came before him.

He starts to ease the pressure and I catch myself pulling him against me, not wanting him to stop. But he does. Slowly. He gives me a small peck on the corner of my mouth before pulling back.

"Wow," I whisper. I open my eyes and he's staring at me. But he's not looking at me in awe like I'm looking at him. There's a very noticeable dejected look on his face.

He shakes his head slowly, his eyes narrowing. "I can't believe you never called me. We could have been kissing like this for months."

His comment throws me off. So much so, I stumble over my words when I attempt a response. "I just . . . I guess I thought being around you would remind me of Ethan too much. Of everything that happened that night."

He nods like he understands. "How many times have you thought of Ethan since seeing me at the restaurant tonight?"

"Once," I say. "Just now."

"Good. Because I'm not Ethan." He lifts me, carrying me to the bed. He lays me down and then he backs away, pulling off his shirt. I'm not sure I've ever touched skin that smooth and tight and beautiful and tanned. Graham without a shirt is near perfection.

"I like your . . ." I point at his chest and make a circular motion with my finger. "Your body. It's very nice."

He laughs, pressing a knee into the mattress. He lies down next to me. "Thank you," he says. "But you can't have this body right now." He adjusts the pillow beneath his head, getting comfortable. I lift up onto my elbow and scowl at him.

"Why not?"

"What's the rush? I'll be here all night."

Surely he's kidding. Especially after that kiss. "Well, what are we supposed to do while we wait? *Talk?*"

He laughs. "You sound like conversation with me is the worst idea in the world."

"If we talk too much before we have sex, I might find out things I don't like about you. Then the sex won't be as fun."

He reaches up and tucks my hair behind my ear with a grin. "Or . . . you might find out we're soul mates and the sex will be mind-blowing."

He has a point.

I fold my arms over my pillow and lay my head on them as I roll onto my stomach. "We better get to talking, then. You go first."

Graham runs his hand over my arm. He traces the scar on my elbow. "Where'd you get this scar?"

"My older sister and I were racing through the house when I was fourteen. I didn't know the sliding glass door was shut and I ran through it. Shattered the glass and cut myself in like ten different places. That's the only scar, though."

"Damn."

"You have any scars?"

Graham lifts up a little and points to a spot on his collarbone. There's about a four-inch scar that looks like it must have been pretty bad at the time of the injury. "Car wreck." He scoots closer to me and wraps his leg over both of mine. "What's your favorite movie?"

"Anything by the Coen brothers. My favorite is *Oh Brother, Where Art Thou?*"

He looks at me like maybe he has no clue what movie I'm talking about. But then he says, "We thought . . . you was . . . a toad."

I laugh. "Damn! We're in a tight spot!"

"Jesus Saves, George Nelson withdraws!" We're both laughing now. My laughter ends with a sigh, and then Graham smiles at me appreciatively. "See? We like the same movie. Our sex is going to be amazing."

I grin. "Next question."

"Name something you hate."

"Infidelity and most vegetables."

Graham laughs. "Do you live off chicken nuggets and French fries?"

"I love fruit. And tomatoes. But I'm not really a fan of anything green. I've tried to love vegetables but I finally decided last year to accept that I hate them and force nutrition into my diet in other ways."

"Do you like to work out?"

"Only in emergencies," I admit. "I like doing stuff outdoors, but not if it's routine exercise."

"I like to run," he says. "It clears my head. And I love every single vegetable *except* tomatoes."

"Uh-oh. Not looking good, Graham."

"No, it's perfect. You'll eat my tomatoes, I'll eat every other vegetable on your plate. Nothing goes to waste. It's a perfect match."

I like his way of looking at it. "What else? Movies and food only scratch the surface."

"We could talk politics and religion but we should probably save those two for after we're in love."

He says that so confidently, but also like he's kidding. Either way, I agree we should avoid politics and religion. Those lead to arguments even when people agree. "Definitely cool with not touching those two."

Graham grabs my wrist and slides it out from under my head. He threads his fingers through mine and rests our hands between us. I try not to focus too much on how sweet I think it is. "What's your favorite holiday?" he asks.

"All of them. But I'm partial to Halloween."

"Not what I expected you to say. Do you like it for the costumes or the candy?"

"Both, but mostly the costumes. I love dressing up."

"What's the best costume you ever wore?"

I think about it for a moment. "Probably when my friends and I went as Milli Vanilli. Two of us talked the whole night while the other two stood in front of us and mouthed everything we said."

Graham rolls onto his back and laughs. "That's pretty spectacular," he says, staring up at the ceiling.

"Do you dress up for Halloween?"

"I'm not opposed to it but I never dressed up with Sasha

because she always went as something typical and slutty. A slutty cheerleader. A slutty nurse. A slutty prude." He pauses for a second. "Don't get me wrong, I love a slutty costume. Nothing wrong with a woman showing off her assets if that's what she wants to do. It's just that Sasha never really asked me to dress up. I think she wanted all the attention and didn't really want to do the couples costume thing."

"That sucks. So much missed opportunity."

"Right? I could have dressed up as her slutty quarterback."

"Well, if we're still talking when Halloween rolls around, we can wear matching slutty costumes."

"*Still* talking? Quinn, Halloween is over two months away. We'll practically be living together by then."

I roll my eyes. "You're way too confident."

"You could call it that."

"Most men push for sex right away. But you turn me down one night and show up six months later just to turn me down again and force me into conversation. I can't tell if I should be worried."

Graham raises an eyebrow. "Don't mistake me for something I'm not. I'm normally all for the sex up front, but you and I have an eternity to get to it."

I can tell he's kidding by the straight face he tries to keep. I lift up on my pillow and raise my brow. "Sex I'm okay with. Eternal commitment is pushing it."

Graham slides an arm beneath me and pulls me against him so that my head is now resting on his chest. "Whatever you say, Quinn. If you want us to pretend for a few more months that we aren't soul mates, that's fine with me. I'm a great actor."

I laugh at his sarcasm. "Soul mates don't exist."

"I know," he says. "We aren't soul mates. Soul mates are dumb."

"I'm serious."

"Me too. Completely serious."

"You're an idiot."

He presses his lips into my hair, kissing me on top of the head. "What is today's date?"

He is so random. I lift my head and look at him. "The eighth of August. Why?"

"Just want to make sure you never forget the date the universe brought us back together."

I lay my head against him again. "You're coming on way too strong. It's probably going to scare me away."

His chest moves with his quiet laughter. "No, it won't. You'll see. Ten years from now on August eighth, I'm going to roll over in our bed at midnight and whisper, *'I told you so'* in your ear."

"Are you that petty?"

"The pettiest."

I laugh. I laugh a lot while we talk. I don't know how long we lay in the same position talking, but I still have a million questions left when I start yawning. I fight it because talking to him is somehow even more relaxing than sleep and I want to ask him questions all night.

Graham eventually goes to the kitchen to get a glass of water. When he comes back to the bedroom, he turns off the lamp and climbs in bed behind me, spooning me. It's honestly not what I expected tonight. Especially with the way he approached me at the restaurant and then showed up at my apartment. I thought he had one thing on his mind.

I couldn't have been more wrong.

I wrap my arms over his and close my eyes. "I thought you were kidding about the no sex," I whisper.

I feel him laugh a little. "Keeping my pants on is not as easy as I'm making it look." He pushes against my ass to let me know how serious he is. I can feel him straining against his jeans.

"That must be painful," I tease. "You sure you don't want to change your mind?"

He squeezes me tighter, pressing a kiss close to my ear. "I've never been more comfortable."

His words make me blush in the dark, but I don't respond to him. I don't have a reply good enough. I'm quiet for several minutes as I listen to his breathing slow into a peaceful pattern. Right before I fall asleep, Graham whispers against my ear. "I thought you were the one that got away."

I smile. "I still could be."

"Don't be."

I try to say, *"I won't be,"* but he puts his hand between my cheek and the pillow and tilts my head until his mouth reaches mine. We kiss just enough. Not too short, but not too long that it leads to something else. It's the perfect kiss for the perfect moment.

Chapter Ten

Now

"Two more lipsticks," Gwenn says. She slides the bright red tube of lipstick over my top lip but goes so far outside of the edges, I feel it touch my nose.

"You're really good at this," I say with a laugh.

We're at Graham's parents' house, having dinner with his family. Graham is on the floor playing with his sister Caroline's five-year-old daughter, Adeline. The three-year-old, Gwenn, is on the couch next to me, putting makeup on me. Graham's parents are in the kitchen, cooking.

This is how most of our Sundays are spent. I've always enjoyed Sundays here, but lately they've become my favorite days of the month. I don't know why things are easier here, surrounded by Graham's family, but they are. It's easier for me to laugh. It's easier for me to look happy. It's even easier for me to let Graham love me.

I've noticed there's a difference with how I am toward Graham in public compared to when we're at home. At home, when it's just the two of us, I'm more withdrawn. I avoid his touch and his kiss because in the past, those things have always led to sex. And now that I dread sex so much, I dread the stuff that leads up to it, too.

But when we're in a setting like this, when his affection leads to nothing, I crave it. I like it when he puts his hands on me. When he kisses me. I love snuggling up to him on the couch. I don't know if he notices the difference in me between our house and other places. If he does, he's never let on.

"I finish," Gwenn says. She struggles putting the cap back on the lipstick she just applied to my mouth. I take it from her and help her close it.

Graham looks up at me from the floor. "Hot damn, Quinn. That is . . . yeah."

I smile at Gwenn. "Did you make me pretty?"

She starts giggling.

I make my way to the bathroom and laugh when I look in the mirror. I'm convinced they only make blue eye shadow for this exact purpose. So three-year-olds can put it on adults.

I'm washing my face when Graham walks into the bathroom. He looks at me in the mirror and makes a face.

"What? You don't like it?"

He kisses my shoulder. "You look beautiful, Quinn. Always."

I finish washing the makeup from my face, but Graham's lips don't leave my shoulder. He traces a soft trail of kisses up my neck. Knowing that this kiss won't lead to *sexhopedevastation* makes me enjoy it more than if this were happening in our own bathroom at our own house.

It sounds so fucked up. I don't understand how his actions can elicit different responses from me depending on the setting. But right now, I'm not going to question it, because he doesn't seem to be questioning it. He seems to be enjoying it.

He remains behind me, pressing me against the sink as his hand runs over my hip and slides around to the front of my thigh. I grip the sink and watch him in the mirror. He lifts his eyes and stares at my reflection as he begins to bunch up the front of my dress with his fingers, crawling it up the front of my thighs.

It's been over a month and a half now since he's initiated sex. The longest we've ever gone. I know, based on how things ended the last time we had sex, he's waiting for me to initiate it. But I haven't.

It's been so long since he's touched me, my reaction seems to be intensified.

I close my eyes when his hand slips inside my panties. I'm covered in chills from head to toe, and knowing this can't go too far makes me want him and his mouth and his hands all over me.

The door is open and someone could walk down the hall at any moment, but that only serves as further affirmation that this make-out session will stop any second now. Which is why my mind is allowing me to enjoy it as much as I am.

He slips a finger inside of me and runs his thumb down the center of me and it's the most I've felt from his touch in over a year. My head falls back against his shoulder and he tilts my mouth toward his. I moan, just as his lips cover mine. He kisses me with hunger and impatience, like he's desperate to get all he can out of this moment before I push him away.

Graham kisses me with urgency the whole time he touches me. He kisses me until I come, and even as I whimper and tremble in his arms, he doesn't stop kissing and touching me until the moment passes completely.

He slowly pulls his hand out of my panties, diving his tongue into my mouth one last time before pulling back. I grip the sink in front of me, breathing heavily. He kisses me on the shoulder, grinning as he walks out of the bathroom, smiling like he just conquered the world.

I take several minutes to collect myself. I make sure my face is no longer flushed before I walk back to the living room. Graham is lying on the couch, watching television. He makes room for me on the couch, pulling me against him. Every now and then, he'll kiss me or I'll kiss him and it feels just like it used to. And I pretend that everything is okay. I pretend every other day of the week is just like Sundays at Graham's parents' house. It's like everything else falls away when we're here, and it's just me and Graham without a single trace of failure.

After dinner, Graham and I offer to do the dishes. He turns on the radio and we stand at the sink together. I wash and he rinses. He talks about work and I listen. When an Ed Sheeran song starts to play, my hands are covered in soapy suds, but Graham pulls me to him anyway and starts dancing with me. We cling to each other and barely move while we dance—his arms around my waist and mine around his neck. His forehead is pressed to mine and even though I know he's watching me, I keep my eyes closed and pretend we're perfect. We dance alone until the song almost comes to an end, but Caroline walks into the kitchen and catches us.

She's due with her third child in a few weeks. She's holding a paper plate with one hand and holding her lower back with the other. She rolls her eyes at the sight of us. "I can't imagine what it must be like when you're in private if you two are this handsy in public." She throws the plate in the trash can and heads back toward the living room. "You're probably that annoyingly perfect couple who has sex twice a day."

When the door to the kitchen closes, we're alone and the song is over and Graham is just staring at me. I know his sister's comment has made him think about my affection. I can tell he wants to ask me why I love his touch so much in public, but recoil from it in private.

He doesn't say anything about it, though. He hands me a towel to dry my hands. "You ready to go home?"

I nod, but I also feel it start to happen. The nerves building in my stomach. The worry that being so affectionate with him at his mother's will make him think I want his affection at the house.

It makes me feel like the worst wife in the world. I don't do this because I don't love him. But maybe if I could somehow love him better, I wouldn't do this.

Even knowing how unfair I am to him doesn't stop me from lying to him on our way home. "I feel like I'm getting a migraine," I say, pressing my forehead to the passenger window of our car.

When we make it home, Graham tells me to go to bed and get some rest. Five minutes later, he brings me a glass of water and some aspirin. He turns out my lamp and leaves the room and I cry because I hate what I've turned this marriage into.

My husband's heart is my saving grace, but his physical touch has become my enemy.

Chapter Eleven

Then

I can feel the heat of his body next to me. I like that the sun is up and he's still here.

I feel Graham move before I open my eyes. His hand finds mine beneath my pillow and he threads our fingers together. "Good morning."

When I open my eyes, I'm smiling. He lifts his other arm and brushes his thumb across my cheek. "What'd I miss while you were asleep? Did you dream?"

I think that might be the sweetest thing anyone has ever said to me. I don't know if that's good or bad. "I had kind of a strange dream. You were in it."

He perks up, releasing my hand and lifting onto his elbow. "Oh yeah? Tell me about it."

"I had a dream that you showed up here in head-to-toe scuba gear. And you told me to put my scuba gear on because we were going to swim with sharks. I told you I was scared of sharks and you said, *'But Quinn. These sharks are actually cats!'* And then I said, *'But I'm scared of the ocean.'* And you said, *'But Quinn. This ocean is actually a park.'"*

Graham laughs. "What happened next?"

"I put on my scuba gear, of course. But you didn't take me to an ocean or a park. You took me to meet your mother. And I was so embarrassed and so mad at you because I was wearing a scuba-diving suit at her dinner table."

Graham falls onto his back with laughter. "Quinn, that is the best dream in the history of dreams."

His reaction makes me want to tell him every dream I ever have for the rest of my life.

I like that he rolls toward me and looks at me like there's nowhere else he'd rather be. He leans forward and presses his mouth to mine. I want to stay in bed with him all day, but he pulls away and says, "I'm hungry. You got anything to eat?"

I nod, but before he can climb out of bed, I pull him back and press my lips against his cheek. "I like you, Graham." I roll off him and head to my bathroom.

He calls out after me. "Of course you like me, Quinn! I'm your soul mate!"

I laugh as I close the door to the bathroom. And then I want to scream when I look in the mirror. Holy shit. I have mascara smeared everywhere. A pimple that appeared on my forehead overnight. My hair is a mess, but not in that sexy, come-hither way. It's just a mess. Like a rat slept in it all night.

I groan and then yell, "I'm taking a shower!"

Graham yells back from the kitchen. "I'm looking for food!"

I doubt he finds much. I don't keep a lot of groceries at my house because I rarely cook since I live alone.

I step into the shower. I have no idea if he's staying after breakfast, but while I shower, I make sure to pay special attention to certain areas just in case.

I've been in the shower all of three minutes when I hear the bathroom door open.

"You don't have anything to eat."

The sound of his voice in my bathroom surprises me so much, I almost slip and fall. I grip the shower bar and steady myself, but immediately let go of the bar and cover my breasts when I see the shower curtain move.

Graham peeks his head inside the shower. He looks straight at my face and nowhere else, but I'm still doing everything I can to shield myself.

"You have absolutely no food. Crackers and a stale box of cereal." He says this like it's not at all unusual that he's looking at me naked. "Want me to go grab breakfast?"

"Um . . . okay." I'm wide-eyed, still shocked from his confident intrusion.

Graham grins, pulling his bottom lip in with his teeth. His eyes begin to slowly trail down my body. "My God, Quinn," he whispers. He closes the shower curtain and says, "I'll be back in a little while." Right before he walks out of my bathroom I hear him whisper, "Fuck."

I can't help but smile. I love how that just made me feel.

I turn back around and face the shower spray as I close my eyes and let the warm water beat down on my face. I can't figure Graham out. He's just the right amount of confident and cocky. But he balances that out with his reverent side. He's funny and smart and he comes on way too strong, but it all feels genuine.

Genuine.

If I had to describe him in one word, that would be it.

It surprises me because I never thought of Ethan as genuine. There was always a part of me that felt his seeming perfection was part of an act. Like he had been taught how to say all the right things but it wasn't inherent with him. It was as if he studied how to be the version of himself he presented to everyone.

But with Graham, I have a feeling he's been who he is all his life.

I wonder if I'll learn to trust him. After what I went through with Ethan, I've felt like that would never happen.

When I'm finished in the shower, I dry off and pull on a T-shirt and a pair of yoga pants. I have no idea if Graham has intentions of hanging out today, but until I find that out, I'll be dressing for comfort.

When I walk back into the bedroom, I grab my phone off the nightstand and notice several missed texts.

I saved my contact in your phone. This is Graham. Your soul mate.

What do you want for breakfast?

McDonald's? Starbucks? Donuts?

Are you still in the shower?

Do you like coffee?

I can't stop thinking about you in the shower.

Okay, then. I'll get bagels.

I'm in my bedroom hanging up laundry when I hear Graham walk through the front door. I walk to the living room and he's at the table, laying out breakfast. *A lot* of breakfast.

"You didn't specify what you wanted, so I got everything."

My eyes scan the box of donuts, the McDonald's, the Chick-fil-A. He even got bagels. And Starbucks. "Are you trying to replicate the breakfast scene from *Pretty Woman* when Richard Gere orders everything off the menu?" I smile and take a seat at the table.

He frowns. "You mean this has been done before?"

I take a bite of a glazed donut. "Yep. You're gonna have to be more original if you want to impress me."

He sits down across from me and pulls the lid off a Starbucks cup. He licks the whipped cream. "I guess I'll have to cancel the white limo that's supposed to pull up to your fire escape this afternoon."

I laugh. "Thank you for breakfast."

He leans back in his seat, placing the lid back on his coffee. "What are your plans today?"

I shrug. "It's Saturday. I'm off work."

"I don't even know what you do for a living."

"I write for an advertising firm downtown. Nothing impressive."

"Nothing about you is unimpressive, Quinn."

I ignore his compliment. "What about you?"

"Nothing impressive. I'm an accountant for a company downtown."

"A math guy, huh?"

"My first choice was an astronaut, but the idea of leaving the earth's atmosphere is kind of terrifying. Numbers don't really pose a threat to my life, so I went with that." He opens one of the bags and pulls out a biscuit. "I think we should have sex tonight." He takes a bite of the biscuit. "All night," he says with a mouthful.

I almost choke on the bite I just swallowed. I pull the extra coffee toward me and take a sip. "You do, huh? What's so different about tonight than last night?"

He tears off a piece of the biscuit and pops it into his mouth. "I was being polite last night."

"So your politeness is just a façade?"

"No, I really am a decent guy. But I'm also extremely attracted to you and want to see you naked again." He smiles at me. It's a shy smile and it's so cute, it makes *me* smile.

"Some men get cheated on and they become revengeful. You get cheated on and become brutally honest."

He laughs, but he doesn't bring up the potential sex again. We both eat in silence for a minute and then he says, "What'd you do with your engagement ring?"

"I mailed it to Ethan's mother."

"What'd you do with the one I left here?"

A reserved smile creeps across my lips. "I kept it. Sometimes I wear it. It's pretty."

He watches me for a moment and then he says, "You want to know what I kept?"

I nod.

"Our fortunes."

It takes me a moment before I realize what he's talking about. "From the Chinese food and infidelity?"

"Yep."

"You kept those?"

"Sure did."

"Why?"

"Because." He looks down at his coffee and moves the cup in small circles. "If you saw what was on the back of them, you wouldn't be questioning it."

I lean back in my seat and eye him suspiciously. Ethan and I got those fortune cookies all the time. I know exactly what's on the back of them because I always thought it was odd. Most fortunes have a set of numbers, but this place only puts a single number on the fortunes. "The backs of those fortune cookies just have a number on them."

"Yep." He has a mischievous gleam in his eyes.

I tilt my head. "What? Did they have the same number or something?"

He looks at me seriously. "The number eight."

I hold his stare and think about that for a few seconds. Last night he asked me the date. August 8.

8/8.

The day we reconnected.

"Are you serious?"

Graham holds his resolve for a moment, but then he relaxes and lets out a laugh. "I'm kidding. Yours had a seven on the back of it and mine had like a five or something." He stands up and takes his trash to the kitchen. "I kept them because I'm a neat freak and I didn't like littering on the floor of the hallway. I forgot they were in my pocket until I got home that night."

I wonder how much of that is true. "Do you really still have them, though?"

He steps on the trash can lever and the lid pops open. "Of course." He walks back to the table and pulls me out of my chair. He slides his arms around my waist and kisses me. It's a sweet kiss and he tastes like caramel and sugar. He moves his mouth to my cheek and kisses it, then pulls me against his chest. "You know I'm only teasing you, right? I don't actually believe we'll spend the rest of our lives together. *Yet.*"

I kind of like his teasing. A lot. I open my mouth to respond to him, but his phone rings. He holds up a finger and pulls it out of his pocket, then immediately answers it. "Hey, beautiful," he says. He covers his phone and whispers, "It's my mother. Don't freak out."

I laugh and leave him to his phone call while I walk to the table to gather all the breakfast he brought. I don't think it'll all fit in the fridge.

"Not much," Graham says. "Is Dad golfing today?" I watch him chat with his mother. He does it with such ease. When I chat with my mother, I'm tense and on edge and rolling my eyes through most of the conversation. "Yeah, dinner sounds good. Can I bring a date?" He covers his phone and looks at me. "Get your scuba gear ready, Quinn."

I don't know whether to laugh at his joke or start freaking out. I don't even know the guy's last name yet. I don't want to meet his parents. I just mouth, "No" very firmly.

He winks at me. "Her name is Quinn," he says, answering his mother's question. He's watching me while he continues the conversation. "Yeah, it's pretty serious. Been seeing her for a while now."

I roll my eyes at his lies. He's unrelenting.

"Hold on, I'll ask her." He doesn't cover his phone this time. Actually, he yells louder than he needs to because we're just a few feet apart. "Babe! Do you want pie or cobbler for dessert?"

I step closer to him so he can hear the seriousness in my voice. "We haven't even been on a *date* yet," I whisper. "I don't want to meet your mother, Graham."

He covers his phone this time and motions at the table. "We just had like five dates," he whispers. "Chick-fil-A, McDonald's, donuts, Starbucks . . ." He pulls his phone back to his ear. "She prefers pie. We'll see you around six?" There's a pause. "Okay. Love you, too."

He ends the call and slides the phone into his pocket. I'm glaring at him, but it doesn't last long because he walks up to me and tickles me until I laugh. Then he pulls me against him. "Don't worry, Quinn. Once you taste her cooking, you won't ever want to leave."

I sigh heavily. "You are nothing like I expected."

He presses a kiss to the top of my head. "Is that good or bad?"

"I honestly have no idea."

Chapter Twelve

Now

When I pull onto Caroline's street, I see Graham's car parked in her driveway. But it looks like other than his sister and her husband, we're the only ones here. I'm relieved by that.

Caroline had her baby boy yesterday morning. A home birth. It's the first boy born in Graham's family since him, actually.

Caroline is the only sister of Graham's who lives in Connecticut. Tabitha lives in Chicago with her wife. Ainsley is a lawyer and lives all over. She travels almost as much as Ava and Reid do. Sometimes I'm a little envious of their carefree lifestyles, but I've always had other priorities.

Graham and I are very involved in the lives of Caroline's two daughters. Outside of the time we spend with them on Sundays, we also occasionally take them for outings or to the movies to give Caroline and her husband time alone. I suspect with the birth of their son, we'll be spending even more time with the girls.

I love watching Graham with them. He's playful and loves to make them laugh. But he's also very invested in their mental health and well-being. He answers every "but why" question with patience and honesty. And even though they're only three and five, he treats them as equals. Caroline jokes that when they return home after spending time at our house, they start every sentence with, "But Uncle Graham said . . ."

I love the relationship he has with his nieces so much, seeing him with his baby nephew makes me even more excited to see him as an uncle. I do occasionally let the thoughts get to me in moments like this about what a great father he would make, but I refuse to let our depressing situation dampen Graham's experience with his family. So, I plaster on my happy face and make sure to never allow the sadness to show.

I practice smiling in my rearview mirror. Smiling used to come naturally to me, but almost every smile that appears on my face nowadays is a façade.

When I reach the front door, I don't know whether to ring the bell or just walk in. If the baby or Caroline are sleeping, I'd feel terrible for waking them up. I push open the door and the front of the house is quiet. No one is seated in the living room, although there are unwrapped gifts lining the sofa. I walk to the living room and place Graham's and my gift on the coffee table next to the couch.

I make my way through a quiet kitchen and toward the den where Caroline and her family spend most of their time. It was an add-on they completed right after Gwenn was born.

Half of the room serves as a living room and the other half serves as a playroom for the girls.

I'm almost to the den, but I pause just outside the door when I see Graham. His back is to me and he's standing near the couch, holding his new nephew. He's swaying from side to side with the newborn cocooned in a blanket in his arms. I suppose if our situation were different, this would be a moment where I would have nothing but pure adoration for my husband—watching him hold his newborn nephew. Instead, I ache inside. It makes me question the thoughts that might be going through his head right now. Does a small part of him resent that I haven't been able to create a moment like this for him?

No one can see me from where I'm standing since Graham has his back to me and I'm out of the line of sight of his sister, who is probably seated on the sofa. I hear her voice when she says, "You're such a natural."

I watch Graham's reaction to her words, but he has none. He just continues staring down at his nephew.

And then Caroline says something that makes me grip the wall behind me. "You would make such a good father, Graham." Her words fly through the air and reach me all the way in the next room.

I'm convinced she wouldn't have said what she said if she knew I could hear her. I wait for Graham's response, curious if he'll even have one.

He does.

"I know," he says quietly, looking over at Caroline. "It devastates me that it still hasn't happened yet."

I slip my hand over my mouth because I'm scared of what might happen if I don't. I might gasp, or cry, or vomit.

I'm in my car now.

Driving.

I couldn't face him after that. Those few sentences confirmed all of my fears. Why would Caroline bring it up? Why would he respond to her with such bluntness, but never tell *me* the truth about how he feels?

This is the first moment I've felt like I'm disappointing his family. What do his sisters say to him? What does his mother say? Do they wish he could have children more than they wish he would stay married to me?

I've never thought about this from their perspective. I don't like how these thoughts are making me feel. Ashamed. Like maybe I'm not only preventing Graham from ever having a child, but I'm preventing his family from being able to love a child that Graham would be perfectly capable of creating if not for me.

I pull into a parking lot to gather myself. I wipe my tears and tell myself to forget I ever heard that. I pull my phone out of my purse to text Graham.

Traffic is terrible. Tell Caroline I won't be able to stop by until tomorrow.

I hit send and lean back in my seat, trying so hard to get their conversation out of my head, but it plays over and over again.

"You would make such a good father, Graham."

"I know. It devastates me that it still hasn't happened yet."

I'm standing at the refrigerator two hours later when Graham finally returns home from Caroline's. I know I'm stressed when I clean out the refrigerator and that's exactly what I've spent the last half hour doing. He lays his things on the kitchen counter. His keys, his briefcase, a bottle of water. He walks over to me and leans in, kissing me on the cheek. I force a smile and when I do, I notice this is the hardest I've ever had to force a smile.

"How was the visit?" I ask him.

He reaches around me into the refrigerator. "Good." He grabs a soda. "The baby is cute."

He's acting so casual about it all, like he didn't admit out loud today that he's devastated he isn't a father.

"Did you get to hold him?"

"No," Graham says. "He was sleeping the whole time I was there."

I snap my eyes back to his. *Why did he just lie to me?*

It feels like the inside walls of my chest are being torched as I try to keep my emotions from surfacing but I can't let go of his admission that he's devastated he hasn't become a father yet. *Why does he stay?*

I close the refrigerator door even though I haven't cleaned out the side drawers. I need to get out of this room. I feel too much guilt when I look at him. "I'll be up late tonight. I have a lot of work to catch up on in my office. Dinner's in the microwave if you're hungry." I walk toward my office. Before I close the door all the way, I glance back into the kitchen.

Graham's hands are pressed against the counter and his head is hanging between his shoulders. He stays like this for almost an entire minute, but then he pushes off the bar with force, as if he's angry at something. Or someone.

Before I can close the door to my office, he looks in my

direction. Our eyes meet. We stare at each other for a few seconds and it's the first time I've ever felt like he was a complete stranger. I have absolutely no clue what he's thinking right now.

This is the moment when I know I should ask him what he's thinking. This is the moment when I should tell him what I'm thinking. This is the moment I should be honest with him and admit that maybe we should open that box.

But instead of being brave and finally speaking truth, I choke on my inner coward. I look away from him and close the door.

We resume the dance.

Chapter Thirteen

Then

Every minute I've spent with him today surprises me more than the last.

Every time he opens his mouth or smiles or touches me, all I can think is, "What would possess Sasha to cheat on this man with *Ethan*?"

Her trash, my treasure.

His childhood home is everything I imagined it would be. Full of laughter and stories and parents who look at him like he was sent straight from heaven. He's the youngest of four kids and the only boy. I didn't get to meet any of his sisters today because two of them live out of state and one of them had to cancel dinner.

Graham gets his looks from his father. His father is a solid man with sad eyes and a happy soul. His mother is petite.

Shorter than me, but carries herself with a confidence even bigger than Graham's.

She's cautious of me. I can tell she wants to like me, but I can also tell she doesn't want to see her son get his heart broken again. She must have liked Sasha at one point. She tries to pry about our "relationship" but Graham feeds her nothing but fiction.

"How long have you two been seeing each other?"

He puts his arm around my shoulders and says, "A while."

A day.

"Has Graham met your parents yet, Quinn?"

Graham says, "A few times. They're great."

Never. And they're terrible.

His mother smiles. "That's nice. Where did you meet?"

"In my office building," he says.

I don't even know where he works.

Graham is having fun with this. Every time he makes up a story about us, I squeeze his leg or nudge him as I try to stifle my laughter. At one point, he tells his mother we met at a vending machine. He says, "Her Twizzlers were stuck in the machine, so I put a dollar in and bought Twizzlers so that hers would get unstuck. But you wouldn't believe what happened." He looks at me and urges me to finish the lie. "Tell them what happened next, Quinn."

I squeeze his leg so hard he winces. "His Twizzlers got stuck in the machine, too."

Graham laughs. "Can you believe it? Neither one of us got Twizzlers. So I took her to lunch in the food court and the rest is history."

I have to bite my cheek to keep from laughing. Luckily, he was right about his mother's food, so I spend most of the meal with my mouth full. His mother is an amazing cook.

When she goes to the kitchen to finish the pie, Graham says, "You want a tour of the house?"

I grab his hand as he leads me out of the dining room. As soon as we're in private, I shove him in the chest. "You lied to your parents like twenty times in under an hour!"

He grabs my hands, pulling me to him. "But it was fun, wasn't it?"

I can't deny the smile that's breaking through. "Yeah. It really was."

Graham lowers his mouth to mine and kisses me. "You want a typical tour of a typical house or do you want to go to the basement and see my childhood bedroom?"

"That's not even a question."

He leads me to the basement and flips on the light. There's a faded poster of the table of elements hanging on the wall of the stairwell. He flips on another light when we reach the bottom of the stairs, revealing a teenage boy's bedroom that looks like it hasn't been touched since he moved out. It's like a secret portal straight into the mind of Graham Wells. *I finally learned his last name over dinner.*

"She refuses to redecorate it," he says, walking backward into the room. "I still have to sleep in here when I visit." He kicks at a basketball lying on the floor. It's flat, so it barely rolls away from him. "I hate it. It reminds me of high school."

"You didn't like high school?"

He makes a quick gesture around the room. "I liked science and math more than I liked girls. Imagine what high school was like for me."

His dresser is covered in science trophies and picture

frames. Not a single sports award in sight. I pick up one of his family photos and bring it in closer for inspection. It's a picture of Graham and his three older sisters. They all favor their mother heavily. And then there's the lanky preteen with braces in the middle. "Wow."

He's standing right behind me now, looking over my shoulder. "I was the poster child for awkward phases."

I place the picture back on the dresser. "You'd never know it now."

Graham walks to his bed and takes a seat on the Star Wars comforter. He leans back on his hands and admires me as I continue to look around the room. "Did I already tell you how much I like that dress?"

I look down at my dress. I wasn't prepared to meet the parents of a man I'm not even dating, so I didn't have a whole lot of clean laundry. I chose a simple navy blue cotton dress and paired it with a white sweater. When I walked out of my bedroom before we left my apartment, Graham saluted me like I was in the navy. I immediately turned around to go change, but he grabbed me and told me I looked really beautiful.

"You did tell me that," I say, leaning back on my heels.

His eyes drag up my legs, slowly. "I'm not gonna lie, though. I really wish you would have worn your scuba gear."

"I'm never telling you my dreams again."

Graham laughs and says, "You have to. Every day for as long as I know you."

I smile and then spin around to read some of the awards on his wall. There are so many awards. "Are you smart?" I glance over at him. "Like *really* smart?"

He shrugs. "Just a little above average. A by-product of

being a nerd. I had absolutely no game with the girls so I spent most of my time in here studying."

I can't tell if he's kidding because if I had to guess what he was like in high school based off what I know about him now, I'd say he was the high school quarterback who dated the head cheerleader.

"Were you still a virgin when you graduated high school?"

He crinkles up his nose. "Sophomore in college. I was nineteen. Hell, I was eighteen before I even kissed a girl." He leans forward, clasping his hands between his knees. "In fact, you're the first girl I've ever brought down here."

"No way. What about Sasha?"

"She came to dinner a few times, but I never showed her my old bedroom. I don't know why."

"Whatever. You probably tell that to all the girls you bring down here. Then you seduce them on your Star Wars comforter."

"Open that top drawer," he says. "I guarantee you there's a condom in there that's been there since I was sixteen."

I pull open the drawer and push things out of the way. It looks like a junk drawer. Old receipts, file folders, loose change. *A condom in the back.* I laugh and pull it out, flipping it over in my fingers. "It expired three years ago." I look at Graham and he's staring at the condom in my hand like he's wondering how accurate expiration dates are. I slip the condom into my bra. "I'm keeping it."

Graham smiles appreciatively at me. I like the way he looks at me. I've felt cute before. Beautiful, even. But I'm not sure I've ever known what sexy felt like until him.

Graham leans forward again, scooting to the edge of his bed. He crooks his finger, wanting me to come closer. He has that look in his eyes again. The look he had that night in the restaurant when he touched my knee. That look sends the same heat through me now, just like it did then.

I take a few steps, but stop a couple of feet from him. He sits up straight. "Come closer, Quinn." The desire in his voice whirls through my chest and stomach.

I take another step. He slides his hand around the back of my knee and pulls me the last step toward him. Chills break out on my legs and arms from his touch.

He's looking up at me and I'm looking down at him. His bed sits low to the floor, so his mouth is dangerously close to my panty line. I swallow when the hand he has wrapped around my leg begins to slide slowly up the back of my thigh.

I'm not prepared for the sensation his touch sends through me. I close my eyes and sway a little, steadying myself with two firm hands on his shoulders. I look down at him again, just as he presses his lips against the dress covering my stomach.

He holds eye contact with me as he slides his other hand to the back of my other thigh. I'm completely engulfed by my own heartbeat. I feel it everywhere, all at once.

Graham begins to bunch my dress up in his hands, little by little, crawling it up my thighs. He slides his hands and the dress up to my waist, then presses his mouth to the top of my thigh. I move my hands to his hair, gasping quietly as his lips move over my panties.

Holy shit.

I can feel the intense heat from his mouth as he kisses me there. It's a soft kiss, right against the front of my panties, but it doesn't matter how soft it is. I feel it all the way to my core and it makes me shudder.

I clench my fingers in his hair, pressing myself closer to his mouth. His hands are on my ass now, pulling me toward him. The soft kisses begin to turn into firm kisses and before he even has the chance to pull down my panties, a tremor starts to rush through me, unexpected, sudden, explosive.

I pull away from him with a whimper, but he pulls me back to his mouth, kissing me there harder until I'm gripping his shoulders, needing his strength to continue standing. My whole body begins to shudder and I struggle to remain quiet and remain upright as the whole bedroom spins around me.

My arms are shaking and my legs are weak as his kisses come to a stop. He slides his mouth against my thigh and looks up at me. It takes everything in me to hold eye contact with him as he pushes my dress up a little more and presses a kiss against the bare skin of my stomach.

Graham grips me at the waist. I'm completely out of breath and a little in shock at what just happened. And how fast it happened. And the fact that I want more of him. I want to lower myself on top of him and put this condom to use.

As if he can read my mind, Graham says, "How accurate do you think that expiration date is?"

I lower myself onto his lap and straddle him, feeling just how serious his question was. I brush my lips across his. "I'm sure the expiration date is just a precaution."

Graham grabs the back of my head and dips his tongue inside my mouth, kissing me with a groan. He slips his fingers in my bra and pulls out the condom, then stops kissing me long enough to tear it open with his teeth. He turns me, pushing me onto his Star Wars comforter. I hook my thumbs inside my panties and slide them off as he unzips his jeans.

I'm lying back on the bed as he kneels onto the mattress and puts the condom on. I don't even get a good look at him before he lowers himself on top of me.

He kisses me as he begins to slowly push himself into me. My whole body tenses and I moan. Maybe a little too loudly, because he laughs against my mouth. "Shh," he says against my lips with a smile. "We're supposed to be touring the house right now. Not each other."

I laugh, but as soon as he begins to push into me again, I hold my breath.

"Jesus, Quinn." He breathes against my neck and then thrusts against me. We're both a little too loud now. He holds still once he's inside me, both of us doing our best to stay as quiet as we can. He begins to move, causing me to gasp, but he covers my mouth with his, kissing me deeply.

He alternates between kissing me and watching me, doing both things with an intensity I'm not sure I've ever experienced. He pauses his lips so that they hover just above mine, occasionally brushing them as we fight to remain silent. He keeps his eyes focused on mine while he moves inside of me.

He's kissing me again when he starts to come.

His tongue is deep inside my mouth and the only reason I know he's about to finish is because he holds his breath and stops moving for a few seconds. It's so subtle as he fights to remain as quiet as possible. The muscles in his back clench beneath my palms and he never once breaks eye contact when he finally does pull away from my lips.

I wait for him to collapse on top of me, out of breath, but he doesn't. He somehow holds himself up after it's over, watching me like he's scared he might miss something. He dips his head and kisses me again. And even when he pulls out of me, he still doesn't collapse on top of me. He puts all his weight on his side as he eases down beside me without breaking the kiss.

I slide my hand through his hair and hold him against my mouth. We kiss for so long, I almost forget where I am.

When he breaks for air, he watches me silently for a moment, his hand still on my cheek, and then he dips his head and kisses me again like he doesn't know how to stop. I don't think I know how to stop this, either. I wish more than anything we were somewhere else. My place . . . his place . . . anywhere other than a place where we have to stop and go back upstairs eventually.

I am not inexperienced when it comes to sex. But I think I am inexperienced when it comes to this. The feeling of not wanting it to be over long after it's over. The feeling of wishing I could bury myself inside his chest so I could be closer to him. Maybe this isn't new for him, but based on the way he's looking at me between all the kissing, I would say there's more confusion in his expression than familiarity.

Several seconds pass as we stare at each other. Neither of us speaks. Maybe he doesn't have anything to say, but I can't speak because of the severe intensity building inside my chest. The sex was great. Quick, but incredible.

But this thing that's happening right now . . . the not being able to let go . . . the not wanting to stop kissing . . . the not being able to look away . . . I can't tell if this is just a side to sex I've never experienced or if this goes deeper than that. Like maybe sex isn't as deep as it gets. Maybe there's a whole level of connection I didn't know could exist.

Graham closes his eyes for a few seconds, then presses

his forehead against mine. After releasing a quick sigh, he pushes himself off me, almost as if he had to force his eyes shut in order to separate us. He helps me up and I look for my panties while he disposes of the condom and zips up his jeans.

It's quiet while I dress. We don't look at each other. He picks up the empty condom wrapper from the floor and tosses it into the trash can beside his bed.

Now we're facing each other. My arms are crossed over my chest and he's looking at me like he isn't sure if the last fifteen minutes actually happened. I'm looking at him like I wish it could happen again.

He opens his mouth like he's about to say something, but then he just gives his head a quick shake and steps forward, grabs my face and kisses me again. It's a rough kiss, like he isn't finished with me. I kiss him back with just as much intensity. After a minute of the kiss, he starts to walk me backward toward the stairs. We break for air and he just laughs, pressing his lips into my hair.

We make it up two steps before I realize I haven't looked in a mirror. I just had sex with this man and I'm about to have to go smile at his parents. I frantically comb my fingers through my hair and straighten out my dress. "How do I look?"

Graham smiles. "Like you just had sex."

I try to shove him in the chest, but he's faster than me. He grabs my hands and turns us until my back is against the wall of the stairwell. He straightens out a few strands of hair and then wipes his thumbs under my eyes. "There," he says. "You look beautiful. And innocent, like you just took a typical tour of the house." He kisses me again and I know he probably means for it to be short and sweet, but I grab his head and pull him closer. I can't get enough of the taste of him. I just want to be back at my apartment, in my bed with him, kissing him. I don't want to have to go upstairs and pretend I want pie when all I want is Graham.

"Quinn," he whispers, grabbing my wrists and pushing them against the wall. "How fast do you think you can eat a slice of pie?"

It's good to know our priorities are aligned. "Pretty damn fast."

Chapter Fourteen

Now

Despite all the Thursday nights that Graham has returned home smelling like beer, I've never actually seen him drunk. I think he chooses not to drink more than one or two beers at a time because he's still so full of guilt over losing his best friend, Tanner, all those years ago. The feeling of being drunk probably reminds him of his devastation. Much like how sex reminds me of *my* devastation.

I wonder what he's devastated about tonight?

This is the first time he's ever had to be escorted home by a coworker on a Thursday night. I watch from the window as Graham stumbles toward the front door, one arm thrown haphazardly around a guy who is struggling to get him to the house.

I move to the front door and unlock it. As soon as I open it, Graham looks up and smiles widely at me. "Quinn!"

He waves toward me; turning his head to the guy he's with. "Quinn, this is my good friend Morris. He's my good friend."

Morris nods apologetically.

"Thanks for getting him home," I say. I reach out and pull Graham from him, wrapping his arm around my shoulders. "Where is his car?"

Morris throws a thumb over his shoulder, just as Graham's car pulls into the driveway. Another of Graham's co-workers steps out of the car. I recognize him from Graham's office. I think his name is Bradley.

Bradley walks toward the front door while Graham puts both arms around me, placing even more of his weight on me. Bradley hands me the keys and laughs.

"First time we could get him to drink more than two," he says, nudging his head toward Graham. "He's good at a lot of things, but the man can't hold his alcohol."

Morris laughs. "Lightweight." They both wave goodbye and walk toward Morris's car. I step into the house with Graham and close the front door.

"I was gonna take a cab," Graham mutters. He releases me and walks toward the living room, falling onto the sofa. I would laugh and find this humorous if I weren't so worried that the reason he decided to drink too much tonight might have something to do with how upset he was after holding his new nephew. Or maybe it's his feelings about our marriage as a whole that he wanted to numb for a while.

I walk to the kitchen to get him a glass of water. When I take it back to him in the living room, he's sitting up on the couch. I hand him the water, noticing how different his eyes look. He's smiling at me as he takes a sip. He hasn't looked this happy or content in a very long time. Seeing him drunk makes me realize just how sad he looks now when he's sober. I didn't notice his sadness consumed him even more than it used to. I probably didn't notice because sadness is like a spiderweb. You don't see it until you're caught up in it, and then you have to claw at yourself to try to break free.

I wonder how long Graham has been trying to break free. I stopped trying years ago. I just let the web consume me.

"Quinn," Graham says, letting his head fall back against the couch. "You are so fucking beautiful." His eyes scroll down my body and then stop at my hand. He wraps his fingers around my wrist and pulls me to him. I'm stiff. I don't give in to the pull. I wish he were drunk enough that he would pass out on the couch. Instead, he's just drunk enough to forget he hasn't initiated sex since that night he slept in the guest room. He's just drunk enough to pretend we haven't been struggling as much as we have.

Graham leans forward and grabs me by my waist, pulling me down onto the couch next to him. His kiss is inebriated and fluid as he pushes me onto my back. My arms are above my head and his tongue is in my mouth and he tastes so good that I forget to be turned off by him for a moment. That moment turns into two and soon he has my T-shirt pushed up around my waist and his pants undone. Every time I open my eyes and look at him, he's looking back at me with eyes so different from my own. So far from the despondence I've permanently acquired.

The lack of sadness in him is intriguing enough for me to let him have me, but not intriguing enough for me to respond to him with as much need as he's taking me.

In the beginning of our marriage, we used to have sex

almost daily, but Thursdays were the day I looked forward to the most. It was one of my favorite nights of the week. I'd put on lingerie and wait for him in the bedroom. Sometimes I would throw on one of his T-shirts and wait for him in the kitchen. It really didn't matter what I was wearing. He'd walk in the door and I'd suddenly not be wearing it anymore.

We've had so much sex in our marriage, I know every inch of his body. I know every sound he makes and what those sounds mean. I know that he likes to be on top the most, but he's never minded when I wanted to take over. I know he likes to keep his eyes open. I know that he loves to kiss during sex. I know that he likes it in the mornings but prefers it late at night. I know everything there is to know about him sexually.

Yet in the last two months . . . we haven't had sex at all. The closest we've come until now is when he made out with me in the bathroom at his parents' house.

He hasn't initiated it since then and neither have I. And we haven't talked about the last time we had sex since it happened. I haven't had to keep up with my ovulation cycle since then and honestly it's been a big relief. After finally going a couple of months without tracking my cycle, I realize how much I would prefer never having sex again. That way, every month when my period comes, it would be completely expected and not at all devastating.

I try to reconcile my need to avoid sex with my need for Graham. Just because I don't desire sex doesn't mean I don't desire him. I've just forced it to be a different kind of desire now. An emotional one. It's my physical desires that never end well. I desire his touch, but if I allow it, it leads to sex. I desire his kiss, but if I kiss him too much, it leads to sex. I desire his flirtatious side, but if I enjoy it too much, it leads to sex.

I want so much to enjoy my husband without the one thing I know he needs the most and the one thing I want the least. But he makes so many sacrifices for me; I know I should sometimes do the same for him. I just wish sex wasn't a sacrifice for me.

But it is. And it's one I decide to make for him tonight. It's been too long, and he's been way too patient.

I lift one leg over the back of the couch and lower one to the floor, just as he pushes into me. His warm breath rolls down my throat as he thrusts into me repeatedly.

Today is the thirteenth.

What is fourteen days from today?

"Quinn," he whispers, his lips barely touching mine. I keep my eyes closed and my body limp, allowing him to use me to fuck the drunkenness out of himself. "Kiss me, Quinn."

I open my mouth but keep my eyes closed. My arms are resting loosely above my head and I'm counting on my fingers how many days it's been since I last had a period. Am I even ovulating? I'm almost finished counting when Graham grabs my right hand and wraps it around his neck. He buries his face into my hair while gripping one of my legs, wrapping it around his waist.

I'm not.

I'm five days past ovulation.

I sigh heavily; disappointed that there won't even be a chance this leads to anything. It's difficult enough bringing myself to make love at all anymore, so the fact that this time doesn't even count fills me with regret. Why couldn't this have happened last week, instead?

Graham pauses above me. I wait for his release, but nothing about him tenses. He just pulls his face away from my hair and looks down at me. His eyebrows are drawn together and he shakes his head, but then drops his face to my neck again, thrusting against me. "Can't you at least pretend you still want me? Sometimes I feel like I'm making love to a corpse."

His own words make him pause.

Tears are falling down my cheeks when he pulls out of me with regret.

His breath is hot against my neck, but this time I hate the way it feels. The way it smells just like the beer that gave him the uninhibited nerve to say those words to me. "Get off me."

"I'm sorry. I'm sorry."

I press my hands against his chest, ignoring the immediate and intense regret in his voice. "Get the fuck off me."

He rolls onto his side, grabbing my shoulder, attempting to roll me toward him. "Quinn, I didn't mean it. I'm drunk, I'm sorry . . ."

I push off the couch and practically run out of the living room without entertaining his apologies. I go straight to the shower and wash him out of me while I let the water wash away my tears.

"Can't you at least pretend you still want me?"

I squeeze my eyes shut as the mortification rolls through me.

"Sometimes I feel like I'm making love to a corpse."

I swipe angrily at my tears. Of course he feels like he's making love to a corpse. It's because he *is*. I haven't felt alive inside in years. I've slowly been rotting away, and that rot is now eating at my marriage to the point that I can no longer hide it.

And Graham can no longer stand it.

When I finish in the shower, I expect to find him in our bed, but he isn't there. He's probably so drunk; he just passed out on the sofa. As angry as I am at him for saying what he said, I also feel enough compassion to check on him and make sure he's okay.

When I walk through the dark kitchen toward the living room, I don't even see him standing at the counter until I pass him and he grabs my arm. I gasp from the unexpectedness of it.

I look up at him, ready to yell at him, but I can't. It's hard to yell at someone for speaking their truth. The moon is casting just enough light into the windows and I can see the sadness has returned to his eyes. He doesn't say anything. He just pulls me to him and holds me.

No . . . he *clings* to me.

The back of my T-shirt is clenched into two solid fists as he tightens his grip around me. I can feel his regret for allowing those words to slip from his mouth, but he doesn't tell me he's sorry again. He just holds me in silence because he knows at this point, an apology is futile. Apologies are good for admitting regret, but they do very little in removing the truth from the actions that caused the regret.

I allow him to hold me until my hurt feelings put a wedge between us. I pull away and look down at my feet for a moment, wondering if I want to say anything to him. Wondering if he's going to say anything to me. When the room remains silent, I turn and walk to our bedroom. He follows me, but all we do is crawl into bed, turn our backs toward each other and avoid the inevitable.

Chapter Fifteen

Then

I ate the slice of pie in five bites.

Graham's parents seemed a little confused by our hasty exit. He told his mother we had tickets to a fireworks show and we needed to go before we missed the grand finale. I was relieved she didn't catch the metaphorical part of his lie.

We do very little speaking on the way home. Graham says he likes to drive with the windows down at night. He turns the music up and grabs my hand, holding it all the way back to my place.

When we reach my apartment, I open the door and make it halfway across the living room before I realize he hasn't followed me inside. I turn around and he's leaning against the frame of the door like he has no intention of coming in.

There's a look of concern in his eye, so I walk back to the door. "Are you okay?"

He nods, but his nod is unconvincing. His eyes flitter around the room and then lock on mine with way too much seriousness. I was getting used to the playful, sarcastic side of Graham. Now the intense, serious side has reappeared.

Graham pushes off the door and runs a hand through his hair. "Maybe this is . . . too much. Too fast."

Heat immediately rises to my cheeks, but not the good kind of heat. It's the kind when you get so angry, your chest burns. "Are you kidding me? You're the one who forced me to meet your parents before I even knew your last name." I press a hand to my forehead, completely blown away that he decides to back down now. *After* he fucks me. I laugh incredulously at my own stupidity. "This is unreal."

I step back to close the door, but he steps forward and pushes it open, pulling me to him by my waist. "No," he says, shaking his head adamantly. "No." He kisses me, but pulls back before I would even have the chance to deny him. "It's just . . . *God,* I feel like I can't even find words right now." His head falls back like he can't figure out how to process his confusion. He releases me and steps out into the hallway. He starts pacing back and forth while he gathers his thoughts. He looks just as torn as he did the first time I saw him. He was pacing then, too, outside of Ethan's door.

Graham takes a step toward me, gripping the doorframe. "We've spent one day together, Quinn. *One.* It's been perfect and fun and you are so beautiful. I want to pick you up and carry you to your bed and stay inside you all night and tomorrow and the next day and it's . . ." He runs a hand through his unruly hair and then grips the back of his neck. "It's making my head swim and I feel like if I don't back off now, I'm gonna be real disappointed when I find out you don't feel the same way."

I take at least ten seconds to catch up to everything he just said. My mouth opens and before I can tell him he's right, that it's too soon and too fast, I say, "I know what you mean. It's terrifying."

He steps closer. "It is."

"Have you ever felt like this before? This fast?"

"Never. Not even close."

"Me neither."

He slips his hand against my neck and slides his fingers through my hair. His other hand presses against my lower back as he pulls me to him. He asks the question in a whisper against my lips. "Do you want me to leave?"

I answer him with a kiss.

Everything that happens next isn't questioned by either of us. There's no second-guessing as he kicks my door shut. No worrying if this is too fast when we tear away each other's clothes. Neither of us hesitates on the way to my bedroom.

And for the next hour, the only question he asks me is, "Do you want to be on top now?"

He only needs my answer once, but I say yes at least five times before we're finished.

Now he's lying on his back and I'm wrapped around him like there's not two feet of mattress on either side of us. My legs are intertwined with his and my hand is tracing circles over his chest. We've been mostly quiet since we finished, but not because we don't have anything to say. I think we're just reflecting on what life was like two days ago compared to what it's like now.

It's a lot to take in.

Graham trails his fingers up and down my arm. His lips meet the top of my head in a quick kiss. "Did Ethan ever try to get you back?"

"Yeah, he tried for a few weeks." I think it goes without saying that he wasn't successful. "What about Sasha?"

"Yep," he says. "She was relentless. She called me three times a day for a month. My voice mail stayed full."

"You should have changed your number."

"I couldn't. It's the only form of contact you had for me."

His admission makes me smile. "I probably never would have called you," I admit. "I kept your number on my wall because I liked how it made me feel. But I didn't think it was a good idea, given how we met."

"Do you still feel that way?"

I slide on top of him and his concerned expression is won over by a smile. "At this point I don't really care how we met. I only care that we met."

Graham kisses the corner of my mouth, threading our hands together. "I actually thought you took Ethan back and that's why you never called me."

"There's no way I would have taken him back. Especially after he tried to blame the whole affair on Sasha. He painted her out to be some kind of temptress who seduced him. He actually called her a whore once. That was the last time I spoke to him."

Graham shakes his head. "Sasha isn't a whore. She's a relatively good person who sometimes makes terrible and selfish decisions." He rolls me onto my back and begins to run a lazy finger over my stomach in circles. "I'm sure they did it because they thought they wouldn't get caught."

I have no idea how he talks so calmly about it. I was so

angry in the weeks following Ethan's affair. I took it personally, like they had the affair just to spite us. Graham looks at the affair like they did it *despite* us.

"Do you still talk to her?"

"Hell, no," he says with a laugh. "Just because I don't think she's a malicious person doesn't mean I want anything to do with her."

I smile at that truth.

Graham kisses the tip of my nose and then pulls back. "Are you relieved it happened? Or do you miss him?"

His questions don't seem to come from a place of jealousy at all. Graham just seems curious about the things that have happened in my life. Which is why I answer him with complete transparency. "I missed him for a while, but now that I've had a chance to reflect, we really had nothing in common." I roll onto my side and prop my head up on my hand. "On paper we had a lot in common. But in here," I touch my chest. "It didn't make sense. I loved him, but I don't think it was the kind of love that could withstand a marriage."

Graham laughs. "You say that like marriage is a Category 5 hurricane."

"Not all the time. But I definitely think there are Category 5 *moments* in every marriage. I don't think Ethan and I could have survived those moments."

Graham stares up at the ceiling in thought. "I know what you mean. I would have disappointed Sasha as a husband."

"Why in the world do you think that?"

"It's more a reflection of her than myself." Graham reaches up to my cheek and wipes something away.

"Then that would make her a disappointing wife. It wouldn't make you a disappointing husband."

Graham smiles at me appreciatively. "Do you remember what your fortune cookie said?"

I shrug. "It's been a while. Something about flaws, accompanied by a grammatical error."

Graham laughs. "It said, *If you only shine light on your flaws, all your perfects will dim.*"

I love that he kept my fortune. I love it even more that he has it memorized.

"We're all full of flaws. Hundreds of them. They're like tiny holes all over our skin. And like your fortune said, sometimes we shine too much light on our own flaws. But there are some people who try to ignore their own flaws by shining light on other people's to the point that the other person's flaws become their only focus. They pick at them, little by little, until they rip wide open and that's all we become to them. One giant, gaping flaw." Graham makes eye contact with me, and even though what he's saying is kind of depressing, he doesn't seem disappointed. "Sasha is that type of person. If I had married her, no matter how much I would have tried to prevent it, she would eventually be disappointed in me. She was incapable of focusing on the positive in other people."

I'm relieved for Graham. The thought of him being in an unhappy marriage makes me sad for him. And the thought of potentially being in an unhappy marriage hits a little too close to home. I frown, knowing I almost went through with that same type of marriage. I stare down at my hand, unconsciously rubbing my naked ring finger. "Ethan used to do that. But I didn't notice until after we broke up. I realized I felt better about myself without him than I did with him." I look back up at Graham. "For so long, I thought he was good for me. I feel so naive. I no longer trust my own judgment."

"Don't be so hard on yourself," he says. "Now you know exactly what to look for. When you meet someone who is good for you, they won't fill you with insecurities by focusing on your flaws. They'll fill you with inspiration, because they'll focus on all the best parts of you."

I pray he can't feel the intense pounding of my heart right now. I swallow hard and then choke out a pathetic sentence. "That's . . . really beautiful."

His pointed stare doesn't waver until he closes his eyes and presses his mouth to mine. We kiss for a quiet moment, but it's so intense, I feel like I can't breathe when we separate. I look down and suck in a quiet breath before looking him in the eye again. I force a grin in an attempt to ease the intensity in my chest. "I can't believe you kept that fortune."

"I can't believe you kept my number on your wall for six months."

"Touché."

Graham reaches to my face and runs his thumb over my lips. "What do you think is one of your biggest flaws?"

I kiss the tip of his thumb. "Does family count as a flaw?"

"Nope."

I think on it a moment longer. "I have a lot. But I think the one I would like to change if I could is my inability to read people. It's hard for me to look at someone and know exactly what they're thinking."

"I don't think many people can read people. They just think they can."

"Maybe."

Graham readjusts himself, wrapping my leg over him

while his eyes fill with playfulness. He leans forward and brushes his lips across mine, teasing me with a swipe of his tongue. "Try to read me right now," he whispers. "What am I thinking?" He pulls back and looks down at my mouth.

"You're thinking you want to move to Idaho and buy a potato farm."

He laughs. "That is *exactly* what I was thinking, Quinn." He rolls onto his back, pulling me on top of him. I push against his chest and sit up, straddling him.

"What about you? What's your biggest flaw?"

The smile disappears from Graham's face and his eyes are suddenly sad again. The variance in his expressions is so extreme. When he's sad, he looks sadder than anyone I've ever known. But when he's happy, he looks happier than anyone I've ever known.

Graham threads his fingers through mine and squeezes them. "I made a really stupid choice once that had some devastating consequences." His voice is quieter and I can tell he doesn't want to talk about it. But I love that he does anyway. "I was nineteen. I was with my best friend, Tanner. His sixteen-year-old brother, Alec, was with us. We had been at a party and I was the least drunk of the three of us, so I drove us the two miles home."

Graham squeezes my hands and inhales a breath. He's not looking me in the eye, so I know his story doesn't end well and I hate it for him. It makes me wonder if this is the flaw that makes him look as sad as he does sometimes.

"We had a wreck half a mile from my house. Tanner died. Alec was thrown from the vehicle and broke several bones. The wreck wasn't our fault. A truck ran a stop sign, but it didn't matter because I wasn't sober. They charged me with a DUI and I spent a night in jail. But since I didn't have a record, I was only charged with injury to a child and put on a year of probation for what happened to Alec." Graham releases a heavy sigh. "Isn't that fucked up? I got charged for the injuries Alec received in the wreck, but wasn't charged in the death of my best friend."

I can feel the weight of his sadness in my chest as I stare at him. There's so much of it. "You say that like you feel guilty you weren't charged for his death."

Graham's eyes finally meet mine. "I feel guilty every day that I'm alive and Tanner isn't."

I hate that he felt he had to tell me this. It's obviously hard to talk about, but I appreciate that he did. I bring one of his hands up to my mouth and I kiss it.

"It does get better with time," Graham says. "When I tell myself it could have just as easily been me in that passenger seat and Tanner behind the wheel. We both made stupid decisions that night. We were both at fault. But no matter what consequences I suffer as a result, I'm alive and he isn't. And I can't help but wonder if my reactions could have been faster had I not been drinking. What if I hadn't decided I was sober enough to drive? What if I'd been able to swerve and miss that truck? I think that's what feeds most of my guilt."

I don't even try to offer him reassuring words. Sometimes situations don't have a positive side. They just have a whole lot of sad sides. I reach down and touch his cheek. Then I touch the corners of his sad eyes. My fingers move to the scar on his collarbone that he showed me last night. "Is that where you got this scar?"

He nods.

I lower myself on top of him and press my lips to his scar. I kiss it from one end to the other and then lift up and look Graham in the eye. "I'm sorry that happened."

He forces a smile, but it fades as fast as it appeared. "Thank you."

I move my lips to his cheek and kiss him there, softly. "I'm sorry you lost your best friend."

I can feel Graham release a rush of air as his arms wrap around me. "Thank you."

I drag my lips from his cheek to his mouth and I kiss him gently. Then I pull back and look at him again. "I'm sorry," I whisper.

Graham watches me in silence for a few brief seconds, then he rolls me over so that he's on top of me. He presses his hand against my throat, gripping my jaw with gentle fingers. He watches my face as he pushes inside me, his mouth waiting in eagerness for my gasp. As soon as my lips part, his tongue dives between them and he kisses me the same way he fucks me. Unhurried. Rhythmic. Determined.

Chapter Sixteen

Now

The first time I dreamt Graham was cheating on me, I woke up in the middle of the night drenched in sweat. I was gasping for air because in my dream, I was crying so hard I couldn't breathe. Graham woke up and immediately put his arms around me. He asked me what was wrong and I was so mad at him. I remember pushing him away because the anger from my dream was still there, as if he'd actually cheated on me. When I told him what happened, he laughed and just held me and kissed me until I was no longer angry. Then he made love to me.

The next day he sent me flowers. The card said, *"I'm sorry for what I did to you in your nightmare. Please forgive me tonight when you dream."*

I still have the card. I smile every time I think about it. Some men can't even apologize for the mistakes they make in reality. But my husband apologizes for the mistakes he makes in my dreams.

I wonder if he'll apologize tonight.

I wonder if he actually has anything to apologize for.

I don't know why I'm suspicious. It started the night he came home too drunk to remember it the next morning and the suspicion continued to last Thursday, when he came home and didn't smell like beer at all. I've never been suspicious of him before this month, even after the trust issues Ethan left me with. But something didn't feel right this past Thursday. He came straight home and changed clothes without kissing me. And it hasn't felt right since that night.

The fear hit me hard today, right in the chest. So hard, I gasped and covered my mouth.

It's as if I could feel his guilt from wherever he was in that second. I know that's impossible—for two people to be so connected that they can feel each other even when they aren't in each other's presence. I think it was more of my denial inching its way forward until it was finally front and center in my conscience.

Things are at their worst between us. We hardly communicate. We aren't affectionate. Yet still, we walk around every other room in our house and pretend we're still husband and wife. But since that drunken night, it seems like Graham stopped sacrificing. The goodbye kisses started becoming more infrequent. The hello kisses have stopped completely. He's finally stooped to my level in this marriage.

He either has something to feel guilty for or he's finally done fighting for the survival of this marriage.

Isn't that what I wanted, though? For him to stop fighting so hard for something that will only bring him more misery?

I don't drink very often but I keep wine on hand for emergencies. This certainly feels like an emergency. I drink the first glass in the kitchen while I watch the clock.

I drink the second glass on the couch while I watch the driveway.

I need the wine to still the doubts I'm having. My fingers are trembling as I stare down at the wine. My stomach feels full of worry, like I'm inside one of my nightmares.

I'm sitting on the far-right side of the couch with my feet curled beneath me. The TV isn't on. The house is dark. I'm still watching the driveway when his car finally pulls in at half past seven. I have a clear view of him as he turns off the car and the headlights fade to black. I can see him, but he can't see me.

Both of his hands are gripping the steering wheel. He's just sitting in the car like the last place he wants to be is inside this house with me. I take another sip of wine and watch as he rests his forehead against his steering wheel.

One, two, three, four, five . . .

Fifteen seconds he sits like this. Fifteen seconds of dread. Or regret. I don't know what he's feeling.

He releases the steering wheel and sits up straight. He looks in his rearview mirror and wipes his mouth. Adjusts his tie. Wipes his neck. *Breaks my heart.* Sighs heavily and then finally exits his car.

When he walks through the front door, he doesn't notice me right away. He crosses the living room, heading for the kitchen, which leads to our bedroom. He's almost to the kitchen when he finally sees me.

My wineglass is tilted to my lips. I hold his stare as I take another sip. He just watches me in silence. He's probably wondering what I'm doing sitting in the dark. Alone. Drinking wine. His eyes follow the path from me to the living room window. He sees how visible his car is from my position. How visible his actions must have been to me as he was sitting in his car. He's wondering if I saw him wipe the remnants of her off his mouth. Off his neck. He's wondering if I saw him adjust his tie. He's wondering if I saw him press his head to the steering wheel in dread. Or regret. He doesn't bring his eyes back to mine. Instead, he looks down.

"What's her name?" I somehow ask the question without it sounding spiteful. I ask it with the same tone I often use to ask him about his day.

How was your day, dear?

What's your mistress's name, dear?

Despite my pleasant tone, Graham doesn't answer me. He lifts his eyes until they meet mine, but he's quiet in his denial.

I feel my stomach turn like I might physically be sick. I'm shocked at how much his silence angers me. I'm shocked at how much more this hurts in reality than in my nightmares. I didn't think it could get worse than the nightmares.

I somehow stand up, still clenching my glass. I want to throw it. Not at him. I just need to throw it at *something*. I hate him with every part of my soul right now, but I don't blame him enough to throw the glass at him. If I could throw it at myself, I would. But I can't, so I throw it toward our wedding photo that hangs on the wall across the room.

I repeat the words as my wineglass hits the picture, shattering, bleeding down the wall and all over the floor. "What's her *fucking* name, Graham?!"

My voice is no longer pleasant.

Graham doesn't even flinch. He doesn't look at the wedding photo, he doesn't look at the bleeding floor beneath it, he doesn't look at the front door, he doesn't look at his feet. He looks me right in the eye and he says, "Andrea."

As soon as her name has fallen from his lips completely, he looks away. He doesn't want to witness what his brutal honesty does to me.

I think back to the moment I was about to have to face Ethan after finding out he cheated on me. That moment when Graham held my face in his hands and said, *"The worst thing we could do right now is show emotion, Quinn. Don't get angry. Don't cry."*

It was easier then. When Graham was on *my* side. It's not so easy being over here alone.

My knees meet the floor, but Graham isn't here to catch me. As soon as he said her name, he left the room.

I do all the things Graham told me not to do the last time this happened to me. I show emotion. I get angry. I cry.

I crawl over to the mess I made on the floor. I pick up the smaller glass shards and I place them into a pile. I'm crying too hard to see them all. I can barely see through my tears as I grab a roll of napkins to soak up the wine from the wood floor.

I hear the shower running. He's probably washing off remnants of Andrea while I wash away remnants of red wine.

The tears are nothing new, but they're different this time. I'm not crying over something that never came to be. I'm crying for something that's coming to an end.

I pick up a shard of the glass and scoot to the wall, leaning against it. I stretch my legs out in front of me and I stare down at the piece of glass. I flip my hand over and press the glass against my palm. It pierces my skin, but I continue to press harder. I watch as it goes deeper and deeper into my palm. I watch as blood bubbles up around the glass.

My chest still somehow hurts worse than my hand. *So much worse.*

I drop the shard of glass and wipe the blood away with a napkin. Then I pull my legs up and hug my knees, burying my face in them. I'm still sobbing when Graham walks back into the room. I hug myself tighter when he kneels next to me. I feel his hand in my hair, his lips in my hair. His arms around me. He pulls me against him and sits against the wall.

I want to scream at him, punch him, run from him. But all I can do is curl up into myself even tighter as I cry.

"Quinn." His arms are clasped firmly around me and his face is in my hair. My name is full of agony when it falls from his lips. I've never hated it so much. I cover my ears because I don't want to hear his voice right now. But he doesn't say another word. Not even when I pull away from him, walk to our bedroom, and lock the door.

Chapter Seventeen

Then

Inseparable.

That's what we are.

It's been two and a half months since I supposedly gave him a "look" that night at the restaurant.

Even after spending every waking moment together outside of our respective jobs, I still miss him. I have never been this wrapped up in someone in my life. I never thought it was possible. It's not an unhealthy obsession, because he gives me my space if I want it. I just don't want the space. He's not possessive or overprotective. I'm not jealous or needy. It's just that the time we spend together feels like this euphoric escape and I want as much of it as I can get.

We've only slept apart once in the ten weeks we've been seeing each other. Ava and Reid got into a fight, so I let her stay with me and we talked shit about guys and ate junk food all night. It was depressingly fun, but five minutes after she walked out the door I was calling Graham. Twenty minutes after she left, he was knocking on my door. Twenty-one minutes after she left, we were making love.

That's basically what it's been. Ten weeks of nothing but sex, laughter, sex, food, sex, laughter, and more sex.

Graham jokes that we have to plateau at some point. But that point is not today.

"Jesus, Quinn." He groans against my neck as he collapses on top of me. He's out of breath and I'm no help because I can't catch mine, either.

This wasn't supposed to happen. It's Halloween and we're supposed to be at a party at Ava and Reid's house, but as soon as I pulled on my slutty T-shirt dress, Graham couldn't keep his hands off me. We almost had sex in the hallway, near the elevator, but he carried me back inside to save our dignity.

He held me to the Halloween costumes I suggested back in August. We decided to go as ourselves, only sluttier. We couldn't really figure out what a slutty slut costume of ourselves should look like, so we decided to just barely wear clothes. I have a ton of makeup on. Graham says his job is to just feel me up all night and make sure we have plenty of public displays of affection.

Our clothes are on the floor now, though, with the addition of a new rip in my shirt. The wait for that damn elevator gets us every time.

Graham leans in to me and buries his head against my neck again, kissing me until I break out in chills. "When am I going to meet your mother?"

That one question rips a hole in the moment and I feel all my joy seep out. "Never, if I can pull it off."

Graham pulls away from my neck and looks down at me. "She can't be that bad."

I release a halfhearted laugh. "Graham, she's the one who put the word *prestigious* in my wedding invitations."

"Did you judge me based on my parents?"

I loved his parents. "No, but I met them the first day we were together. I didn't even know you enough to judge you."

"You knew me, Quinn. You didn't know anything about me, but you knew *me*."

"You sound so sure of yourself."

He laughs. "I am. We figured each other out the night we met in that hallway. Sometimes people meet and none of the surface-level stuff matters because they see past all that." Graham lowers his mouth to my chest and places a kiss over my heart. "I knew everything I needed to know the first night I met you. Nothing external could ever influence my opinion of you. Even my judgment of the woman who raised you."

I want to kiss him. Or marry him. Or *fuck* him.

I settle on a kiss, but I keep it fairly quick because I'm scared if I don't pull away from him I might tell him I'm in love with him. It's right there on the tip of my tongue and it's harder keeping it in than letting it out. But I don't want to be the first one to say it. Not yet, anyway.

I quickly roll off the bed and pick up our costumes. "Fine. You can meet my mother next week." I toss him his clothes. "But tonight you're meeting Ava. Get dressed, we're late."

When I get my costume situated, Graham is still sitting on the bed, staring at me.

"What about your panties?" he asks.

My skirt is really short, and any other night I wouldn't be caught dead in it. I look down at my panties on the floor and think about how crazy it would drive him if he knew I wasn't wearing anything under this already-too-short skirt all night. I leave them on the floor and grin at him. "They don't really go with my costume."

Graham shakes his head. "You're killing me, Quinn." He stands up and gets dressed while I touch up my makeup.

We make it out the door.

We make it down the hallway.

But once again, we get distracted while we wait for the elevator.

———

"You're late." It's the only thing Ava says when she opens the door and sees me standing there with Graham. She's dressed in a two-piece pantsuit and her hair is styled like she's straight out of *Stepford Wives*. She waits until we're inside her house and then she slams the door shut. "Reid!" She yells his name and turns to look for him, but he's standing right next to her. "Oh." She tosses a hand toward Graham. "He's here."

Reid reaches out and shakes Graham's hand. "Nice to meet you."

Ava gives Graham the once-over. Then me. "Your costumes are so undignified." She walks away without looking back.

"What the hell?" I say, looking at Reid. "Why is she being so rude?"

Reid laughs. "I tried to tell her it wasn't an obvious costume."

"What is she supposed to be? A bitch?"

Reid's face reddens. He leans in to Graham and me. "She's dressed up as your mother."

Graham immediately starts to laugh. "So she's not normally that . . . unpleasant?"

I roll my eyes and grab his hand. "Come on, I need to reintroduce you to my sister."

Ava is actually nice to Graham the second time she meets him. But then she goes into character the rest of the night and pretends to be our mother. The funniest part is that no one at the party has any idea who she's supposed to be. That's just a secret among the four of us, which makes it even better every time I hear her tell someone how tired they look or how much she hates children.

At one point, she walked up to Graham and said, "How much money do you make?"

Then Ava said, "Make sure you sign a prenup before you marry my daughter."

She's so good at being our mother, I'm relieved the party is winding down because I don't think I could take another second of it.

I'm in the kitchen with her now, helping her wash dishes. "I thought you and Reid used to have a dishwasher. Have I lost my mind?" Ava lifts her foot and points toward the mini-fridge with the glass door a few feet away. "Is that a wine refrigerator? Where your dishwasher used to be?"

"Yep," she says.

"But . . . *why?*"

"Downside of marrying a French guy. He thinks an ample supply of chilled wine is more important than a dishwasher."

"That's terrible, Ava."

She shrugs. "I agreed to it because he promised he'd do most of the dishes."

"Then why are we doing the dishes?"

Ava rolls her eyes. "Because your boyfriend is a shiny new toy and my husband is enamored."

It's true. Graham and Reid have spent most of the night chatting. I hand Ava the last plate. "Reid pulled me aside earlier and told me he already likes Graham more than he ever liked Ethan."

"That makes two of us," Ava says.

"*Three* of us."

When we finish with the dishes, I peek into the living room and Graham is saying something to Reid that's requiring a lot of arm movement. I don't think I've ever seen him so animated. Reid is doubled over with laughter. Graham catches my eye and the smile that appears on his face during our quick glance sends a warmth through me. He holds my stare for a couple of seconds and then focuses his attention back on Reid. When I turn around, Ava is standing in the doorway, watching as I try to wipe the smile off my face.

"He's in love with you."

"Shh." I walk back into the kitchen and she follows me.

"That *look*," she says. She picks up a paper plate and fans herself. "That man is in love with you and he wants to marry you and he wants you to have all his babies."

I can't help but smile. "God, I hope so."

Ava stands up straight and straightens out her pantsuit. "Well, Quinn. He is very decent-looking, but as your mother, I must admit that I think you can do much richer. Now where is my martini?"

I roll my eyes. "Please stop."

Chapter Eighteen

Now

I don't know if Graham slept in the guest room or on the couch last night, but wherever he slept, I doubt he actually got any sleep. I tried to imagine what he looked like with his sad eyes and his hands in his hair. Every now and then I'd feel sorry for him, but then I'd try to imagine what Andrea looks like. What she looked like through my husband's sad eyes while he kissed her.

I wonder if Andrea knows that Graham is married. I wonder if she knows he has a wife at home who hasn't been able to get pregnant. A wife who has spent the entire night and the entire day locked inside her bedroom. A wife who finally pulled herself out of bed long enough to pack a suitcase. A wife who is . . . *done*.

I want to be gone before Graham returns home.

I haven't called my mother to tell her I'm coming to stay

with her yet. I probably won't call her. I'll just show up. I dread the conversation with her enough to put as much time between now and having to speak with her about it.

"*I warned you,*" she'll say.

"*You should have married Ethan,*" she'll say. "*They all eventually cheat, Quinn. At least Ethan would have been a* rich *cheater.*"

I unlock my bedroom door and walk to the living room. Graham's car isn't in the driveway. I walk around the house to see if there's anything I want to take with me. It feels reminiscent of when I was cleaning Ethan out of my apartment. I wanted nothing to do with him. Not even the things that reminded me of him.

I scour my home as my eyes fall over the years of stuff Graham and I have accumulated. I wouldn't even know where to start if I wanted to take anything. So I start nowhere. I just need clothes.

When I make it back to the bedroom, I close my suitcase and zip it up. As I'm pulling it off the bed, my eyes lock on the wooden box on the bottom shelf of my bookcase. I immediately walk to the bookcase and grab the box, then take it back to the bed. I jiggle the lock, but it doesn't budge. I remember Graham taping the key to it so we'd never lose it. I flip the box over and dig my nail beneath the piece of tape. I guess I'll finally get to see what's inside of it after all.

"Quinn."

I jump when I hear his voice. But I don't look at him. I cannot look at him right now. I keep my eyes downcast and finish pulling at the tape until I can pry the key loose.

"*Quinn.*" Graham's voice is full of panic. I freeze, waiting for him to say whatever it is he needs to say. He walks into the room and sits down on the bed next to me. His hand clasps my hand that's gripping the key. "I did the absolute worst thing I could possibly do to you. But please give me a chance to make things right before you open this."

I can feel the key in the palm of my hand.

He can keep it.

I grab his hand and flip it over. I place the key in his palm and then close his fist. I look him in the eye. "I won't open the box. But only because I don't give a *fuck* what's inside of it anymore."

I don't even remember the grief between leaving my house and driving over here, but I'm now parked in my mother's driveway.

I stare up at it. At the huge Victorian-style home that means more to my mother than anything outside of it. Including me.

She'd never admit to that, though. It would look bad, admitting out loud that she never really wanted to be a mother. Sometimes I resent her for that. She was able to get pregnant—by accident—and carry a child to term. Twice. And neither of those times was exciting for her. She talked for years about the stretch marks my sister and I left on her. She hated the baby weight she never lost. On the days we were really stressing her out, she'd call the nanny she had on speed dial and she'd say, *"Honestly, Roberta. I can't take this another minute. Please come as soon as you can, I need a spa day."*

I sit back in my seat and stare up at the bedroom that used to be mine. Long before she turned it into a spare closet for her empty shoeboxes. I remember standing at my window once, staring out over our front yard. Graham was with me. It was the first time I'd ever taken him home to meet her.

I'll never forget what he said that day. It was the most

honest and beautiful thing he's ever said to me. And it was that moment—standing with him at my bedroom window—that I fell in love with him.

That's the best memory I have inside my mother's house and it isn't even a memory I share with her. It's a memory I share with Graham. The husband who just cheated on me.

I feel like being inside my mother's house would be worse than being inside my own. I can't face her right now. I need to figure out my shit before I allow her to stick her nose in it.

I begin to back out of the driveway, but it's too late. The front door opens and I see her step outside, squinting to see who is in her driveway.

I lean my head back against the seat. So much for escaping.

"Quinn?" she calls out.

I get out of the car and walk toward her. She holds the front door open, but if I go inside, I'll feel trapped. I take a seat on the top step and look out over the front yard.

"You don't want to go inside?"

I shake my head and then fold my arms over my knees and I just start crying. She eventually takes a seat next to me. "What's the matter?"

It's times like these when I wish I had a mother who actually cared when I was crying. She just goes through the motions, patting a stiff hand against my back.

I don't even tell her about Graham. I don't say anything because I'm crying too hard to speak at first. When I finally do calm down enough to catch my breath, all I can ask her is something that comes out way worse than I mean for it to.

"Why would God give someone like you children but not me?" My mother stiffens when I say that. I immediately lift up and look at her. "I'm sorry. I didn't mean for that to sound so heartless."

She doesn't look all that offended. She just shrugs. "Maybe it isn't God's fault," she says. "Maybe reproductive systems just work or they don't." That would make more sense. "How did you know I never wanted kids?"

I laugh halfheartedly. "You said it. Many times."

She actually looks guilty. She glances away from me and stares out over the front yard. "I wanted to travel," she says. "When your father and I got married, we had plans to move to a different country every year for five years before buying a house. Just so we could experience other cultures before we died. But one crazy night, we weren't careful and it turned into your sister, Ava." She looks at me and says, "I never wanted to be a mother, Quinn. But I've done my best. I truly have. And I'm grateful for you and Ava. Even if it's hard for me to show it." She grabs my hand and squeezes it. "I didn't get my first choice at the perfect life, but I sure as hell did the best I could with my second choice."

I nod, wiping a tear away. I can't believe she's admitting all of this to me. And I can't believe I can sit here and be okay with her telling me my sister and I weren't what she wanted in life. But the fact that she's being honest and even said she's grateful is more than I ever imagined I'd get from her. I put my arms around her.

"Thank you."

She hugs me back, albeit stiffly and not like I would hug my own children if I had any. But she's here and she's hugging me and that should count for something.

"Are you sure you don't want to come inside? I could put on some hot tea."

I shake my head. "It's late. I should probably get back home."

She nods, although I can tell she's hesitant to leave me out here alone. She just doesn't know what to do or say beyond what she's already said without it becoming too awkward. She eventually goes inside, but I don't leave right away. I sit on her porch for a while because I don't want to go back home yet.

I also don't want to be here.

I kind of wish I didn't have to be anywhere at all.

Chapter Nineteen

Then

"I miss you." I try not to pout, but it's a phone conversation and he can't see me, so I push my lip out.

"I'll see you tomorrow," he says. "Promise. I just worry I'm smothering you but you're too nice to tell me."

"I'm not. I'm mean and blunt and I would tell you to leave if I wanted you to leave." It's true. I would tell him if I wanted space. And he would give it to me without question.

"I'll come over as soon as I get off work tomorrow and pick you up. Then I meet your mother."

I sigh. "Okay. But let's have sex before we go to her house because I'm already stressed."

Graham laughs and I can tell by his laugh he's thinking dirty thoughts because of my sentence. He has different laughs for different reactions and it's been one of my favorite things, differentiating them all. My favorite laugh is in the morning when I tell him about what I dreamt the night before. He always thinks my dreams are funny and there's a dry throatiness to his morning laugh because he's not fully awake yet.

"See you tomorrow." He says it quietly, like he already misses me.

"Goodnight." I hang up in a hurry. I don't like talking to him on the phone because he still hasn't told me he loves me yet. I haven't told him, either. So when we're saying goodbye to each other, I'm always scared that's when he'll choose to say it. I don't want him to say it for the first time during a phone conversation. I want him to say it when he's looking at me.

I spend the next two hours trying to remember what my life was like before Graham. I take a shower alone, watch TV alone, play on my phone alone. I thought maybe it would be nice, but I'm mostly just bored with it.

It's odd. I was with Ethan for four years and probably spent one or two nights a week with him. I loved my alone time when Ethan and I were dating. Even in the beginning. Being with him was nice, but being alone was just as nice.

It's not like that with Graham. After two hours, I'm bored out of my mind. I finally turn off the television, turn off my phone, turn off the lamp. When all is dark, I try to clear my thoughts so I'll fall asleep and be able to dream about him.

———

My alarm starts to buzz, but it's too bright, so I grab a pillow and throw it over my face. Graham is normally here and he always cuts off the alarm for me and gives me a couple of minutes to wake up. Which means my alarm will go off forever if I don't adult.

I move the pillow and just as I'm about to reach for the alarm, it cuts off. I open my eyes and Graham is rolling back over to face me. He's not wearing a shirt and it looks like he just woke up.

He smiles and pecks me on the lips. "I couldn't sleep," he says. "Finally gave up and came over here after midnight."

I smile, even though it's way too early for me to feel like smiling. "You missed me."

Graham pulls me against him. "It's weird," he says. "I used to be fine when I was alone. But now that I have you, I'm *lonely* when I'm alone."

Sometimes he says the sweetest things. Words I want to write down and keep forever so that I'll never forget them. But I never write them down because every time he says something sweet, I take off his clothes and need him inside me more than I need to write down his words.

That's exactly what happens. We make love and I forget to write down his words. We've been trying to catch our breath for the last minute when he turns to me and says, "What did I miss while you were sleeping?"

I shake my head. "It's too weird."

He lifts up onto his elbow and looks at me like I'm not getting out of this. I sigh and roll onto my back. "Okay, fine. We were at your apartment in the dream. Only your apartment was a really tiny shit-hole in Manhattan. I woke up before you because I wanted to do something nice and make you breakfast. But I didn't know how to cook and all you had were boxes of cereal, so I decided to make you a bowl of Lucky Charms. But every time I would pour the cereal into the bowl, the only thing that would come out of the box were tiny little comedians with microphones."

"Wait," Graham says, interrupting me. "Did you say *comedians*? Like as in people who tell jokes?"

"I told you it was weird. And yes. They were telling knock-knock jokes and yo-momma jokes. I was getting so angry because all I wanted to do was make you a bowl of Lucky Charms, but there were hundreds of tiny, annoying comedians climbing all over your kitchen, telling lame jokes. When you woke up and walked into the kitchen, you found me crying. I was a sobbing mess, running around your kitchen, trying to squash all the little comedians with a mason jar. But instead of being freaked out, you just walked up behind me and wrapped your arms around me. You said, 'Quinn, it's okay. We can have toast for breakfast.'"

Graham immediately drops his face into the pillow, stifling his laughter. I shove him in the arm. "Try and decipher that one, smartass."

Graham sighs and pulls me to him. "It means that I should probably cook breakfast from now on."

I like that plan.

"What do you want? French toast? Pancakes?"

I lift up and kiss him. "Just you."

"Again?"

I nod. "I want seconds."

I get exactly what I want for breakfast. Then we shower together, drink coffee together, and leave for work.

We couldn't even spend an entire night apart, but I don't think this means we live together. That's a huge step neither of us are willing to admit we took. I think if anything, this just means we no longer live alone. If there's a difference.

His mother probably thinks we already live together since she thinks we've been dating a lot longer than we have. I've been to Graham's parents' house at least once a week since the first night he took me there. Luckily, he stopped with the fictional stories. I was worried I wouldn't be able to keep up with everything he told her the first night.

His mother absolutely loves me now and his father already refers to me as his daughter-in-law. I don't mind it. I know we've only been together three months, but Graham will be my husband one day. It's not even a question. It's what happens when you meet your future husband. You eventually marry him.

And eventually . . . you introduce him to your mother.

Which is what is happening tonight. Not because I want him to meet her, but because it's only fair since I've met his. *I show you mine, you show me yours.*

"Why are you so nervous?" Graham reaches across the seat and puts pressure on my knee. The knee I've been bouncing up and down since we got in the car. "I'm the one meeting your mother. I should be the nervous one."

I squeeze his hand. "You'll understand after you meet her."

Graham laughs and brings my hand to his mouth, kissing it. "Do you think she'll hate me?"

We're on my mother's street now. So close. "You aren't Ethan. She already hates you."

"Then why are you nervous? If she already hates me, I can't disappoint her."

"I don't care if she hates you. I'm scared you'll hate *her*."

175

Graham shakes his head like I'm being ridiculous. "I could never hate the person who gave you life."

He says that now . . .

I watch Graham's expression as he pulls into the driveway. His eyes take in the massive home I grew up in. I can feel his thoughts from where I'm sitting. I can also hear them because he speaks them out loud.

"Holy shit. You grew up here?"

"Stop judging me."

Graham puts the car in park. "It's just a home, Quinn. It doesn't define you." He turns in his seat to face me, placing his hand on the seat rest behind my head as he leans in closer. "You know what else doesn't define you? Your mother." He leans forward and kisses me, then reaches around me and pushes open my door. "Let's get this over with."

No one greets us at the door, but once we're inside, we find my mother in the kitchen. When she hears us, she turns around and assesses Graham from head to toe. It's awkward because Graham goes in for a hug at the same time she goes in for a handshake. He falters a little, but that's the only time he falters. He spends the entire dinner as the adorably charming person he is.

The whole time, I watch him, completely impressed. He's done everything right. He greeted my mother as if he were actually excited to meet her. He's answered all her questions politely. He's talked just enough about his own family while making it seem he was more interested in ours. He complimented her décor, he laughed at her lame jokes, he ignored her underhanded insults. But even as I watch him excel, I've seen nothing but judgment in her eyes. I don't even have to hear what she's thinking because she's always worn her thoughts in her expressions. Even through years of Botox.

She hates that he drove up in his Honda Accord and not something flashier.

She hates that he dared to show up for his first introduction in a T-shirt and a pair of jeans.

She hates that he's an accountant, rather than the millionaires he does the accounting *for*.

She hates that he isn't Ethan.

"Quinn," she says as she stands. "Why don't you give your friend a tour of the house."

My friend.

She won't even dignify us with a label.

I'm relieved to have an excuse to leave the sitting room, even if it's just for a few minutes. I grab Graham's hand and pull him out of the sitting room as my mother returns the tea tray to the kitchen.

We start in the great room, which is just a fancier name for a living room no one is allowed to sit in. I point to the wall of books and whisper, "I've never even seen her read a book. She just pretends to be worldly."

Graham smiles and pretends to care while we walk slowly through the great room. He pauses in front of a wall of photos. Most of them are of my mother and us girls. Once our father died and she remarried, she put away most of the photos of him. But she's always kept one. It's a picture of our father with Ava on one knee and me on the other. As if Graham knows the exact photo I'm studying, he pulls it off the wall.

"You and Ava look more alike now than you did here."

I nod. "Yeah, we get asked if we're twins every time we're together. We don't really see it, though."

"How old were you when your father died?"

"Fourteen."

"That's so young," he says. "Were you very close?"

I shrug. "We weren't *not* close. But he worked a lot. We only saw him a couple of times a week growing up, but he made the most of the times we did see him." I force a smile. "I like to imagine that we'd be a lot closer now if he were alive. He was an older father, so I think it was just hard for him to connect with little girls, you know? But I think we would have connected as adults."

Graham places the picture back on the wall. He pauses at every single picture and touches my photo, as if he can learn more about me through the pictures. When we finally make it through the sitting room, I lead him toward the back door to show him the greenhouse. But before we pass the stairs, he rests his hand against the small of my back and whispers against my ear. "I want to see your old bedroom first."

His seductive voice makes his intentions clear. I get excited at the thought of recreating what happened in his childhood bedroom. I grab his hand and rush him up the stairs. It's probably been a year or more since I actually came up to my old bedroom. I'm excited for him to see it because after being in his, I feel like I learned a lot more about him as a person.

When we reach my bedroom, I push open the door and let him walk in first. As soon as I flip on the light, I'm filled with disappointment. This experience won't be the same as the one we had in Graham's old bedroom.

My mother has boxed up everything. There are empty designer shoe boxes stacked up against two of the walls, floor to ceiling. Empty designer purse boxes cover a third wall. All of my things that once covered the walls of my bedroom are now boxed up in old moving boxes with my name sprawled across them. I walk over to the bed and run my hands over one of the boxes.

"I guess she needed the spare bedroom," I say quietly.

Graham stands next to me and rubs a reassuring hand against my back. "It's a tiny house," he says. "I can see why she'd need the extra room."

I laugh at his sarcasm. He pulls me in for a hug and I close my eyes as I curl into his chest. I hate that I was so excited for him to see my old bedroom. I hate that it makes me this sad to know my mother will never love me like Graham's mother loves him. There are two guest bedrooms in this house, yet my mother chooses to use my old bedroom as the storage room. It embarrasses me that he's witnessing this.

I pull back and suck up my emotions. I shrug, hoping he can't tell how much it bothers me. But he can. He brushes my hair back and says, "You okay?"

"Yeah. I just . . . I don't know. Meeting your family was an unexpected quality about you. I was kind of hoping you could have the same experience." I laugh a little, embarrassed I even said that. "Wishful thinking."

I walk over to my bedroom window and stare outside. I don't want him to see the disappointment on my face. Graham walks up behind me and slips his arms around my waist.

"Most people are products of their environment, Quinn. I come from a good home. I grew up with two great, stable parents. It's expected that I would grow up and be relatively normal." He spins me around and puts his hands on my shoulders. He dips his head and looks at me with so much sincerity in his eyes. "Being here . . . meeting your mother and seeing where you came from and who you somehow turned out to be . . . it's *inspiring*, Quinn. I don't know how you did it, you selfless, amazing, incredible woman."

A lot of people can't pinpoint the exact moment they fall in love with another person.

I can.

It just happened.

And maybe it's coincidence or maybe it's something more, but Graham chooses this exact moment to press his forehead to mine and say, "I love you, Quinn."

I wrap my arms around him, grateful for every single part of him. "I love you, too."

Chapter Twenty

Now

I turn off my car and scoot my seat back, propping my leg against the steering wheel. The only light on inside the house is the kitchen light. It's almost midnight. Graham is probably sleeping because he has to work tomorrow.

This morning when I woke up, I expected Graham to still be outside our bedroom door, knocking, begging for forgiveness. It made me angry that he left for work. Our marriage is crumbling, he admitted to seeing another woman, I holed myself up in our bedroom all night . . . but he woke up, got dressed, and traipsed off to work.

He must work with Andrea. He probably wanted to warn her that I knew in case I flew off the handle and showed up at his office to kick her ass.

I wouldn't do that. I'm not mad at Andrea. She's not the one who made a commitment to me. She has no loyalty to me or I to her. I'm only mad at one person in this scenario and that is my husband.

The living room curtain moves. I debate ducking, but I know from experience what a clear view it is from the living room to our driveway. Graham sees me, so there's no point in hiding. The front door opens and Graham steps outside. He begins to head toward my car.

He's wearing the pajama pants I bought him for Christmas last year. His feet are covered in two mismatched socks. One black, one white. I always thought that was a conflicting personality trait of his. He's very organized and predictable in a lot of ways, but for some reason, he never cares if his socks match. To Graham, socks are a practical necessity, not a fashion statement.

I stare out my window as he opens the passenger door and takes a seat inside the car. When he closes the door, it feels as though he cuts off my air supply. My chest is tight and my lungs feel like someone took a knife and ripped a hole in them. I roll down my window so I can breathe.

He smells good. I hate that no matter how much he hurt my heart, the rest of me never got the memo that it's supposed to be repulsed by him. If a scientist could figure out how to align the heart with the brain, there would be very little agony left in the world.

I wait for his apologies to start. The excuses. Possibly even the blame. He inhales a breath and says, "Why did we never get a dog?"

He's sitting in the passenger seat, his body half facing me as his head rests against the headrest. He's staring at me very seriously despite the unbelievable question that just fell from his lips. His hair is damp, like he just got out of the shower.

His eyes are bloodshot. I don't know if it's from lack of sleep or if he's been crying, but all he wants to know is why we never got a *dog*?

"Are you kidding me, Graham?"

"I'm sorry," he says, shaking his head. "It was just a thought I had. I didn't know if there was a reason."

His first *I'm sorry* since he admitted to having an affair and it's an apology unrelated to his infidelity. It's so unlike him. Having an *affair* is so unlike him. It's like I don't even know this man sitting next to me. "Who *are* you right now? What did you do with my husband?"

He faces forward and leans back against his seat, covering his eyes with his arm. "He's probably somewhere with my wife. It's been a while since I've seen her."

So this is how it's going to be? I thought he'd come out here and make this entire ordeal a little easier to bear, but instead, he's giving me every reason in the world to justify my rage. I look away from him and focus my attention out my window. "I hate you right now. So much." A tear slides down my cheek.

"You don't hate me," he says quietly. "In order to hate me you'd have to love me. But you've been indifferent toward me for a long time now."

I wipe away a tear. "Whatever helps you excuse the fact that you slept with another woman, Graham. I'd hate for you to feel guilty."

"I never slept with her, Quinn. We just . . . it never got that far. I swear."

I pause with his confession.

He didn't sleep with her? Does that make a difference?

Does it hurt less? No. Does it make me less angry at him?

No. Not even a little bit. The fact is, Graham was intimate with another woman. It wouldn't matter if that consisted of a conversation, a kiss, or a three-day fuck-a-thon. Betrayal hurts the same on any level when it's your husband doing the betraying.

"I never slept with her," he repeats quietly. "But that shouldn't make you feel any better. I thought about it."

I clasp my hand over my mouth and try to stifle a sob. It doesn't work because everything he's saying, everything he's doing . . . it's not what I expected from him. I needed comfort and reassurance and he's giving me nothing but the opposite. "Get out of my car." I unlock the doors, even though they're already unlocked. I want him far away from me. I grip the steering wheel and pull my seat up straighter, waiting for him to just go. I start the engine. He doesn't move. I look at him again. "Get out, Graham. *Please*. Get out of my car." I press my forehead to the steering wheel. "I can't even look at you right now." I squeeze my eyes shut and wait for the door to open, but instead, the engine cuts off. I hear him pull my keys out of the ignition.

"I'm not going anywhere until you know every detail," he says.

I shake my head, swiping at more tears. I reach for my door but he grabs my hand. "Look at me." He pulls me toward him, refusing to let me out of the car. "Quinn, *look* at me!"

It's the first time he's ever yelled at me.

It's actually the first time I've ever heard him *yell*.

Graham has always been a silent fighter. The strength of his voice and the way it reverberates inside the car makes me freeze. "I need to tell you why I did what I did. When I'm finished, you can decide what to do, but *please*, Quinn. Let me speak first."

I close my door and lean back in my seat. I squeeze my eyes shut and the tears continue to fall. I don't want to listen to him. But part of me needs to know every detail because if I don't get the facts, I'm scared my imagination will make it even worse. "Hurry," I whisper. I don't know how long I can sit here without completely losing it.

He inhales a calming breath. It takes him a moment to figure out where to start. Or how to start. "She was hired on by our firm a few months ago."

I can hear the tears in his voice. He tries to keep it steady, but the regret is there. It's the only thing that helps ease the pain—knowing he's suffering, too.

"We interacted a few times, but I never looked at her as anything more than a coworker. I've never looked at any woman how I look at you, Quinn. I don't want you to think that's how it started."

I can feel him looking at me, but I keep my eyes shut. My pulse is pounding so hard, I feel like the only thing that could make it stop is getting out of this claustrophobic car. But I know he won't let me until I hear him out, so I focus on breathing steadily while he speaks.

"There were things she would do sometimes that would catch my attention. Not because I found her intriguing or attractive, but because . . . her mannerisms reminded me of you."

I shake my head and open my mouth to speak. He can tell I'm about to interrupt, so he whispers, "Just let me finish."

I close my mouth and lean forward, crossing my arms over the steering wheel. I press my forehead against my arms and pray he gets this over with.

"Nothing happened between us until last week. We were assigned to work on a job together Wednesday, so we spent a lot of the day together. I noticed as the hours passed that I was . . . drawn to her. Attracted to her. But not because she had something you didn't. I was drawn to her because of how much she reminded me of you."

I have so much I want to scream at him right now, but I hold back.

"Being around her all day Wednesday made me miss you. So I left work early, thinking maybe if I just took you out for a nice dinner or did something to make you happy, you would smile at me like you used to. Or you'd be interested in my day. Or *me*. But when I got home and walked through the front door, I saw you walking out of the living room. I know you heard me opening the door. But for some reason, instead of being excited to see me come home an hour early, you went to your office so you could avoid me."

I'm not only full of anger now. I'm also full of shame. I didn't think he noticed all the times I try to avoid him.

"You spoke one word to me Wednesday night. *One*. Do you remember what it was?"

I nod, but I keep my head buried against my arms. "Goodnight."

I can hear the tears in his voice when he says, "I was so angry at you. Figuring you out is like a fucking riddle sometimes, Quinn. I was tired of trying to figure out how to be around you the right way. I was so mad at you, I didn't even kiss you goodbye when I left for work Thursday."

I noticed.

"When we finished up the project on Thursday, I should have come home. I should have left, but instead . . . I stayed.

And we talked. And . . . I kissed her." Graham runs his hands down his face. "I shouldn't have done it. And even after it started, I should have stopped it. But I couldn't. Because the whole time I had my eyes closed, I pretended it was you."

I lift my head off my arms and look at him. "So it's *my* fault? Is that what you're saying?" I turn my whole body toward him in my seat. "You don't get the attention you want from me, so you find someone who reminds you of me? I guess as long as you pretend it's your wife, it shouldn't count." I roll my eyes and fall back against my seat. "Graham Wells, first man in the world to find an ethical way around an affair."

"Quinn."

I don't let him speak. "You obviously didn't feel very guilty if you had the entire fucking weekend to think about it, but then went back to work and did it all over again."

"It was twice. Last Thursday and last night. That's it. I swear."

"What if I wouldn't have caught on? Would you have even stopped it?"

Graham runs his hand over his mouth, squeezing his jaw. His head shakes a little and I'm hoping it's not an answer to my question. I'm hoping he's just shaking it in regret.

"I don't know how to answer that," he says, looking out his window. "Nobody deserves this. Especially you. Before I left tonight, I swore to myself that it would never happen again. But I also never believed I would be capable of something like this to begin with."

I look up at the roof of the car and press my palm to my chest, blowing out a quick breath. "Then why did you do it?" My question comes out in a sob.

Graham turns to me as soon as I start crying. He leans

across the seat and grips my face, silently pleading for me to look at him. When I finally do meet his desperate stare, it makes me cry even harder. "We walk around inside that house like everything is okay, but it's *not*, Quinn. We've been broken for years and I have no idea how to fix us. I find solutions. It's what I do. It's what I'm good at. But I have no idea how to solve me and you. Every day I come home, hoping things will be better. But you can't even stand to be in the same room with me. You hate it when I touch you. You hate it when I talk to you. I pretend not to notice the things you don't want me to notice because I don't want you to hurt more than you already do." He releases a rush of air. "I am not blaming you for what I did. It's my fault. It's *my* fault. *I* did that. *I* fucked up. But I didn't fuck up because I was attracted to *her*. I fucked up because I miss *you*. Every day, I miss you. When I'm at work, I miss you. When I'm home, I miss you. When you're next to me in bed, I miss you. When I'm *inside* you, I miss you."

Graham presses his mouth to mine. I can taste his tears. Or maybe they're my tears. He pulls back and presses his forehead to mine. "I miss you, Quinn. So much. You're right here, but you aren't. I don't know where you went or when you left, but I have no idea how to bring you back. I am so alone. We live together. We eat together. We sleep together. But I have never felt more alone in my entire life."

Graham releases me and falls back against his seat. He rests his elbow against the window, covering his face as he tries to compose himself. He's more broken than I've ever seen him in all the years I've known him.

And I'm the one slowly tearing him down. I'm making him unrecognizable. I've strung him along by allowing him to believe there's hope that I'll eventually change. That I'll miraculously turn back into the woman he fell in love with.

But I can't change. We are who our circumstances turn us into.

"Graham." I wipe at my face with my shirt. He's quiet, but he eventually looks at me with his sad, heartbroken eyes. "I haven't gone anywhere. I've been here this whole time. But you can't see me because you're still searching for someone I used to be. I'm sorry I'm no longer who I was back then. Maybe I'll get better. Maybe I won't. But a good husband loves his wife through the good *and* the bad times. A good husband stands at his wife's side through sickness *and* health, Graham. A good husband—a husband who *truly* loves his wife—wouldn't cheat on her and then blame his infidelity on the fact that he's *lonely*."

Graham's expression doesn't change. He's as still as a statue. The only thing that moves is his jaw as he works it back and forth. And then his eyes narrow and he tilts his head. "You don't think I love you, Quinn?"

"I know you used to. But I don't think you love the person I've become."

Graham sits up straight. He leans forward, looking me hard in the eye. His words are clipped as he speaks. "I have loved you every single second of every day since the moment I laid eyes on you. I love you more now than I did the day I married you. I love you, Quinn. I fucking *love* you!"

He opens his car door, gets out and then slams it shut with all his strength. The whole car shakes. He walks toward the house, but before he makes it to the front door, he spins around and points at me angrily. "I *love* you, Quinn!"

He's shouting the words. He's angry. *So* angry.

He walks toward his car and kicks at the front bumper with his bare foot. He kicks and he kicks and he kicks and then pauses to scream it at me again. "I *love* you!"

He slams his fist against the top of his car, over and over, until he finally collapses against the hood, his head buried in his arms. He remains in this position for an entire minute, the only thing moving is the subtle shaking of his shoulders. I don't move. I don't even think I breathe.

Graham finally pushes off the hood and uses his shirt to wipe at his eyes. He looks at me, completely defeated. "I love you," he says quietly, shaking his head. "I always have. No matter how much you wish I didn't."

Chapter Twenty-one

Then

I never ask my mother for favors for obvious reasons. Which is precisely why I called my stepfather to ask permission to use his beach house in Cape Cod. He only uses it as a rental property now and it stays booked up in the summers. But it's February and the house has been sitting empty for most of the winter. It took a lot to swallow my pride and ask him, but it was a lot easier than if I'd asked her. She has stated numerous times since she met Graham that she thinks I could do better. In her eyes, better means meeting someone with his own beach house so that I'll never have to ask to borrow theirs for the weekend.

Graham walked around for an hour after we got here, pointing things out with the excitement of a kid on Christmas morning.

Quinn, come look at this view!

Quinn, come look at this bathtub!
Quinn, did you see the fire pit?
Quinn, they have kayaks!

His excitement has waned a little since we got here earlier today. We just ate dinner and I took a shower while Graham built a fire in the fire pit. It's an unusually warm day for a February in Massachusetts, but even on a warmer winter day, it barely tops out in the fifties during the day and the thirties at night. I bring a blanket to the fire pit with me and curl up next to Graham on the patio sofa.

He pulls me even closer, wrapping an arm around me while I rest my head on his shoulder. He tucks the blanket around both of us. It's cold, but the warmth from both him and the fire make it bearable. Comfortable, even.

I've never seen Graham more at peace than when he's out here, listening to the sounds of the ocean. I love how he looks out over the water as if it holds all the answers to every question in the world. He looks at the ocean with the respect it deserves.

"What a perfect day," he says quietly.

I smile. I like that a perfect day to him includes me. It's been six months since we started dating. Sometimes I look at him and feel such an overwhelming appreciation for him, I almost want to write thank-you notes to our exes. It's the best thing that's ever happened to me.

It's funny how you can be so happy with someone and love them so much, it creates an underlying sense of fear in you that you never knew before them. The fear of losing them. The fear of them getting hurt. I imagine that's what it's like when you have children. It's probably the most incredible kind of love you'll ever know, but it's also the most terrifying.

"Do you want kids?" I practically blurt the question out. It was so quiet between us and then I sliced through that quiet with a question whose answer could determine our future. I don't know how to do anything with subtlety.

"Of course. Do you?"

"Yeah. I want a lot of kids."

Graham laughs. "How many is a lot?"

"I don't know. More than one. Less than five." I lift my head off his shoulder and look at him. "I think I would make a great mom. I don't brag on myself, but if I had kids, I'm pretty sure they would be the best kids ever."

"I have no doubt."

I lay my head back on his shoulder. He covers my hand that's pressed against his chest. "Have you always wanted to be a mom?"

"Yes. It's kind of embarrassing how excited I am to be a mother. Most girls grow up dreaming of a successful career. I was always too embarrassed to admit that I wanted to work from home and have a bunch of babies."

"That's not embarrassing."

"Yes it is. Women nowadays are supposed to want to amount to more than just being a mother. Feminism and all that."

Graham scoots me off his chest to tend to the fire. He grabs two small logs and walks them over to the fire pit, then reclaims his seat next to me. "Be whatever you want to be. Be a soldier if you want. Or a lawyer. Or a CEO. Or a housewife. The only thing you shouldn't be is embarrassed."

I love him. I love him so much.

"A mom isn't the only thing I want to be. I want to write a book someday."

"Well you certainly have the imagination for it based on all the crazy dreams you have."

"I should probably write them down," I laugh.

Graham is smiling at me with an unfamiliar look on his face. I'm about to ask him what he's thinking, but he speaks first.

"Ask me again if I want kids," he says.

"Why? Are you changing your answer?"

"I am. Ask me again."

"Do you want kids?"

He smiles at me. "I only want kids if I can have them with you. I want to have lots of kids with you. I want to watch your belly grow and I want to watch you hold our baby for the first time and I want to watch you cry because you're so deliriously happy. And at night I want to stand outside the nursery and watch you rock our babies to sleep while you sing to them. I can't think of anything I want more than to make you a mother."

I kiss his shoulder. "You always say the sweetest things. I wish I knew how to express myself like you do."

"You're a writer. You're the one who's good with words."

"I'm not arguing about my writing skills. I could probably write down what I feel for you, but I could never put it into words verbally like you do."

"Then do that," he says. "Write me a love letter. No one's ever written me a love letter before."

"I don't believe that."

"I'm serious. I've always wanted one."

I laugh. "I'll write you a love letter, you sappy man."

"It better be more than a page long. And I want you to tell me everything. What you thought of me the first time you saw me. What you felt when we were falling in love. And I want you to spray your perfume on it like the girls in high school do."

"Any other requests?"

"I wouldn't be opposed to you slipping a nude pic in the envelope."

I can probably make that happen.

Graham tugs me onto his lap so that I'm straddling him. He pulls the blanket over us, cocooning us inside of it. He's wearing a pair of cotton pajama pants, so I get a clear sense of what he's thinking right now. "Have you ever made love outdoors in thirty-degree weather before?"

I grin against his mouth. "Nope. But funny enough, that's precisely why I'm not wearing any underwear right now."

Graham's hands fall to my ass and he groans as he lifts my nightgown. I rise a little so that he can free himself, and then I lower myself on top of him, taking him in. We make love, cocooned under a blanket with the sound of the ocean as our background song. It's the perfect moment in a perfect place with the perfect person. And I know without a doubt that I'll be writing about this moment when I write my love letter to him.

Chapter Twenty-two

Now

He kissed another woman.

I stare at the text I'm about to send Ava, but then I remember she's several hours ahead where she lives. I would feel bad, knowing this is the text she'll wake up to. I delete it.

It's been half an hour since Graham gave up and went back inside, but I'm still sitting in my car. I think I'm too wounded to move. I have no idea if any of this is my fault or if it's his fault or if it's no one's fault. The only thing I know is that he hurt me. And he hurt me because I've been hurting him. It doesn't make what he did right in any sense, but a person can understand a behavior without excusing it.

Now we're both full of so much pain, I don't even know where to go from here. No matter how much you love someone—the capacity of that love is meaningless if it outweighs your capacity to forgive.

Part of me wonders if we'd even be having any of these problems if we would have been able to have a baby. I'm not sure that our marriage would have taken the turn it did because I would have never been as devastated as I've been the last few years. And Graham wouldn't have had to walk on eggshells around me.

But then part of me wonders if this was inevitable. Maybe a child wouldn't have changed our marriage and instead of just being an unhappy couple, we would have been an unhappy family. And then what would that make us? Just another married couple staying together for the sake of the children.

I wonder how many marriages would have survived if it weren't for the children they created together. How many couples would have continued to live together happily without the children being the glue that holds their family together?

Maybe we should get a dog. See if that fixes us.

Maybe that's exactly what Graham was thinking when he sat in my car earlier and said, *"Why did we never get a dog?"*

Of course, that's what he was thinking. He's just as aware of our problems as I am. It only makes sense our minds would head in the same direction.

When it grows too cold in the car, I walk back into our house and sit on the edge of the sofa. I don't want to go to my bedroom where Graham is sleeping. A while ago he was screaming that he loves me at the top of his lungs. He was so loud, I'm sure all the neighbors woke up to the sound of him yelling and the pounding of his fist against metal.

But right now, our house is silent. And that silence between us is so loud; I don't think I'll ever be able to fall asleep.

We've tried therapy in the past, hoping it would help with the infertility issues we struggled with. I got bored with it. *He* got bored with it. And then we bonded over how boring therapy was. Therapists do nothing but try to make you recognize the wrongs within yourself. That's not Graham's issue and it's not my issue. We know our faults. We recognize them. My fault is that I can't have a baby and it makes me sad. Graham's fault is that he can't fix me and it makes *him* sad. There's no magical cure that therapy will bring us. No matter how much we spend on trying to fix our issue, no therapist in the world can get me pregnant. Therefore, therapy is just a drain on a bank account that has already had one too many leaks.

Maybe the only cure for us is divorce. It's weird, having thoughts of divorcing someone I'm in love with. But I think about it a lot. I think about how much time Graham is wasting by being with me. He would be sad if I left him, but he'd meet someone new. He's too good not to. He'd fall in love and he could make a baby and he'd be able to rejoin that circle of life that I ripped him out of. When I think about Graham being a father someday, it always makes me smile . . . even if the thought of him being a father doesn't include me being a mother.

I think the only reason I never completely let him go is because of the miracles. I read the articles and the books and the blog posts from the mothers who tried to conceive for years and then just as they were about to give up, *voilà! Pregnant!*

The miracles gave me hope. Enough hope to hang on to Graham just enough in case we ever got a miracle of our own. Maybe that miracle would have fixed us. Put a Band-Aid on our broken marriage.

I want to hate him for kissing someone else. But I can't, because part of me doesn't blame him. I've been giving him every excuse in the world to walk out on me. We haven't had sex in a while, but I know that's not why he strayed outside of our marriage. Graham would go a lifetime without sex if I needed him to.

The reason he allowed himself to fuck up is because he gave up on us.

Back when I was in college, I was assigned to do an article on a couple who had been married for sixty years. They were both in their eighties. When I showed up to the interview, I was shocked at how in tune they were with each other. I assumed, after living with someone for sixty years, you'd be sick of them. But they looked at each other like they still somehow respected and admired each other, even after all they'd been through.

I asked them a number of questions during the interview, but the question I ended the interview with left such an impact on me. I asked, "What's the secret to such a perfect marriage?"

The old man leaned forward and looked at me very seriously. "Our marriage hasn't been perfect. *No* marriage is perfect. There were times when she gave up on us. There were even more times when *I* gave up on us. The secret to our longevity is that we never gave up at the same time."

I'll never forget the honesty in that man's answer.

And now I truly feel like I'm living that. I believe that's why Graham did what he did. Because he finally gave up on us. He's not a superhero. He's human. There isn't a person in this world who could put up with being shut out for as long as Graham has put up with it. He has been our strength in the past and I've continually been our weakest link. But now the tables have turned and Graham was momentarily our weakest link.

The problem is—I feel like I've given up, too. I feel like we've both given up at the same time and there may be no turning back from that. I know I could fix it by forgiving him and telling him I'll try harder, but part of me wonders if that's the right choice.

Why fight for something that will likely never get better? How long can a couple cling to a past they both prefer in order to justify a present where neither of them is happy?

There is no doubt in my mind that Graham and I used to be perfect for each other. But just because we used to be perfect for each other doesn't mean we're perfect together now. We're far from it.

I look at the clock, wishing it would magically fast forward through tomorrow. I have a feeling tomorrow is going to be so much worse than today was. Because tomorrow I feel like we'll be forced to make a decision.

We'll have to decide if it's finally time to open that wooden box.

The thought of it makes my stomach turn. A pain rips through me and I clench at my shirt as I lean forward. I am so heartbroken; I can actually physically feel it. But I don't cry, because in this situation, my tears cause me even more pain.

I walk to our bedroom with dry eyes. It's the longest stretch of time I've gone in the last twenty-four hours without crying. I push open our bedroom door, expecting Graham to be asleep. Instead, he's sitting up against the headboard. His reading glasses are at the tip of his nose and he's holding a book in his lap. His bedside lamp is on and we make eye contact for a brief second.

I crawl in bed beside him, my back turned to him. I think we're both too broken tonight to even continue the argument. He continues reading his book and I do my best to try to fall asleep. My mind runs, though. Several minutes pass and just knowing he's right next to me prevents me from relaxing. He must realize I'm still awake because I hear him as he closes his book and places it on the nightstand. "I quit my job today."

I don't say anything in response to his confession. I just stare at the wall.

"I know you think I left for work this morning and that I just left you here, locked up in this bedroom."

He's right. That's exactly what I thought.

"But I only left the house because I needed to quit my job. I can't work in the place where I made the worst mistake of my life. I'll start looking for a new job next week."

I squeeze my eyes shut and pull the covers up to my chin. He turns out the lamp, indicating he doesn't need a response from me. After he rolls over, I let out a quiet sigh, knowing he won't be working around Andrea anymore. He stopped giving up. He's trying again. He still believes there's a possibility that our marriage will go back to how it used to be.

I feel sorry for him. What if he's wrong?

These thoughts plague me for the next hour. Graham somehow falls asleep—or I think he's asleep. He's playing the part well.

But I can't sleep. The tears keep threatening to fall and the pain in my stomach gets worse and worse. I get up and take some aspirin, but when I'm back in the bed I start to question whether emotional turmoil can actually manifest as physical pain.

Something isn't right.

It shouldn't hurt this much.

I feel a sharp pain. A deep pain. A pain strong enough to force me onto my side. I clench my fists around my blanket and curl my legs up to my stomach. When I do this, I feel it. Slippery and wet, all over the sheets.

"Graham." I try to reach for him, but he's rolling over to turn on the light. Another pain, so profound it makes me gasp for breath.

"Quinn?"

His hand is on my shoulder. He pulls the covers away. Whatever he sees sends him flying off the bed, the lights are on, he's picking me up, telling me it'll be okay, he's carrying me, we're in the car, he's speeding, I'm sweating, I look down, I'm covered in blood. "Graham."

I'm terrified and he takes my hand and he squeezes it and he says, "It's okay, Quinn. We're almost there. We're almost there."

Everything after that runs together.

There are glimpses of things that stick out to me. The fluorescent light over my head. Graham's hand around mine. Words I don't want to hear, like, *miscarriage* and *hemorrhaging* and *surgery*.

Words Graham is saying into the phone, probably to his mother, while he holds my hand. He whispers them because he thinks I might be asleep. Part of me is, most of me isn't. I know these aren't things he's saying *might* happen. They've *already* happened. I'm not going into surgery. I've just come out of it.

Graham ends the call. His lips are against my forehead and he whispers my name. "Quinn?" I open my eyes to meet his. His eyes are red and there's a deep wrinkle between his brows that I've never noticed before. It's new, probably brought on by what's currently happening. I wonder if I'll think of this moment every time I look at that wrinkle.

"What happened?"

The crease between his eyes deepens. He brushes his hand over my hair and carefully releases his words. "You had a miscarriage last night," he confirms. His eyes search mine, preparing for whatever reaction I might have.

It's weird that my body doesn't feel it. I know I'm probably heavily medicated, but it seems like I would know that there was a life growing inside of me that is no longer there. I put a hand on my stomach, wondering how I missed it. How long had I been pregnant? How long has it been since we last had sex? Over two months. Closer to three.

"Graham," I whisper. He takes my hand and squeezes it. I know I should be full of so much devastation right now that not even a sliver of happiness or relief could find its way into my soul. But somehow, I don't feel the devastation that should accompany this moment. I feel hope. "I was pregnant? We finally got pregnant?"

I don't know how I'm focusing on the only positive thing about this entire situation, but after years of constant failure, I can't help but take this as a sign. *I got pregnant. We had a partial miracle.*

A tear slips out of Graham's eye and lands on my arm. I look down at the tear and watch it slide over my skin. My eyes flick back up to Graham's and not a single part of him is able to see the positive in this situation.

"Quinn . . ."

Another tear falls from his eye. In all the years I've known him, I've never seen him look this sad. I shake my head, because whatever has him this terrified to speak is not something I want to hear.

Graham squeezes my hand again and looks at me with so much devastation in his eyes, I have to turn away from him when he speaks. "When we got here last night . . ."

I try to stop listening, but my ears refuse to fail me.

"You were hemorrhaging."

The word *no* is repeating and I have no idea if it's coming from my mouth or if it's inside my head.

"You had to have a . . ."

I curl up and hug my knees, squeezing my eyes shut. As soon as I hear the word *hysterectomy* I start crying. *Sobbing.*

Graham crawls into the hospital bed and wraps himself around me, holding me as we let go of every single ounce of hope that was left between us.

Chapter Twenty-three

Then

It's our last night at the beach house. We leave in the morning to head back to Connecticut. Graham has a meeting he has to be back for tomorrow afternoon. I have laundry to do before I go back to work on Tuesday. Neither of us is ready to leave yet. It's been peaceful and perfect and I'm already looking forward to coming back here with him. I don't even care if I have to kiss my mother's ass for the next month in order to plan our next getaway. It's a price I'll gladly pay for another weekend of perfection.

It's a little bit colder tonight than the last two nights we've been here, but I kind of like it. I have the heater turned up high in the house. We freeze our asses off for hours near the fire pit and then cuddle up in bed to thaw out. It's a routine I would never get bored of.

I just finished making us both cups of hot chocolate. I

take them outside and hand Graham his, then sit down next to him.

"Okay," he says. "Next question."

Graham found out this morning that, even though I love looking at it, I've never actually stepped foot in the ocean. He spent the majority of the day trying to figure out other things about me that he didn't know. It's become a game to us now and we're alternating questions so we can find out everything there is to know about each other.

He mentioned the first night we were together that he doesn't talk about religion or politics. But it's been six months now and I'm curious to know his opinions. "We've still never discussed religion," I say. "Or politics. Are those still topics that are off the table?"

Graham edges the cup with his lips and sucks a marshmallow into his mouth. "What do you want to know?"

"Are you a Republican or a Democrat?"

He doesn't even hesitate. "Neither. I can't stand the extremists on either side, so I sort of hover in the middle."

"So you're one of *those* people."

He tilts his head. "What people?"

"The kind who pretend to agree with every opinion just to keep the peace."

Graham arches an eyebrow. "Oh, I have opinions, Quinn. Strong ones."

I pull my legs up and tuck them under me, facing him. "I want to hear them."

"What do you want to know?"

"Everything," I challenge. "Your stance on gun control. Immigration. Abortion. *All* of it."

I love the look of excitement on his face, as if he's preparing for a presentation. It's adorable that a presentation would even excite him.

He sets his mug of hot chocolate on the table beside him. "Okay . . . let's see. I don't think we should take away a citizen's right to own a gun. But I do think it should be one hell of a difficult process to get your hands on one. I think women should decide what to do with their own bodies, as long as it's within the first trimester or it's a medical emergency. I think government programs are absolutely necessary but I also think a more systematic process needs to be put in place that would encourage people to get off of welfare, rather than to stay on it. I think we should open up our borders to immigrants, as long as they register and pay taxes. I'm certain that life-saving medical care should be a basic human right, not a luxury only the wealthy can afford. I think college tuition should automatically be deferred and then repaid over a twenty-year period on a sliding scale. I think athletes are paid way too much, teachers are paid way too little, NASA is underfunded, weed should be legal, people should love who they want to love, and Wi-Fi should be universally accessible and free." When he's finished, he calmly reaches for his mug of hot chocolate and brings it back to his mouth. "Do you still love me?"

"More than I did two minutes ago." I press a kiss to his shoulder and he wraps his arm around me, tucking me against him.

"Well, that went better than I thought it would."

"Don't get too comfortable," I warn. "We still haven't discussed religion. Do you believe in God?"

Graham breaks eye contact and looks out at the ocean. He caresses my shoulder and thinks about my question for a moment. "I didn't used to."

"But you do now?"

"Yeah. I do now."

"What changed your mind?"

"A few things," he says. He nudges his head toward the ocean. "*That* being one of them. How can something exist that is that magnificent and powerful without something even more magnificent and powerful creating it?"

I stare out at the water with him when he asks me what I believe. I shrug. "Religion isn't one of my mother's strong suits, but I've always believed there was something out there greater than us. I just don't know exactly what it is. I don't think anyone knows for sure."

"That's why they call it faith," he says.

"So how does a man of math and science reconcile his knowledge with his faith?"

Graham smiles when I ask him that question, like he's been dying to discuss it. I love that about him. He has this adorable inner nerd that appears sometimes and it makes him even more attractive.

"Do you know how old the earth is, Quinn?"

"No, but I bet I'm about to find out."

"Four and a half *billion* years old," he says. His voice is full of wonder, like this is his absolute favorite thing to talk about. "Do you know how long ago our specific species appeared?"

"No idea."

"Only two hundred thousand years ago," he says. "Only two hundred thousand years out of four and a half *billion* years. It's unbelievable." He grabs my hand and lays it palm down on his thigh. He begins tracing over the back of my hand with a lazy finger. "If the back of your hand represented the age of this earth and every species that has ever lived, the entire human race wouldn't even be visible to the naked eye. We are that insignificant." He drags his fingers to the center of the back of my hand and points to a small freckle. "From the beginning of time until now, we could combine every single human that has ever walked this earth, and all their problems and concerns as a whole wouldn't even amount to the size of this freckle right here." He taps my hand. "Every single one of your life experiences could fit right here in this tiny freckle. So would mine. So would Beyoncé's."

I laugh.

"When you look at the earth's existence as a whole, we're nothing. We haven't even been here long enough to earn bragging rights. Yet humans believe we're the center of the universe. We focus on the stupidest, most mundane issues. We stress about things that mean absolutely nothing to the universe, when we should be nothing but grateful that evolution even gave our species a chance to *have* problems. Because one of these days . . . humans won't exist. History will repeat itself and earth will move on to a different species altogether. Me and you . . . we're just two people out of an entire race that, in retrospect, is still way less impressive at sustainability than a dinosaur. We just haven't reached our expiration date yet." He slides his fingers through mine and squeezes my hand.

"Based on all the scientific evidence that proves how insignificant we are, it was always hard for me to believe in God. The more appropriate question would have been, '*Could a God believe in me?*' Because a lot has happened on this earth in four and a half billion years to think that a God would give a shit about me or my problems. But, I recently concluded that there's no other explanation for how you and I could end up on the same planet, in the same species, in the same century, in the same country, in the same state, in the same town, in the same hallway, in front of the same door for the same reason at the exact same time. If God didn't believe in me, then I'd have to believe you were just a coincidence. And you being a coincidence in my life is a lot harder for me to fathom than the mere existence of a higher power."

Oh.

Wow. I'm breathless.

Graham has said so many sweet things to me, but this wasn't sweet. This was pure poetry. This was beyond an expression of his intelligence, because I know he's incredibly smart. This was sacrificial. He gave me purpose. He made me incredibly relevant—crucial—to him, when I've never felt relevant, vital, or crucial to anyone else before. "I love you so much, Graham Wells." It's all I can say because I can't compete with what he just said. I don't even try.

"Do you love me enough to marry me?"

I lift off his arm and sit up straight, still facing him.

Did he seriously just ask me that?

It was so spontaneous. He probably hasn't even thought it through. He's still smiling but in a few seconds I think he's probably going to laugh because he accidentally blurted it out without even thinking. He doesn't even have a ring, which proves it was an accident.

"Graham . . ."

He slips his hand under the blanket. When he pulls his hand back out, he's holding a ring. No box, no gift wrap, no pretenses. It's just a ring. A ring he's been carrying in his pocket for a moment he obviously *did* think through.

I bring my hands up to my mouth. They're shaking because I wasn't expecting this and I'm speechless and I'm scared I won't be able to answer him out loud because everything is caught in my throat but I somehow still whisper the words, "Oh my God."

Graham pulls my left hand from my mouth and he holds the ring near my ring finger, but he doesn't attempt to slip it on. Instead, he dips his head to bring my focus back to him. When our eyes meet, he's looking at me with all the clarity and hope in the world. "Be my wife, Quinn. Weather the Category 5 moments with me."

I'm nodding before he's even finished speaking. I'm nodding, because if I try to say *yes*, I'll start crying. I can't even believe he somehow made this perfect weekend even better.

As soon as I start nodding, he laughs with a heavy sigh of relief. And when he slips the ring on my finger, he bites his lip because he doesn't want me to see that he's getting choked up, too. "I didn't know what ring to get you," he says, looking back up at me. "But when the jeweler told me that the wedding ring symbolizes an endless loop without a beginning, middle, or end, I didn't want to break up that endless loop with diamonds. I hope you like it."

The ring is a delicate, thin gold band with no stones. It's not a reflection of how much money Graham has or doesn't have. It's a reflection of how long he believes our love will last. An eternity.

"It's perfect, Graham."

Chapter Twenty-four

Now

". . . cervical ectopic pregnancy," she says. "Very rare. In fact, the chances of a woman experiencing this type of ectopic pregnancy are less than one percent."

Graham squeezes my hand. I lay back in the hospital bed, wanting nothing more than for the doctor to leave the room so I can go back to sleep. The medicine has me so drowsy, it's hard to pay attention to everything she's saying. I know I don't have to though, because Graham is focused on every word that comes out of her mouth. "Bed rest for two weeks," is the last thing I hear her say before I close my eyes. I know Graham is the one who loves math, but I feel like I'm going to be obsessing over that less than one percent. The chances of me getting pregnant after so many years of trying were greater than the chances of a pregnancy resulting in a cervical ectopic abruption.

"What was the cause?" Graham asks.

"More than likely the endometriosis," she replies. She goes into a little more detail, but I tune her out. I tilt my head toward Graham and open my eyes. He's staring at the doctor, listening to her response. But I can see the worry in him. His right hand is covering his mouth, his left hand still has a grip on mine.

"Could . . ." He glances down at me and there is so much worry in his eyes. "Could stress have caused the miscarriage?"

"Miscarriage was inevitable with this type of pregnancy," she says. "Nothing could have been done to prolong it. It ruptured because ectopic pregnancies aren't viable."

My miscarriage happened nineteen hours ago. It isn't until this moment that I realize Graham has spent the last nineteen hours thinking he was somehow responsible. He's been afraid that the stress from our fight led to this.

After the doctor leaves the room, I brush my thumb across his hand. It's a small gesture, and one that is very hard to make due to the amount of anger I still hold, but one he notices immediately. "You have a lot to feel guilty for, but my miscarriage is not one of them."

Graham stares at me a moment with vacant eyes and a broken soul. Then he releases my hand and walks out of the room. He doesn't come back for half an hour, but it looks like he's been crying.

He's cried a few times during our marriage. I've never actually seen him cry until yesterday, but I've seen him in the aftermath.

Graham spends the next few hours making sure I'm comfortable. My mother comes to visit, but I pretend to be asleep. Ava calls, but I tell Graham to tell her I'm asleep. I spend most of the day and night trying not to think about everything that's happening, but every time I close my eyes I find myself wishing I would have just known. Even if the pregnancy would have ended the same way, I'm angry with myself for not paying more attention to my body so I could have enjoyed it while it lasted. If I had paid more attention, I would have suspected I was pregnant. I would have taken a test. It would have been positive. And then, just once, Graham and I would have known what it felt like to be parents. Even if it would have been a fleeting feeling.

It's a little morbid that I would go through this entire thing again if I could have just known I was pregnant for one single day. After so many years of trying, it seems cruel that our payoff was a miscarriage followed by a hysterectomy without the cushion of feeling like parents, if even for a moment.

The entire ordeal has been unfair and painful. More so than my recovery will be. Because of the rupture and the hemorrhaging, the doctors had to perform an emergency abdominal hysterectomy, rather than a vaginal one. Which means a longer recovery time. I'll likely be in the hospital another day or two before I'll be discharged. Then I'll be confined to our bed for two weeks.

Everything feels so unfinished between us. We hadn't resolved anything before the miscarriage and now it just feels like the decision we were about to make has been put on hold. Because I'm in no place to discuss the future of our marriage right now. It'll probably be weeks before things are back to normal.

As normal as things can get without a uterus.

"You can't sleep?" Graham asks. He hasn't left the hospital all day. He only left the room earlier for half an hour, but then he returned and has been alternating between the couch and the chair next to my bed. Right now he's in the chair, seated on the edge of it, waiting for me to speak. He looks exhausted, but I know Graham and he isn't going anywhere until I do. "Do you want something to drink?"

I shake my head. "I'm not thirsty." The only light on in the room is the one behind my bed and it makes it look like Graham is in a spotlight on a lonely stage.

His need to console me is warring with his awareness of the tension that's been between us for so long. But he fights the tension and reaches for the rail. "Do you mind if I lay with you?" He already has the rail down and is crawling into the bed with me when I shake my head. He's careful to turn me so that my IV doesn't pull. He fits himself into less than half the bed next to me and slips a hand under my head, sacrificing his comfort for mine. He kisses me on the back of my head. Part of me wasn't sure I wanted him in the bed with me, but I soon realize that falling asleep in our shared sadness is somehow more comforting than falling asleep alone.

"I'm flying home," Ava blurts out, before I even have the chance to say hello.

"No you aren't. I'm fine."

"Quinn, I'm your sister. I want to come stay with you."

"No," I repeat. "I'll be fine. You're pregnant. The last thing you need is to spend all day on an airplane."

She sighs heavily.

"Besides," I add. "I'm thinking about coming to visit you,

instead." It's a lie. I haven't thought about it until this very moment. But my impending two weeks on bed rest makes me realize how much I'll need to put space between our house and myself when I'm finally recovered.

"Really? Can you? When do you think you'll be released to fly?"

"I'll ask the doctor when she discharges me."

"Please don't say that if you aren't serious."

"I am serious. I think it'll do me some good."

"What about Graham? Won't he be using all his vacation time during your recovery?"

I don't talk about my marriage troubles to anyone. Not even Ava. "I want to come alone," I say. I don't elaborate. I haven't told her Graham quit his job and I didn't tell her about him kissing another woman. But by the pause Ava gives me, I can tell she knows something is up. I'll wait to tell her about everything until I actually see her in person.

"Okay," she says. "Talk to your doctor and let me know a date."

"Okay. Love you."

"Love you, too."

After I end the call, I look up from the hospital bed to see Graham standing in the doorway. I wait for him to tell me it's not a good idea to plan travel after just having surgery. Instead, he just looks down at the coffee cup in his hand. "You're going to visit Ava?"

He doesn't say *we*. Part of me feels guilty. But surely he understands that I need space.

"Not until I get cleared to fly. But yeah. I need to see her."

He doesn't look up from his cup. He just nods a little and says, "Are you coming back?"

"Of course."

Of course.

I don't say it with a lot of conviction, but there's enough in my voice to assure him that this isn't a separation. It's just a break.

He swallows heavily. "How long will you be gone?"

"I don't know. Maybe a couple of weeks."

Graham nods and then takes a sip from his cup while kicking off the door. "We have some airline miles on our card. Let me know when you want to leave and I'll book your flight."

Chapter Twenty-five

Then

I don't remember Ethan's and my wedding plans being this stressful.

That might have been because I let my mother take the reins back then and had very little to do with the planning. But this is different. I want Graham and I to decide on what flavor of cake we want. I want Graham and I to decide who to invite and where it should be and what time of day we want to commit to each other for the rest of our lives. But my mother won't stop making decisions that I don't want her to make, no matter how many times I ask her to stop.

"I just want your day to be perfect, Quinn," she says.

"Graham can't afford these things, so I'm only trying to help out," she says.

"Don't forget to have him sign a prenup," she says.

"You never know if your stepfather will leave you an inheritance," she says. *"You need to protect your assets."*

She says things that make me feel like marriage is nothing more than a loan to her, rather than a commitment of love. She's brought up the idea of a prenuptial agreement so many times, she forgets that as it stands, I have no assets to protect. Besides, I know Graham isn't marrying me for the money or property my stepfather may or may not leave me one day. Graham would marry me even if I were up to my eyeballs in debt.

I feel myself starting to resent the whole idea of a lavish wedding. I would vent my frustration to Graham, but if I did that, I'd have to tell him why my mother is frustrating me. The last thing I want to do is share with Graham all the underhanded things my mother says about him.

I look down at my phone as another text comes through from my mother.

You should rethink the buffet, Quinn. Evelyn Bradbury hired a private chef for her wedding and it was so much classier.

I roll my eyes and flip my phone over so I won't be subjected to more of her texts.

I hear the front door to my apartment close, so I grab my brush. I pretend I'm just brushing my hair rather than moping in the bathroom when Graham walks in. The sight of him alone instantly calms me. My frustration is now long gone and replaced with a smile. Graham wraps his arms around me from behind and kisses me on the neck. "Hey, beautiful." He smiles at me in the mirror.

"Hey, handsome."

He spins me around and gives me an even better kiss. "How was your day?"

"Fine. How was yours?"

"Fine."

I push against his chest because he's staring at me too hard and I might accidentally let my true emotions out and then he'll ask me what's wrong and I'll have to tell him how much this wedding is stressing me out.

I turn around and face the mirror, hoping he'll go to the living room or the kitchen or anywhere that isn't somewhere he can stare at me like he's staring at me right now.

"What's bothering you?"

Sometimes I hate how well he knows me.

Except during sex. It comes in handy during sex.

"Why can't you be oblivious to a woman's emotional state like most men?"

He smiles and pulls me to him. "If I was oblivious to your emotional state, I would merely be a man in love with you. But I'm more than that. I'm your soul mate and I can feel everything you're feeling." He presses his lips to my forehead. "Why are you sad, Quinn?"

I sigh, exasperated. "My *mother*." He releases me and I walk to the bedroom and sit on my bed. I fall backward and stare up at the ceiling. "She's trying to turn our wedding into the wedding she had planned for me and Ethan. She's not even asking me what we want, Graham. She's just making decisions and telling me after the fact."

Graham crawls onto the bed and lays beside me, propping his head up on his hand. He rests his other hand on my stomach.

"Yesterday she told me she put down a deposit at the Douglas Whimberly Plaza for the date of our wedding. She's not even asking what we want, but because she's paying for everything, she thinks it earns her the right to make all the decisions. Today she texted and said she ordered the invitations."

Graham makes a face. "You think that means our wedding invitations will have the word *prestigious* in them?"

I laugh. "I'd be more shocked if they didn't." My head flops to the side and I give him the most pathetic look, short of pouting. "I don't want a huge wedding in a fancy plaza with all my mother's friends there."

"What *do* you want?"

"At this point I don't even know that I *want* a wedding." Graham tilts his head, a little concerned by my comment. I quickly rectify it. "I don't mean I don't want to marry you. I just don't want to marry you in my mother's dream wedding."

Graham gives me a reassuring smile. "We've only been engaged for three months. We still have five months before the wedding date. There's plenty of time to put your foot down and make sure you get what you want. If it'll make things easier for you, just blame everything on me. Tell her I said no and she can hate me for ruining her dream wedding while keeping the peace between the two of you."

Why is he so perfect? "You really don't care if I blame you?"

He laughs. "Quinn, your mother already hates me. This will give her a little more justification for her hatred and then everyone wins." He stands up and slips off his shoes. "We going out tonight?"

"Whatever you want to do. Ava and Reid are ordering some kind of fight on Pay-Per-View and invited us over."

Graham undoes his tie. "That sounds fun. I have some emails I need to send but I can be ready in an hour."

I watch as he leaves the room. I fall back onto the bed and

smile because it feels like he just might have come up with a solution to some of my issues in less than two minutes. But even though the solution sounds like a good one—*just blame Graham for everything*—my mother will never go for it. She'll just point out that Graham isn't paying for the wedding, so Graham doesn't get a say.

But still. He *tried* to solve my issues. That's what counts, right? He's willing to take the blame for something just to keep the peace between my mother and me.

I can't believe I get to marry that man in five months. I can't believe I get to spend the rest of my life with him. Even if that life together will start in the Douglas Whimberly Plaza, surrounded by people I barely know and food that's so expensive, it guarantees ample trays full of raw meat and ceviche that no one actually likes to eat, but pretends to because it's fancy.

Oh, well. The wedding may not be ideal, but it will only be a few painful hours, followed by a lifetime of perfection.

I drag myself off the bed, committed to somehow remaining sane for the next five months. I spend the next half hour getting ready for our night out. Graham and I have a handful of friends we sometimes spend time with on the weekends, but we mostly spend our time with Ava and Reid. They got married just before I met Graham. Ava was smart. She married Reid on a whim in Vegas. My mother wasn't able to order her invitations or book her venue or even choose which cake tasted best to her. I was the only one who knew they were jetting off to Vegas to get married and I've secretly been envious of their decision.

I'm buttoning my jeans when Graham walks into the bathroom. "Are you ready?"

"Almost. Let me grab some shoes." I walk to my closet and Graham follows me in there. He leans against the doorway and watches me while I look for a pair of shoes. I have to dress up for work every day, so a lazy night at Ava and Reid's is a nice respite from the heels and business attire I wear daily. I'm looking through all the shoes on my shelf, trying to find my favorite comfy pair. Graham is watching me the whole time. I glance at him a couple of times and I can't help but think he's up to something. There's a smirk on his face. It's barely there, but it's there.

"What is it?"

He unfolds his arms and slides his hands into the pockets of his jeans. "What if I told you I just spent the last half hour reworking the plans for our wedding?"

I stand up straight. He definitely has all my attention now. "What do you mean?"

He inhales a breath, like he's trying to calm his nerves. Knowing he's nervous about whatever he's about to say makes *me* nervous for what he's about to say.

"I don't care about the details of our wedding, Quinn. We can have whatever kind of wedding you want as long as the final result is that you'll be my wife. But . . ." He walks into my closet and pauses a foot away from me. "If the only thing you want from this wedding is me, then why are we waiting? Let's just go ahead and get married. This weekend." Before I can speak, he grabs my hands and squeezes them. "I just booked the beach house through next Monday. I spoke to a minister who is willing to come marry us there. He'll even bring a witness so we don't have to tell anyone. It'll just be you and me. We'll get married by the ocean tomorrow afternoon and then tomorrow night we can sit by the fire where I proposed to you. We'll spend the whole night eating s'mores and asking each other questions, and then we'll make love and fall asleep and wake up married on Sunday."

I'm almost as speechless as I was the moment he proposed to me. And just like three months ago when I was too excited and shocked to say *yes*, I nod. Profusely. And I laugh and I hug him and I kiss him.

"It's perfect, it's perfect, I love you, it's *perfect*."

We grab a suitcase out of my closet and start packing. We decide we aren't telling anyone. Not even his mother.

"We can call them tomorrow, after we're married," Graham says.

I can't stop smiling, even though I know my mother is going to completely lose it when I call her tomorrow night and tell her we're already married. "My mother is going to kill us."

"Yes, she probably will. But it's a lot easier to ask for forgiveness than permission."

Chapter Twenty-six

Now

Tomorrow will mark three weeks since I've been at Ava's and I haven't heard Graham's voice since the day he dropped me off at the airport.

He called me once last week but I didn't answer my phone. I texted him and told him I needed time to think. He responded and said *Call me when you're ready*. He hasn't texted me since then and I'm still not ready to call him.

As miserable as I feel inside, I really do like it here at Ava's. I can't determine if I like it because it's new and different or if I like it because I feel further away from all of my problems. I haven't done a lot of sightseeing because of the recovery. My body is still sore and weaker than what I'm used to. But Ava and Reid's home is beautiful and relaxing, so I don't mind spending most of my time here. It's been so long since Ava and I had quality time together, I've actually been enjoying myself despite the circumstances of my marriage.

I do miss Graham, though. But I miss the Graham that was married to the happier version of myself. We fit together better in the beginning than we do now. I know that's because my piece of the puzzle has changed shape more than his. But even though I feel more at fault over the downfall of our relationship, it still does nothing to change the trajectory.

This trip has been exactly what my soul was craving—a much-needed change of pace. I spoke openly to Ava about everything going on with Graham for the first time. The thing I love most about Ava is that she listens more than she gives advice. I don't really want advice. Advice won't change how I feel. Advice won't change the fact that I can't get pregnant. Advice won't change the fact that Graham said he was devastated he hasn't become a father yet. The only thing advice is good for is to pad the esteem of the person giving it. So instead of advice, she's just given me distraction. Not only from Graham, but from our mother. From work. From infertility. Connecticut. *My whole life.*

"What about this color?" Ava holds up a swatch of yellow paint.

"Too . . . canary," I say.

She looks down at the swatch and laughs. "That's actually what it's called. Canary."

Reid walks to the stove and lifts a lid from a pot, taking a whiff of the sauce he's been cooking. I'm sitting on the bar with Ava, looking through possible wall colors for their nursery. "If we'd just find out what we're having, it would make this process a lot easier," Reid says, putting the lid back on the pot. He turns off the burner.

"Nope," Ava says, sliding off the bar. "We decided we aren't finding out. We only have ten weeks left. Be patient." She gathers three plates from the cabinet and walks them to the table. I take silverware and napkins to the table while Reid brings the pasta.

Neither of them have made me feel as if I'm overstaying my welcome, but I'm starting to worry that I might be. Three weeks is a long time to host someone. "I'll probably fly home this week," I say as I spoon pasta onto my plate.

"Don't leave on our account," Reid says. "I like having you here. Brings me a little peace of mind while I'm traveling."

Reid spends two or three nights a week away from home and with Ava being pregnant, he worries about leaving her alone more than she wants him to. "I don't know why my presence brings you peace of mind. Ava is braver than I am."

"It's true," she says. "One time we went to a haunted house and Freddy Krueger jumped out at us. Quinn pushed me toward him and ran back to the entrance."

"Did not," I say. "I pushed you toward Jason Voorhees."

"Either way, I almost died," Ava says.

"Do you think you'll fly back in two months when Ava has the baby?"

"Of course I will."

"Bring Graham this time," Reid says. "I miss the guy."

Graham and Reid have always gotten along well. But I can tell by the look Ava gives me that she hasn't told Reid about Graham's and my issues. I appreciate that.

I twist my fork in the pasta, reflecting on how lonely I've felt since Ava and Reid moved away from Connecticut, but this is the first time I've realized how much their move probably affected Graham, too. He lost a friend in Reid with their move. Probably his closest friend since Tanner. But he's never once talked about it because my sadness fills our house from wall to wall, leaving no room for his sadness.

For the rest of dinner, all I can think about are all the things Graham probably doesn't tell me because he doesn't want to put his sadness onto me. When we're finished eating, I offer to do the dishes. Reid and Ava are sitting at the table, poring over more color options for the nursery when their doorbell rings.

"That's weird," Ava says.

"Really weird," Reid agrees.

"Do you two never have visitors?"

Reid scoots back from the table. "Never. We don't really know anyone here well enough yet for them to come to our house." He walks to the door and Ava and I are both watching him when he opens it.

The last person I expect to see standing in that doorway is Graham.

My hands are submersed in suds and I remain frozen as Reid and Graham hug hello. Reid helps him with his suitcase and as soon as he walks through the door, Graham's eyes go in search of mine.

When he finally sees me, it's as if his whole body relaxes. Reid is smiling, looking back and forth between us expectantly, waiting on the surprised reunion. But I don't run to Graham and he doesn't run to me. We just stare at each other in silence for a beat. The beat is a little too long. Long enough for Reid to sense the tension in this reunion.

He clears his throat and takes Graham's suitcase. "I'll um . . . put this in the guest room for you."

"I'll help you," Ava says, quickly standing. When they've

both disappeared down the hallway, I finally break out of my shocked trance long enough to pull my hands out of the water and dry them on a dish towel. Graham slowly makes his way into the kitchen, eyeing me carefully the whole time.

My heart is pounding at the sight of him. I didn't realize how much I missed him, but I don't think that's why my heart is pounding. My pulse is out of control because his presence means confrontation. And confrontation means a decision. I'm not sure I was ready for that yet. It's the only reason I've still been hiding out at my sister's house halfway across the world from him.

"Hey," he says. It's such a simple word, but it feels more serious than anything he's ever said to me. I guess that's what almost three weeks of not speaking to your husband feels like.

"Hi." My reply comes out cautious. But not as cautious as the hug I eventually give him. It's quick and meaningless and I want a redo as soon as I pull away from him, but instead I reach toward the sink and remove the drain. "This is a surprise."

Graham shrugs, leaning against the counter next to me. He gives the kitchen and living room a quick once-over before bringing his eyes back to mine. "How are you feeling?"

I nod. "Good. I'm still a little sore, but I've been getting plenty of rest." Surprisingly, I do feel good. "I thought I might be sadder than I am, but I've realized I had already come to terms with the fact that my uterus was useless, so what does it matter that it's no longer in my body?"

Graham stares at me in silence, not really knowing how to respond to that. I don't expect him to, but his silence makes me want to scream. I don't know what he's doing here. I don't know what I'm supposed to say. I'm angry that he showed up without warning and angry that I'm happy to see him.

I wipe my hand across my forehead and press my back into the counter next to him.

"What are you doing here, Graham?"

He leans in to me, looking at me sincerely. "I can't take this another day, Quinn." His voice is low and pleading. "I need you to make a choice. Either leave me for good or come home with me." He reaches for me, pulling me to his chest. "Come home with me," he repeats in a whisper.

I close my eyes and inhale the scent of him. I want so bad to tell him I forgive him. That I don't even blame him for what he did.

Yes, Graham kissing someone who wasn't me is the single worst thing he's done during our relationship. But I'm not completely innocent in this situation.

Forgiving him isn't even what I've been worried about.

I'm worried about what happens *after* I forgive him. We had issues before he kissed another woman. We'll still have those same issues if I forgive him. That night in the car, before the miscarriage, Graham and I fought about the affair. But as soon as we open this floodgate tonight . . . that's when the real fight will happen. That's when we'll talk about the issues that caused all the other issues that lead to our current issues. This is the talk I've been trying to avoid for a couple of years now.

The talk that's about to happen because he just flew halfway around the world to confront me.

I pull away from Graham, but before I can speak, Reid and Ava interrupt us, but only momentarily. "We're going out for dessert," Ava says, pulling on her jacket.

Reid opens the front door. "See you two in an hour."

He closes the door and Graham and I are suddenly alone in their house, half a world away from our home. Half a world away from the comfort of our avoidance.

"You must be exhausted," I say. "Do you want to sleep first? Or eat?"

"I'm fine," he says quickly.

I nod, realizing just how imminent this conversation is. He doesn't even want food or water before we do this. And I can do nothing but stand here like I'm trying to decide if I want to talk it out or run from him so we can continue to avoid it. There's never been so much tension between us as we contemplate our next moves.

He eventually walks to the table. I follow him, taking a seat across from him. He folds his arms over the table and looks at me.

He's so handsome. As many times as I've turned away from him in the past, it's not because I'm not attracted to him. That's never been the issue. Even now after a full day of travel, he looks better than he did the day I met him. It always works that way with men, doesn't it? They somehow look manlier into their thirties and forties than they did in the pinnacle of their youth.

Graham has always taken good care of himself. Still, like clockwork, he wakes up every day and goes for a run. I love that he stays in shape, but not because of the physical attributes it's given him. My favorite part of him is that he never talks about it. Graham isn't the type to prove anything to anyone or turn his fitness routine into a pissing match with his friends. He runs for himself and no one else and I love that about him.

He reminds me a lot in this moment of how he looked the

morning after we got married. *Tired*. Neither of us got much sleep the night of our wedding and by morning, he looked like he'd aged five years overnight. His hair was in disarray; his eyes were slightly swollen from lack of sleep. But at least that morning he looked *happy* and tired.

Right now, he's nothing but sad and tired.

He presses his palms and fingertips together and brings his hands against his mouth. He looks nervous, but also ready to get this over with. "What are you thinking?"

I hate the feeling I'm experiencing right now. It's like all my worries and fears have been bound together in a tight ball and that ball is bouncing around inside of me, pounding against my heart, my lungs, my gut, my throat. It's making my hands shake, so I clasp them together on the table in front of me and try to still them.

"I'm thinking about everything," I say. "About where you went wrong. Where *I* went wrong." I release a quick rush of air. "I'm thinking about how right it used to feel and how I wish it was still like that."

"We can get back to that, Quinn. I know we can."

He's so hopeful when he says it. And naïve. "How?"

He doesn't have an answer for that question. Maybe that's because he doesn't feel broken. Everything broken in our marriage stems from me, and he can't fix me. I'm sure if he could somehow fix our sex life, that would be enough to appease him for a few more years.

"Do you think we should have sex more often?" *Graham almost looks offended by my question.* "That would make you happier, right?"

He traces an invisible line on the table, looking down at it until he begins to speak. "I won't lie and say I'm happy with our sex life. But I'm also not going to pretend that's the only thing I wish were different. What I want more than anything is for you to want to be my wife."

"No, what you want is for me to be the wife I used to be. I don't think you want me as I am now."

Graham stares at me a moment. "Maybe you're right. Is it so bad that I missed it when I was convinced that you were in love with me? When you would get excited to see me? When you wanted to make love to me because you wanted to and not because you just wanted to get pregnant?" He leans forward, pegging me with his stare. "We can't have kids, Quinn. And you know what? I'm okay with that. I didn't marry you for the potential kids we might have had together one day. I fell in love with you and I committed to you because I wanted to spend the rest of my life with you. That's all I cared about when I said my vows. But I'm starting to realize that maybe you didn't marry me for the same reasons."

"That's not fair," I say quietly. He can't insinuate that I wouldn't have married him if I'd known he couldn't have kids. And he can't say he still would have married me if he'd had that knowledge prior to our marriage. A person can't confidently proclaim what they would have done or how they would have felt in a situation they've never been in.

Graham stands up and walks to the kitchen. He grabs a bottle of water out of the fridge and I sit silently as he drinks it. I wait for him to come back to the table to continue the conversation, because I'm not ready to speak again. I need to know everything he's feeling before I decide what to say. What to do. When he takes his seat again, he reaches across the table and puts his hand over mine. He looks at me sincerely.

"I will never put a single ounce of blame on you for what

I did. I kissed someone who wasn't you and that was my fault. But that's only one issue out of a dozen issues we have in this marriage and they are *not* all my fault. I can't help you when I don't know what's going on in your head." He pulls my hand closer and cradles it between both of his. "I know that I have put you through hell these past few weeks. And I am so, so sorry for that. More than you know. But if you can forgive me for putting you through the worst thing imaginable, then I know we can get through the rest of it. I *know* we can."

He's looking at me with so much hope in his expression. I guess that's easy to do when he honestly believes him kissing someone else is the worst thing that's ever happened to me.

If I weren't so outraged, I would laugh. I pull my hand away from him.

I stand up.

I try to suck in a breath, but I had no idea anger settled in the lungs.

When I'm finally able to respond to him, I do it slowly and quietly because if there's anything I need for Graham to understand, it's everything I'm about to say. I lean forward and press my palms against the table, staring directly at him.

"The fact that you think what you did with that woman was the worst thing that could possibly happen to me proves that you have *no* idea what I've been through. You have no idea what it's like to experience infertility. Because *you* aren't experiencing infertility, Graham. *I* am. Don't get that confused. You can fuck another woman and make a baby. *I* can't fuck another man and make a baby." I push off the table and spin around. I planned to take a moment and gather my thoughts, but apparently, I don't need a moment, because I immediately turn and face him again. "And I *loved* making love to you,

Graham. It's not you I didn't want. It was the agony that came afterward. Your infidelity is a walk in the park compared to what I experienced month after month every time we had sex and it lead to nothing but an orgasm. An *orgasm*! Big *fucking* deal! How was I supposed to admit that to you? There was no way I could admit that I grew to despise every hug and every kiss and every touch because all of it would lead to the worst day of my life every twenty-eight fucking days!" I push past the chair and walk away from the table. "Fuck you and your affair. I don't give a *fuck* about your affair, Graham."

I walk into the kitchen as soon as I'm finished. I don't even want to look at him right now. It's the most honest I've ever been and I'm scared of what it did to him. I'm also scared that I don't care what it did to him.

I don't even know why I'm arguing issues that are irrelevant. I can't get pregnant now no matter how much we fight about the past.

I pour myself a glass of water and sip from it while I calm down.

A few silent moments go by before Graham moves from the table. He walks into the kitchen and leans against the counter in front of me, crossing his feet at the ankles. When I work up the courage to look at his eyes, I'm surprised to see a calmness in them. Even after the harsh words that just left my mouth, he somehow still looks at me like he doesn't absolutely hate me.

We stare at each other, both of us dry-eyed and full of years' worth of things we should never have kept bottled up. Despite his calmness and his lack of animosity, he looks deflated by everything I just yelled at him—like my words were safety pins, poking holes in him, letting all the air out.

I can tell by the exhaustion in his expression that he's given up again. I don't blame him. Why keep fighting for someone who is no longer fighting for *you*?

Graham closes his eyes and grips the bridge of his nose with two fingers. He cycles through a calming breath before folding both arms over his chest. He shakes his head, like he's finally come to a realization that he never wanted to come to. "No matter how hard I try . . . no matter how much I love you . . . I can't be the one thing you've always wanted me to be, Quinn. I will never be a father."

A tear immediately falls from my eye. And then another. But I remain stoic as he steps toward me.

"If this is what our marriage is . . . if this is all it will ever be . . . just me and you . . . will that be enough? Am I enough for you, Quinn?"

I'm confounded. Speechless.

I stare at him in utter disbelief, unable to answer him. Not because I can't. I know the answer to his question. I've *always* known the answer. But I stay silent because I'm not sure I *should* answer him.

The silence that lingers between his question and my answer creates the biggest misunderstanding our marriage has ever seen. Graham's jaw hardens. His eyes harden. Everything—even his heart—hardens. He looks away from me because my silence means something different to him than what it means to me.

He walks out of the kitchen, toward the guest room. Probably to get his suitcase and leave again. It takes everything in me not to run after him and beg him to stay. I want to fall to my knees and tell him that if on our wedding day, someone had forced me to choose between the possibility of having children or spending a life with Graham, I would have chosen life with him. Without a doubt, I would have chosen him.

I can't believe our marriage has come to this point. The point where my behavior has convinced Graham that he's not enough for me. He *is* enough for me.

The problem is . . . he could be so much more *without* me.

I blow out a shaky breath and turn around, pressing my palms into the counter. The agony of knowing what I'm doing to him makes my entire body tremble.

When he emerges from the hallway, he's not holding his suitcase. He's holding something else.

The box.

He brought our box with him?

He walks into the kitchen and sets it beside me on the counter. "If you don't tell me to stop, we're opening it."

I lean forward and press my arms into the counter, my face against my arms. I don't tell him to stop, though. All I can do is cry. It's the kind of cry I've experienced in my dreams. The cries that hurt so much, you can't even make a sound.

"Quinn," he pleads with a shaky voice. I squeeze my eyes shut even harder. "*Quinn.*" He whispers my name like it's his final plea. When I still refuse to ask him to stop, I hear him move the box closer to me. I hear him insert the key into the lock. I hear him pull the lock off, but instead of it clinking against the counter, it crashes against the kitchen wall.

He is so angry right now.

"Look at me."

I shake my head. I don't want to look at him. I don't want to remember what it felt like when we closed that box together all those years ago.

He slides his hand through my hair and leans down, bringing his lips to my ear. "This box won't open itself, and I sure as hell am not going to be the one to do it."

His hand leaves my hair and his lips leave my ear. He slides the box over until it's touching my arm.

There have only been a handful of times I've cried this hard in my life. Three of those times were when the IVF rounds didn't take. One of those times was the night I found out Graham kissed another woman. One of those times was when I found out I had a hysterectomy. Out of all the times I've cried this hard, Graham has held me every single time. Even when the tears were because of him.

This time feels so much harder. I don't know if I'm strong enough to face this kind of devastation on my own.

As if he knows this, I feel his arms slide around me. His loving, caring, selfless arms pull me to him, and even though we're on opposite sides of this war, he refuses to pick up his weapons. My face is now pressed against his chest and I am so broken.

So broken.

I try to still the war inside me, but all I hear are the same sentences that have been repeating over and over in my head since the moment I first heard them.

"You would make such a great father, Graham."

"I know. It devastates me that it still hasn't happened yet."

I press a kiss to Graham's chest and whisper a silent promise against his heart. *Someday it'll happen for you, Graham. Someday you'll understand.*

I pull away from his chest.

I open the box.

We finally end the dance.

Chapter Twenty-seven

Then

It's been five hours since we said I do on a secluded beach in the presence of two strangers we met just minutes before our vows. And I don't have a single regret.

Not one.

I don't regret agreeing to spend the weekend with Graham at the beach house. I don't regret getting married five months before we planned to. I don't regret texting my mother when it was over, thanking her for her help, but letting her know it's no longer needed because we're already married. And I don't regret that instead of a fancy dinner at the Douglas Whimberly Plaza, Graham and I grilled hot dogs over the fire pit and ate cookies for dessert.

I don't think I'll ever regret any of this. Something so perfect could never become a regret.

Graham opens the sliding glass door and walks onto the balcony. It was too cold to sit up here when we were here three months ago, but it's perfect tonight. A cool breeze is coming off the water, blowing my hair just enough to keep it out of my face. Graham takes a seat next to me, tugging me toward him. I snuggle against him.

Graham leans forward slightly and places his phone next to mine on the railing in front of us. He's been inside breaking the news to his mother that there won't be a wedding.

"Is your mother upset?" I ask.

"She's pretending to be happy for us but I can tell she would have liked to have been there."

"Do you feel guilty?"

He laughs. "Not at all. She's been through two weddings with two of my sisters and she's in the middle of planning the last one's wedding. I'm sure a huge part of her is relieved. It's my sisters I'm worried about."

I didn't even think about them. I texted Ava on the way here yesterday, but I think she's the only one who knew. Ava and all three of Graham's sisters were going to be bridesmaids in the wedding. We had just told them last week. "What did they say?"

"I haven't told them yet," he says. "I'm sure I won't have to because ten bucks says my mother is on the phone with all three of them right now."

"I'm sure they'll be happy for you. Besides, they met my mother on Easter Sunday. They'll understand why we ended up doing it this way."

My phone pings. Graham reaches forward and grabs it for me. He naturally glances at it as he's handing it to me. When I see the text is from my mom, I try to pull the phone from him, but it's too late. He pulls it back to him and finishes reading the text.

"What is she talking about?"

I read the text and feel panic wash over me. "It's nothing." *Please just let it go, Graham.*

I can tell he isn't, because he urges me to sit up and look at him. "Why did she text you that?"

I look down at my phone again. At her terrible text.

You think he jumped the gun because he was excited to marry you? Wake up, Quinn. It was the perfect way for him to avoid signing.

"Sign what?" Graham asks.

I press my hand against his heart and try to find the words, but they're somehow even harder to find tonight than they have been the last three months I've avoided talking about it.

"She's talking about a prenuptial agreement."

"For what?" Graham says. I can already hear the offense in his voice.

"She's concerned my stepfather has changed the will to add me to it. Or maybe he already has, I don't know. It would make more sense, since she's been wanting me to talk to you about it so bad."

"Why haven't you?"

"I was going to. It's just . . . I don't feel like I need to, Graham. I know that's not why you're marrying me. And even if my mother's husband does leave me money in the future, I don't care that it would go to both of us."

Graham hooks his thumb under my chin. "First, you're right. I don't give a damn about your bank account. Second, your mother is mean to you and it makes me angry. But . . .

as mean as she speaks to you sometimes, she's right. You shouldn't have married me without a prenup. I don't know why you never talked to me about it. I would have signed one without question. I'm an accountant, Quinn. It's the smart thing to do when assets are involved."

I don't know what I was expecting, but I wasn't expecting him to agree with her. "Oh. Well . . . I should have brought it up to you, then. I didn't think the conversation would be this easy."

"I'm your husband. My goal is to make things easier on you, not more difficult." He kisses me, but the kiss is interrupted by my phone going off.

It's another text from my mother. Before I can finish reading it, Graham takes the phone from me. He types out a text to her.

Graham agreed to sign a postnup. Have your lawyer draft
it up. Problem solved.

He sets the phone on the railing and, similar to the first night we met, he pushes the phone over the edge of the balcony. Before my phone lands in the bushes below, Graham's phone receives an incoming text. And then another. And another.

"Your sisters."

Graham leans forward and gives his phone a shove, too. When we hear it land in the bushes below, we both laugh.

"Much better," he says. He stands up and reaches for my hand. "Come on. I have a present for you."

I grab his hand and jump up with excitement. "Really? A wedding present?"

He pulls me behind him, walking me into the bedroom. "Have a seat," he says, motioning to the bed. "I'll be right back."

I hop onto the center of the bed and wait giddily for him to get back with the gift. It's the first gift I've ever received from my husband, so I'm making a way bigger deal out of it than it probably needs to be. I don't know when he would have had time to buy me something. We didn't know we were getting married until half an hour before we came here.

Graham walks back into the room holding a wooden box. I don't know if the box is my present or if there's something inside of it, but the box itself is so beautiful, I wouldn't mind if the actual box was my present. It's a dark mahogany wood and it looks hand-carved, with intricate detailing on the top of the lid.

"Did you make this?"

"A few years ago," he says. "I used to build stuff in my father's garage. I like working with wood."

"I didn't know that about you."

Graham smiles at me. "Side effect of marrying someone you've known less than a year." He takes a seat across from me on the bed. He won't stop smiling, which excites me even more. He doesn't hand me the present, though. He opens the lid and pulls something out of the box. It's familiar. An envelope with his name on it.

"You know what this is?"

I take the envelope from him. The last time we were at this beach house, Graham asked me to write him a love letter. As soon as we got home, I spent an entire evening writing him this letter. I even sprayed it with my perfume and slipped a nude pic in the envelope before I sealed it.

After I gave it to him, I wondered why he never mentioned it again. But I got so caught up in the wedding, I forgot about it. I flip over the envelope and see that it's never even been opened. "Why haven't you opened it?"

He pulls another envelope out of the box, but he doesn't answer me. This one is a larger envelope with my name on it.

I grab it from him, more excited for a love letter than I've ever been in my life. "You wrote me one, too?"

"First love letter I've ever written," he says. "I think it's a decent first attempt."

I grin and use my finger to start to tear open the flap, but Graham snatches it out of my hands before I can get it open.

"You can't read it yet." He holds the letter against his chest like I might fight him for it.

"Why not?"

"Because," he says, putting both envelopes back in the box. "It's not time."

"You wrote me a letter I'm not allowed to read?"

Graham appears to be enjoying this. "You have to wait. We're locking this box and we're saving it to open on our twenty-fifth wedding anniversary." He grabs a lock that goes to the box and he slides it through the attached loop.

"Graham!" I say, laughing. "This is like the worst gift ever! You gave me twenty-five years of torment!"

He laughs.

As frustrating as the gift is, it's also one of the sweetest things he's ever done. I lift up onto my knees and lean forward, wrapping my arms around his neck. "I'm kind of mad I don't get to read your letter yet," I whisper. "But it's a really beautiful gift. You really are the sweetest man I know, Mr. Wells."

He kisses the tip of my nose. "I'm glad you like it, Mrs. Wells."

I kiss him and then sit back down on the bed. I run my

hand over the top of the box. "I'm sad you won't see my picture for another twenty-five years. It required a lot of flexibility."

Graham arches an eyebrow. "Flexibility, huh?"

I grin. I look down at the box, wondering what his letter to me says. I can't believe I have to wait twenty-five years. "There's no way around the wait?"

"The only time we're allowed to open this box before our twenty-fifth anniversary is if it's an emergency."

"What kind of emergency? Like . . . death?"

He shakes his head. "No. A relationship emergency. Like . . . divorce."

"Divorce?" I hate that word. "Seriously?"

"I don't see us needing to open this box for any other reason than to celebrate our longevity, Quinn. But, if one of us ever decides we want a divorce—if we've reached the point where we think that's the only answer—we have to promise not to go through with it until we open this box and read these letters. Maybe reminding each other of how we felt when we closed the box will help change our minds if we ever need to open it early."

"So this box isn't just a keepsake. It's also a marriage survival kit?"

Graham shrugs. "You could say that. But we have nothing to worry about. I'm confident we won't need to open this box for another twenty-five years."

"I'm *more* than confident," I say. "I would bet on it, but if I lose and we get divorced, I won't have enough money to pay out on our bet because you never signed a prenup."

Graham winks at me. "You shouldn't have married a gold digger."

"Do I still have time to change my mind?"

Graham clicks the lock shut. "Too late. I already locked it." He picks up the key to the lock and walks the box to the dresser. "I'll tape the key to the bottom of it tomorrow so we'll never lose it," he says.

He walks around the bed to get closer to me. He grabs me by the waist and lifts me off the bed, throwing me over his shoulder. He carries me over the patio threshold and back outside to the balcony where he slides me down his body as he sits on the swing.

I'm straddling his lap now, holding his face in my hands. "That was a really sweet gift," I whisper. "Thank you."

"You're welcome."

"I didn't get you a gift. I didn't know I was getting married today so I didn't have time to shop."

Graham slides my hair over my shoulder and presses his lips against the skin of my neck. "I can't think of a single gift in the world I would push you off my lap for."

"What if I bought you a huge flat screen TV? I bet you'd push me off your lap for a flat screen."

He laughs against my neck. "Nope." His hand slides up my stomach until he's cupping my breast.

"What about a new car?"

He slowly drags his lips up my throat. When his mouth reaches mine, he whispers *hell no* against my lips. He tries to kiss me, but I pull back just enough.

"What if I bought you one of those fancy calculators that cost like two grand? I bet you'd push me off your lap for math."

Graham slides his hands down my back. "Not even for math." His tongue pushes between my lips and he kisses me with such assurance, my head starts to spin. And for the next half hour, that's all we do. We make out like teenagers on the outdoor balcony.

Graham eventually stands up, holding me against him without breaking our kiss. He carries me inside and lays me down on the bed. He turns out the light and pushes the sliding glass door all the way open so we can hear the waves as they crash against the shore.

When he returns to the bed, he pulls off my clothes, one piece at a time, ripping my shirt in the process. He kisses his way down my neck and down my throat, all the way to my thighs, giving attention to every single part of me.

When he finally makes it back to my mouth, he tastes like me.

I roll him onto his back and return the favor until I taste like him.

When he spreads my legs and connects us, it feels different and new, because it's the first time we've made love as husband and wife.

He's still inside me when the first ray of sun begins to peek out from the ocean.

Chapter Twenty-eight

Now

Graham does nothing after I open the box. He just stands next to me in silence as I grab the envelope with his name on it. I slide it to him and look back down in the box.

I lift the envelope with my name on it, assuming it would be the only thing left inside the box since all we put in it before closing it were these two letters. But beneath our two letters, there are a few more letters, all addressed to me with dates on them. *He's been adding letters.* I look up at him, silently questioning him.

"There were things I needed to say that you never really wanted to hear." He grabs his envelope and walks out the back door, onto Ava and Reid's back porch. I take the box to the guest bedroom and close the door.

I sit alone on the bed, holding the only envelope from him that I expected to find in the box. The one from our wedding night. He wrote the date in the top right corner of the envelope. I open the other envelopes and I pile the pages on top of each other in the order they were written. I'm too scared to read any of it. Too scared not to.

When we locked this box all those years ago, there wasn't a doubt in my mind that we wouldn't need to open it before our twenty-fifth wedding anniversary. But that was back before reality set in. Back before we knew that our dream of having kids would never come true. Back before we knew that the more time that passed and the more devastating moments I experienced and the more Graham made love to me, that it would *all* start to hurt.

My hands are shaking as I press the pages to the blanket, smoothing them out. I lift the first page and begin to read it.

I don't think I'm prepared for this. I don't think anyone who gets married for the right reasons ever expects this moment to come. I stiffen like I'm bracing myself for impact as I begin to read.

Dear Quinn,

> *I thought I would have more time to prepare this letter. We aren't supposed to get married yet, so this gift is all very last minute. I'm not even that great of a writer, so I'm not sure I'm even going to be able to convey what I need to say to you in words. I'm better with numbers, but I don't want to bore you with a bunch of math equations, like Me plus you equals infinity.*
>
> *If you think that's cheesy, you're lucky you met me later in life, rather than when I was in junior high. When I was in the seventh grade, I concocted a love*

*poem that I was going to write down and give to my
first girlfriend. Thank God it was years later before
I actually got my first girlfriend. By then, I realized
what a bad idea it was to rhyme a love poem with the
Periodic Table of Elements.*

*However, I'm so comfortable in my masculinity
around you, I think this is the perfect time to finally
put that Periodic Table of Elements love poem to use.
Because yes, I still remember it. Some of it.*

> *Hey, girl, you're looking mighty fine*
> *Feels like I'm breathing Iodine*
>
> *Your smile gets all up in my head*
> *Feel so heavy, like I'm dragging Lead*
>
> *Your skin is smooth, it looks so sleek*
> *It's like someone dipped you in Zinc*
>
> *Kissing you would never get old*
> *Marry me girl, I'll flank you in Gold*

*That's right. You're the lucky girl who gets to marry
the author of that poem today.*

*Good thing it'll be twenty-five years before you read
it, because as soon as we're married this afternoon, I'm
never letting you out of this marriage. I'm like Hotel
California. You can love Graham any time you like,
but you can never leave.*

*The minister will be here in two hours. You're
upstairs getting ready for our wedding as I write this*

letter. On our way here yesterday, we stopped at a bridal store and you made me wait in the car while you ran inside to pick out a wedding dress. When you got back to the car with the dress hidden inside of a garment bag, you couldn't stop laughing. You said the ladies who were helping you thought you were insane, buying a dress just a day before your wedding. You said they gasped when you told them you're a procrastinator and that you still haven't picked out a groom.

I can't wait to see what you look like walking down that aisle of sand. It'll just be you in your dress on a beach with no decorations, no guests, no fanfare. And the entire ocean will be our backdrop. But let's just pray none of your dream from last night comes true.

This morning when you woke up, I asked what I had missed while you were sleeping. You told me you had a dream that we were getting married on the beach, but right before we said I do, a tsunami came and washed us away. But we didn't die. We both turned into aquatic killers. You were a shark and I was a whale, and we were still in love, even though you were a fish and I was a mammal. You said the rest of your dream was just us trying to love one another in an ocean full of creatures who didn't approve of our interspecies relationship.

That's probably my favorite dream of yours to date.

I'm sitting out here on the patio, writing the love letter I thought I had five more months to write. Part of me is a little nervous because, like I said, I've never been much of a writer. My imagination isn't as wild as yours, as evidenced by the things you dream about.

But writing a letter to you about how much I love you should come pretty easily, so hopefully this letter and this gift to you will serve its purpose.

Honestly, Quinn, I don't even know where to start. I guess the beginning is the most obvious choice, right?

I could begin by talking about the day we met in the hallway. The day I realized that maybe my life was thrown off course because fate had something even better in store for me.

But instead, I'm going to talk about the day we didn't meet. This will probably come as a surprise to you because you don't remember it. Or maybe you do have a memory of it but you just didn't realize it was me.

It was a few months before we met in the hallway. Ethan's father held a Christmas party for their employees and I was Sasha's date. You were Ethan's date. And while I will admit I was still wrapped up in all things Sasha at the time, something about you was engraved in my memory after that night.

We hadn't been formally introduced, but you were just a few feet away and I knew who you were because Sasha had pointed you and Ethan out a few minutes before. She said Ethan was in line to be her next boss and you were in line to be his wife.

You were wearing a black dress with black heels. Your hair was up in a tight bun and I overheard you joking with someone about how you looked just like the caterers. They all wore black and the girls had their hair styled the same way as yours. I don't know if the catering team was shorthanded that night, but I remember seeing someone walk up to you and ask for a refill on his champagne. Rather than correct him, you just walked behind the bar and refilled his champagne. You then took the bottle and started refilling other people's glasses. When you finally made it over to me and Sasha, Ethan walked up and asked what you were doing. You told him you were refilling drinks like it was no big deal, but he didn't like it. I could tell by the look on his face that it embarrassed him. He told you to put down the champagne bottle because there was someone he wanted you to meet. He walked off and I'll never forget what you did next.

You turned to me and you rolled your eyes with a laugh, then held up the champagne bottle and offered me a refill.

I smiled at you and held out my glass. You refilled Sasha's glass and proceeded to offer refills to other guests until the bottle was finally empty.

I don't remember much else about that night. It was a mundane party and Sasha was in a bad mood most of the time so we left early. And to be honest, I didn't think about you much after that.

Not until the day I saw you again in the hallway. When you stepped off the elevator and walked toward Ethan's door, I should have been filled with nothing but absolute dread and disgust over what was happening inside Ethan's apartment. But for a brief moment, I felt myself wanting to smile when I laid eyes on you. Seeing you reminded me of the party and how easy-going you were. I liked how you didn't care if people thought you were a caterer or the girlfriend of the Ethan Van Kemp. And it wasn't until the moment you joined me in the hallway—when your presence somehow brought me to the brink of smiling during the worst moment of my life—that I knew everything would be fine. I knew that my inevitable breakup with Sasha wasn't going to break me.

I don't know why I never told you that. Maybe because I liked the idea of us meeting in a hallway under the same circumstances. Or maybe because I was worried you wouldn't remember that night at the party or refilling my glass of champagne. Because why would you? That moment held no significance.

Until it did.

I would write more about our meeting in the hallway, but you know all about it. Or maybe I could write more about the first night we made love, or the fact that once we finally reconnected, we never wanted to spend a single second apart. Or I could write about the day I proposed to you and you so stupidly agreed to spend the rest of your life with a man who couldn't possibly give you all that you deserve in this world.

But I don't really want to talk about any of that. Because you were there for all of it. Besides, I'm almost positive your love letter to me details every minute of us falling in love, so I'd hate to waste my letter on repeating something you more than likely put into words more eloquently than I ever could.

I guess that means I'm left with talking about the future.

If all goes as planned, you'll be reading this letter on our twenty-fifth wedding anniversary. You might cry a few tears and smear the ink a little. Then you'll lean over and kiss me and we'll make love.

But . . . if for some reason, you're opening this box because our marriage didn't work out how we thought it would, let me first tell you how sorry I am. Because I know we wouldn't read these letters early unless we did absolutely everything we could to prevent it.

I don't know if you'll remember this, but we had a conversation once. I think it was only the second night we spent together. You mentioned how all marriages have Category 5 moments, and how you didn't think your previous relationship would have made it through those moments.

I think about that sometimes. About what could make one couple survive a Category 5 moment, but a different couple might not. I've thought about it enough to come up with a possible reason.

Hurricanes aren't a constant threat to coastal towns. There are more days with great weather and perfect beach days than there are hurricanes.

Marriages are similar, in that there are a lot of great days with no arguments, when both people are filled with so much love for each other.

But then you have the threatening-weather days. There might only be a few a year, but they can do enough damage that it takes years to repair. Some of the coastal towns will be prepared for the bad-weather days. They'll save their best resources and most of their energy so that they'll be stocked up and prepared for the aftermath.

But some towns won't be as prepared. They'll put

all their resources into the good weather days in hopes that the severe weather will never come. It's the lazier choice and the choice with greater consequences.

I think that's the difference in the marriages that survive and the marriages that don't. Some people think the focus in a marriage should be put on all the perfect days. They love as much and as hard as they can when everything is going right. But if a person gives all of themselves in the good times, hoping the bad times never come, there may not be enough resources or energy left to withstand those Category 5 moments.

I know without a doubt that we're going to have so many good moments. No matter what life throws at us, we're going to make great memories together, Quinn. That's a given. But we're also going to have bad days and sad days and days that test our resolve.

Those are the days I want you to feel the absolute weight of my love for you.

I promise that I will love you more during the storms than I will love you during the perfect days.

I promise to love you more when you're hurting than when you're happy.

I promise to love you more when we're poor than when we're swimming in riches.

I promise to love you more when you're crying than when you're laughing.

I promise to love you more when you're sick than when you're healthy.

I promise to love you more when you hate me than when you love me.

And I promise . . . I swear . . . that I love you more as you read this letter than I did when I wrote it.

I can't wait to spend the rest of my life with you. I can't wait to shine light on all your perfects.

I love you.

So much.

Graham

————

Dear Quinn,

I'm going to start this letter off with a little apology. I'm sorry I opened the box again. I'm sorry I needed to write another letter. But I feel like you'll appreciate it more than you'll be upset about it.

Okay, now for math. I know you hate math, but I love it and I need to math for you. It's been exactly one year to the day since we decided to start a family. Which means there have been approximately 365 days between that day and this one.

Of those 365 days, we have had sex an average of about 200 days. Roughly four nights a week. Of those 200 days, you were ovulating only 25% of the time. About fifty days. But the chances of a woman getting pregnant while they ovulate is only twenty percent. That's ten days out of fifty. Therefore, by my calculations, out of the total 365 days that have passed between the day we first started trying and today, only ten of those days counted. Ten is nothing.

It's almost like we just started trying.

I'm only writing this down because I can tell you're starting to get worried. And I know by the time you read this letter on our 25th anniversary, we'll probably be just a few years away from being grandparents and none of this math will even be relevant. But just as I want you to remember the perfect days, I feel like I should probably talk a little about our not so perfect days, too.

You're asleep on the couch right now. Your feet are in my lap and every now and then, your whole body jerks, like you're jumping in your dream. I keep trying to write you this letter, but your feet keep knocking my arm, making the pen slide off the page. If my handwriting is shit, it's your fault.

You never fall asleep on the couch, but it's been a long night. Your mother had another one of her fancy charity events. This one was actually kind of fun. It was casino themed and they had all kinds of tables set up where you could gamble. Of course, it was for charity, so you can't really win, but it was better than a lot of the stuffier events where we have to sit at tables with people we don't like, and listen to speeches from people who do nothing but brag on themselves.

The night was fine, but I noticed pretty early on that you were getting drained from the questions. It's just harmless, casual conversation, but sometimes that casual conversation can be really tiresome. Hurtful, even. I listened, over and over, as people would ask you when we were going to have a baby. Sometimes people just naturally assume pregnancy follows a marriage. But people don't think about the questions they ask others and they don't realize how many times someone has already been forced to answer their question.

The first few times you were asked, you just smiled and said we just started trying.

But by the fifth or sixth time, your smile was becoming more forced. I started answering for you, but even then, I could see in your eyes that the questions were painful. I just wanted to get you out of there.

Tonight was the first time I could see your sadness. You're always so hopeful and positive about it, even when you're worried. But tonight you seemed like you were over it. Like maybe tonight is going to be the last event we'll ever attend until we actually do have a baby in our arms.

But I get it. I'm tired of the questions, too. It's breaking me seeing you so sad. I feel so . . . ineffectual. I hate it. I hate not being in control of this. I hate not being able to fix this for you.

But even though we've been trying for over a year, I have hope. It'll happen someday. It'll just have to happen a different way than we thought it would.

Hell, I don't even know why I'm writing about this, because you'll be a mother when you read this letter. Five times over, maybe.

I guess I'm just processing all of it. And we have so much to be grateful for. You love your job. I tolerate mine. After work we get to spend our evenings together. We make love all the time and we laugh a lot. Life is perfect, really. Of course there's the one element of you getting pregnant that we hope makes life even better, but that will come with time. And honestly, the longer it takes, we might even appreciate it a little more. Gratitude is born in the struggle. And we have definitely struggled.

Our niece Adeline is beautiful and happy and she likes you way more than she likes me. Caroline agreed to let her sleep over last year and it hasn't stopped. And you look so forward to when we get to keep her. I think it has made me fall a little more in love with you. I know how much it hurts that we haven't had a baby of our own yet, but seeing how genuinely happy you are for my sister and her family reaffirms just how selfless you are. You don't equate our struggles with their success and it makes me love that strength about you.

You're still asleep on the couch, but you're snoring now and I need to stop writing this letter so I can go find my phone and record it. You argue with me and tell me you don't snore, so I'm about to get the proof.

I love you, Quinn. And even though the tone of this letter was kind of depressing, the strength of my love for you is at its greatest. This isn't a Category 5 moment. Maybe more of a Category 2. But I promise you I am loving you harder this year than any year that came before it.

I love you.

So much.

Graham

Dear Quinn,

I would apologize for opening the box yet again, but I have a feeling it's going to happen again. Sometimes you don't want to talk about the things that make you sad, but I feel like someday you'll want to know my thoughts. Especially this year. It's been our toughest yet.

We've been married for more than five years now. I don't want to dwell on it too much because I feel like it's all our life has become, but in the last few years, nothing has been successful as far as our fertility issues are concerned. We went through three rounds of IVF before calling it quits. We would have gone a fourth round, despite the doctor advising against it, but we just couldn't afford it.

There are a lot of things I want to document during this marriage, Quinn, but the devastation following each of those failed attempts is not one of them. I'm sure you remember how hard it was for both of us, so there's no point in detailing it.

You know how I always ask you about your dreams? I think I'm going to stop doing that for a while.

Last Sunday when you woke up, I asked you what I missed while you were sleeping. You stared at me with this blank look in your eyes. You were silent for a little while and I thought you were trying to figure out how to relay your dream, but then your chin started to quiver. When you couldn't stop it, you pressed your face into your pillow and you started to cry.

God, Quinn. I felt so guilty. I just put my arm around you and held you until you stopped crying.

I didn't push you to talk about what your dream was because I didn't want you to have to think about it again. I don't know if you dreamt that you were pregnant or that we had a baby but whatever it was, it was something that devastated you when you woke up and realized it was merely a dream.

It's been six days since that happened, and I haven't asked you about your dreams since that morning. I just don't want to put you through that again. Hopefully one day we'll get back to that, but I promise I won't ask you again until you finally are a mother.

It's tough. I know when we got married we didn't expect to face these kinds of hurdles together. And honestly, Quinn, I try to carry you over them but you're so damn independent. You try not to cry in front of me. You force your smiles and your laughter and you pretend to still be hopeful, but it's changing you. It's making you sad and filling you with guilt.

I know you sometimes feel bad because you think you're taking away my opportunity to be a father. But I don't care about that. If you tell me today that you want to stop trying for a baby, I'll be relieved, because that would mean you might stop being sad. I'm only going through this fertility process with you because I know you want to be a mother more than anything. I would walk through fire to see you happy. I'd give up everything I have to see a genuine smile on your face. If we had to forego sex forever, I would. Hell, I'd even give up cheese to see you finally get your dream of becoming a mother. And you know how much I love cheese.

I would never tell you this because I know part

of you would take it the wrong way, but I think my favorite moments in the past year are all the moments when we aren't home. When we go out with our friends or visit our parents. I've noticed when we're home, you've become a little more withdrawn when I touch you or kiss you. It used to be that we couldn't keep our hands off each other, but something changed earlier this year. And I know it's only because sex has become so clinical between us, that it's starting to feel routine to you. Maybe even a little painful, because it never leads to what you hope it leads to. Sometimes when we're alone and I kiss you, you don't kiss me back like you used to. You don't turn away, but you barely reciprocate.

You tend to enjoy me more when you know a kiss has to stop at a kiss. In public, you reciprocate and you lean on me and I know it's a subtle difference, but there's a difference. I think our friends think we're the most affectionate couple they know because we always have our hands all over each other. They probably imagine our private life is even more affectionate.

But it's actually our private life that has stalled. And I am not complaining, Quinn. I didn't marry you just for the good years. I didn't marry you just for the amazing chemistry we have. And I'd be foolish to think our marriage could last an eternity without a few tough moments. So, while this year has been our toughest yet, I know one thing with complete certainty. I love you more this year than any year that came before it.

I know I sometimes get frustrated. Sometimes I miss when we made love on a whim, rather than on a schedule. But I ask that even in the times I get frustrated, please remember that I'm only human. And as much as I promise to be your pillar of strength for as long as you need one, I'm sure I will sometimes fail you. My whole purpose in life is to make you happy, and sometimes I feel like I'm unable to do that anymore. Sometimes I give up on myself.

But I just pray that you don't give up on me, too.

I love you, Quinn. I hope this is the last depressing letter I ever write to you. My hope is that next year, my letter will be full of good news.

Until then, I will continue to love you more and more with every struggle we face than I loved you when all was perfect.

Graham

P.S. I don't know why I only vent about the stressful stuff. So much good has happened in the last couple of years. We bought a house with a big backyard and we spent the first two days christening every room. You got a promotion a few months ago. Now you only have to go into the office one or two days a week. You do most of the writing for the advertising firm from home, which you love. And we've talked about the possibility of me opening my own accounting firm. I'm working on a business plan for that. And Caroline gave us another niece.

All good things, Quinn.

So many good things.

Dear Quinn,

We've been trying.

Trying to have a baby. Trying to adopt a baby. Trying to pretend we're okay. Trying to hide from each other when we cry.

It's all our marriage has become. A whole lot of trying and not much succeeding.

I truly believed we could make it through all the Category 5s we faced, but I think this year has been a Category 6. As much as I hope I'm wrong and as much as I don't want to admit it, I have a feeling we'll be opening this box soon. Which is why I'm on a flight to your sister's house right now as I write this letter. I'm still fighting for something I don't even know that you still want me to fight for.

I know I failed you, Quinn. Maybe it was self-sabotage or maybe I'm not the man I thought I could be for you. Either way, I am so disappointed in myself. I love you so much more than my actions have shown and I could spend this whole letter telling you how sorry I am. I could write an entire novel that's nothing more than an apology and it still wouldn't detail my regret.

I don't know why I did what I did. I can't even explain it, even when I tried to tell you about it that night in the car. It's hard to put into words because I'm still trying to process it. I didn't do it because of some intense attraction I couldn't fight. I didn't do it because

I missed having sex with you. And even though I tried to convince myself that I was doing it because she reminded me of you, I know how stupid that sounds. I never should have said that to you. You're right, in a way it sounded like I was blaming you, and that was never my intention. You had nothing to do with what I did.

I don't want to talk about it, but I need to. You can skip this part of the letter if you don't want to read it, but I need to work through it and for some reason, writing about things in these letters always seems to help sort through my thoughts. I know I should be better at communicating them, but I know you don't always want to hear them.

I think the way I've been feeling started during a moment I had at my sister's house. I guess you could say it was an epiphany, but that sounds like such a positive word for what I was feeling. It was the day we were supposed to meet our new nephew, but you said you got stuck in traffic.

I know that was a lie, Quinn.

I know, because when I was leaving Caroline's house, I saw the gift we bought her in the living room. Which means you had been there at some point during my visit, but for whatever reason, you didn't want me to know.

I thought about it during my whole drive home after leaving her house. And the only thing I can think of that would make you not want to admit you were there is if you saw me standing in Caroline's living room, holding Caleb. And if you saw that, you might have heard what Caroline said to me, and what I said to her in return. About how I was devastated I still hadn't become a father yet. As much as I wish I could take that away, I can't. But I do need you to know why I said it.

I couldn't stop staring at him as I held him because he kind of looks like me. I had never held the girls when they were that young, so Caleb was the tiniest human I had ever held. And it made me wonder, had you been there, what would that have made you feel? Would you have been proud, seeing me with my nephew? Or would you have been disappointed that you would never see me holding a newborn of our own like that?

I think Caroline saw the look on my face while I was holding him and thought I was looking at him with such intensity because I wanted one of my own. But I was actually looking at him and wondering if you would continue to love me if I never became the one thing you wished I could be.

I know Caroline was merely complimenting me when she said I'd make a good father. But the reason I said I was devastated it still hadn't happened yet is because I was devastated for you. For our future. Because it wasn't until that moment that I realized I might never be enough for you.

Not long after that, I was walking out of my sister's house and saw the gift and knew you had been there. I didn't want to go home. I didn't want to confront you because I was afraid you might confirm my fears, so I drove around aimlessly. Later that night when I got home, you asked if I got to hold Caleb. I lied to you because I wanted to see your reaction to my lie. I was hoping maybe I was wrong and you weren't actually at my sister's house. Maybe the gift was from someone else and it was just similar to the one we had bought. But as soon as I saw your reaction, I knew you had been there.

And because you were hiding it, I knew you must have overheard our conversation. Which meant you also saw me holding Caleb. I was worried that the image of me holding a newborn like I was a father would be stuck in your head and it would make you sad every time you looked at me and I wasn't a father. You would realize that the only way to get those images out of your head is if I were out of your life for good.

I've worried about a lot of things since we got married, but I don't think I've ever worried about us until after that moment. I've been fighting for so long to be the strength you need, but that was the first time it occurred to me that I may not be what brings you strength anymore. What if I'm part of what brings you pain?

I wanted you to call me out for lying to you. I wanted you to scream at me for telling Caroline I was devastated I wasn't a father yet. I wanted something from you, Quinn. Anything. But you keep all your thoughts and feelings bottled up so tight; it's becoming impossible to read you anymore.

But you aren't the only one who is impossible to read anymore. I should have been honest with you about it that night. The moment I knew you had been to Caroline's, I should have said so. But somewhere between our wedding day and today, I lost my courage. I became too scared to hear what you truly feel inside that head

273

and heart of yours, so I've done my share of keeping it just below the surface. If I didn't press you to talk about it, I would never have to confront the possibility that our marriage was in trouble. Confrontation leads to action. Avoidance leads to inaction.

I have been an inactive husband for the past few years and I am so sorry for that.

The night I lied to you about holding Caleb, I remember you walking to your office. It was the first moment I ever had the thought that we might need a divorce.

I didn't have that thought because I wasn't happy with you. I had that thought because I felt I was no longer making you happy. I felt like my presence was bringing you down, causing you to sink further and further into yourself.

I walked to the living room and sat down on the couch, wondering if new possibilities would open up for you if I left you. Maybe if you weren't tied to me, somewhere down the line you could meet a man who already had children. You could fall in love with him and be a stepmother to his children and have some semblance of happiness brought back into your life.

I broke down, Quinn. Right there in our living room. It's the moment I realized that I was no longer bringing you happiness. I had become one of the many things adding to your pain.

I think that's been the case for a while now, but for some reason, I wasn't able to recognize it until recently. And even then, it took me a while before I finally allowed myself to believe it.

*I felt like I had failed you. But even knowing that,
I never would have made the decision to leave you.
I knew that about myself. Even if I believed that you
might be happier after I left, I was too selfish to give
that to you. I knew what it would do to me if I left you
and that terrified me. My fear of not having you in my
life sometimes overpowered my desire to see you happy.*

*I think that's why I did what I did. Because I knew
I would never be selfless enough to leave you. I allowed
myself to do something completely out of character for
me because if I felt I was no longer worthy of you, it
would be easier to convince myself that you deserved
better.*

It's so fucked up.

*I don't even know how it got to this point. I can't
look back on our marriage and pinpoint the day that
my love for you became something you resented and not
something you cherished.*

*I used to believe if you loved someone enough, that
love could withstand anything. As long as two people
remained in love, then nothing could tear them apart.
Not even tragedy.*

*But now I realize that tragedy can tear down even
the strongest of things.*

*You could have one of the greatest singing voices
of all time, but one injury to the throat could end your
entire career. You could be the fastest runner in the
world, but one back injury could change all of that.
You could be the most intelligent professor at Harvard,
but one stroke could send you into early retirement.*

You could love your wife more than any man

has ever loved a wife, but one harrowing battle with infertility could turn a couple's love into resentment.

But even after years of tragedy wearing us down, I refuse to give in just yet. I don't know if flying to Europe with the box we closed on our wedding night will make it better or worse. I don't know that a grandiose gesture will convince you of how incomplete my life is without you. But I can't go another day without trying to prove to you how inconsequential children are when it comes to the fate of my future with you. I don't need children, Quinn. I only need you. I don't know how I can stress that enough.

But even still, no matter how content I am with this life, it doesn't mean you are content with yours.

When I get to Europe, a final decision will be made and I have a feeling I'm not going to want to agree to that decision. If I could avoid the conversation with you forever just to keep you from deciding to open the box, I would. But that's where we went wrong. We stopped talking about all the things that should never have been silenced.

I have no idea what's best for us anymore. I want to be with you, but I don't want to be with you when my presence causes you so much pain. So much has changed between us in the time since we closed the box on our wedding night to now. Our circumstances changed. Our dreams changed. Our expectations changed. But the most important thing between us never changed. We lost a lot of ourselves in this marriage, but we have never stopped loving each other. It's the one thing that stood strong against those Category 5 moments. I realize now that sometimes two people can lose their hope or their desire or their happiness, but losing all those things doesn't mean you've lost.

We haven't lost yet, Quinn.

And no matter what has happened since we closed this box or what will happen after we open it, I promise to love you through it all.

I promise to love you more when you're hurting than when you're happy.

I promise to love you more when we're poor than when we're swimming in riches.

I promise to love you more when you're crying than when you're laughing.

I promise to love you more when you're sick than when you're healthy.

I promise to love you more when you hate me than when you love me.

I promise to love you more as a childless woman than I would love you as a mother.

And I promise . . . I swear . . . that if you choose to end things between us, I will love you more as you're walking out the door than on the day you walked down the aisle.

I hope you choose the road that will make you the happiest. Even if it's not a choice I'll love, I will still always love you. Whether I'm a part of your life or not. You deserve happiness more than anyone I know.

I love you. Forever.

Graham

COLLEEN HOOVER

I don't know how long I cry after reading the final letter. Long enough that my head hurts and my stomach aches and I've gone through half a box of Kleenex. I cry for so long, I get lost in the grief.

Graham is holding me.

I don't know when he walked into the room, or when he knelt on the bed, or when he pulled me to his chest.

He has no idea what I've even decided. He has no idea if the words about to come out of my mouth are going to be nice ones or hateful ones. Yet here he is, holding me as I cry, simply because it hurts him to see me cry.

I press a kiss to his chest, right over his heart. And I don't know if it takes five minutes or half an hour, but when I finally stop crying long enough to speak, I lift my head from his chest and look at him.

"Graham," I whisper. "I love you more in this moment than any moment that has come before it."

As soon as the words are out of my mouth, the tears begin to fall from his eyes. "Quinn," he says, holding my face. "*Quinn . . .*"

It's all he can say. He's crying too hard to say anything else. He kisses me and I kiss him back with everything in me in an attempt to make up for all the kisses I denied him.

I close my eyes, repeating the words from his letter that reached me the deepest.

We haven't lost yet, Quinn.

He's right. We might have finally given up at the same time, but that doesn't mean we can't get back that hope. I want to fight for him. I want to fight for him as hard as he's been fighting for me.

"I'm so sorry, Quinn," he whispers against my cheek. "For everything."

I shake my head, not even wanting an apology. But I know he needs my forgiveness, so I give it to him. "I forgive you. With everything I am, Graham. I forgive you and I don't blame you and I am so sorry, too."

Graham wraps his arms around me and holds me. We remain in the same position for so long, my tears have dried, but I'm still clinging to him with everything in me. And I'll do everything I can to make sure I never let go of him again.

Chapter Twenty-nine

Then

I couldn't imagine a better way to end our first anniversary—wrapped up in a blanket outside, listening to the waves crash against the shore. It's the perfect moment for the perfect gift.

"I have something for you," I say to Graham.

He's the one who usually surprises me with gifts, so the fact that I have one for him grabs his attention. He looks at me with anticipation and pulls the blanket away from me, pushing me out of the chair. I run inside and then return with his package. It's wrapped in Christmas paper, even though it's not even close to Christmas.

"It's all I could find," I say. "I didn't have time to wrap it before I left, so I had to wrap it with what was in the closet here."

He begins to open it, but before he even has the wrapping paper off, I blurt out, "It's a blanket. I made it."

He laughs. "You are so terrible at surprises." He pulls away the tissue paper and reveals the blanket I made out of ripped pieces of our clothing. "Are these . . ." He lifts up one of his ripped work shirts and laughs.

We sometimes have issues with keeping our clothing intact when we're pulling them off each other. I think I've ripped a half dozen of Graham's shirts, at least. Graham has ripped several of mine. Sometimes I do it because I love the dramatics of the buttons popping off. I don't remember when it started, but it's become a game to us. A pricey game. Which is why I decided to put some of the discarded clothing to good use.

"This is the best gift anyone has ever given me." He throws the blanket over his shoulder and then picks me up. He carries me inside and lays me on the bed. He rips my nightgown off of me and then he rips his own shirt for show. The whole scene has me laughing until he climbs on top of me and smothers my laugh with his tongue.

Graham lifts my knee and starts to push himself inside me, but I press against his chest. "We need a condom," I whisper breathlessly.

I was on antibiotics last week for a cold I was trying to get over so I haven't been taking my pill. We've had to use condoms all week as a preventative measure.

Graham rolls off me and walks to his duffel bag. He grabs a condom, but he doesn't immediately come back to the bed. He just stares at it. Then he tosses it back onto the bag.

"What are you doing?"

With a heavy amount of assuredness, he says, "I don't want to use one tonight."

I don't respond. He doesn't want to use a condom? Am I reading his intent wrong?

Graham walks back to the bed and lowers himself on top of me again. He kisses me, then pulls back. "I think about it sometimes. About you getting pregnant."

"You do?" I was not expecting that. I hesitate a moment before saying, "Just because you think about it doesn't mean you're ready for it."

"But I am. When I think about it, I get excited." He rolls onto his side and puts his hand on my stomach. "I don't think you should get back on the pill."

I grip the top of his hand, shocked at how much I want to kiss him and laugh and take him inside me. But as sure as I am about having children, I don't want to make that choice unless he's just as certain as I am. "Are you positive?"

The thought of us becoming parents fills me with an overwhelming amount of love for him. So much, I feel a tear fall down my cheek.

Graham sees the tear and he smiles as he brushes it away with his thumb. "I love that you love me so much, it sometimes makes you cry. And I love that the idea of us having a baby makes you cry. I love how full of love you are, Quinn."

He kisses me. I don't think I tell him enough what a great kisser he is. He's the best I've ever had. I don't know what makes his kisses different from the men I've kissed in the past, but it's so much better. Sometimes I'm scared he'll get tired of kissing me someday because of how much I kiss him. I just can't be near him without tasting him. "You're a really good kisser," I whisper.

Graham laughs. "Only because it's you I'm kissing."

We kiss even more than we usually do when we make

love. And I know we've made love a hundred times before tonight. Maybe even a thousand times. But this time feels different. It's the first time we don't have some kind of barrier preventing us from creating a new life together. It's like we're making love with a purpose.

Graham finishes inside of me and it's the most incredible feeling, knowing that our love for each other might be creating something even bigger than our love for each other. I don't know how that can even be possible. How can I possibly love anyone as much or even *more* than I love Graham?

It's been such a perfect day.

I've experienced a lot of perfect moments, but entire perfect days are hard to come by. You need the perfect weather, the perfect company, the perfect food, the perfect itinerary, the perfect mood.

I wonder if things will always be this perfect. Now that we've decided to start a family, part of me wonders if there's a level of perfection that we haven't even reached yet. What will things be like next year when we're possibly parents? Or five years from now? Ten? Sometimes I wish I had a crystal ball that could actually see into the future. I'd want to know everything.

I'm tracing my fingers in an invisible pattern over his chest when I look up at him. "Where do you think we'll be ten years from now?"

Graham smiles. He loves talking about the future. "Hopefully we'll have our own house in ten years," he says. "Not too big, not too small. But the yard will be huge and we'll play outside with the kids all the time. We'll have two—a boy and a girl. And you'll be pregnant with the third."

I smile at that thought. He reacts to the smile on my face and he continues to talk.

"You'll still write, but you'll work from home and you'll only work when you feel like it. I'll own my own accounting firm. You'll drive a minivan because we're totally gonna be those parents who take the kids to soccer games and gymnastics." Graham grins at me. "And we'll make love all the time. Probably not as often as we do now, but more than all of our friends."

I press my hand over his heart. "That sounds like the perfect life, Graham."

Because it does. But *any* life with Graham sounds perfect.

"Or . . ." he adds. "Maybe nothing will change. Maybe we'll still live in an apartment. Maybe we'll be struggling financially because we keep moving from job to job. We might not even be able to have kids, so we won't have a big yard or even a minivan. We'll be driving our same, shitty cars ten years from now. Maybe absolutely nothing will change and ten years from now, our lives will be the same as they are now. And all we'll have is each other."

Just like after he described the first scenario, a serene smile spreads across my face. "That sounds like the perfect life, too." And it does. As long as I have Graham, I don't know that this life could be anything less than what it is now. And right now, it's wonderful.

I relax against his chest and fall asleep with the most peaceful feeling in my heart.

Chapter Thirty

Now

"Quinn."

His voice is raspy against my ear. It's the first morning in a long time that I've been able to wake up with a smile on my face. I open my eyes and Graham looks like a completely different person than the broken man who walked through Ava and Reid's front door last night. He presses his lips to my cheek and then pulls back, pushing my hair off my face. "What did I miss while you were sleeping?"

I've missed those words so much. It's one of the things I've missed the most about us. It means even more to me now, knowing he only stopped asking me because he didn't want me to hurt. I reach my hand out to his face and brush my thumb across his mouth. "I dreamt about us."

He kisses the pad of my thumb. "Was it a good dream or a bad dream?"

"It was good," I say. "It wasn't a typical weird dream, though. It was more of a memory."

Graham slips a hand between his head and the pillow. "I want to know every detail."

I mirror his position, smiling when I begin telling him about the dream. "It was our first anniversary. The night we decided to start a family. I asked you where you thought we'd be ten years from now. Do you remember?"

Graham shakes his head. "Vaguely. Where did I think we'd be?"

"You said we'd have kids and I'd drive a minivan and we'd live in a house with a big yard where we played with our children." Graham's smile falters. I brush his frown away with my thumb, wanting his smile back. "It's strange, because I forgot all about that conversation until I dreamt about it last night. But it didn't make me sad, Graham. Because then you said we might not have any of that. You said there was a chance that we'd be moving from job to job and that we wouldn't be able to have kids. And that maybe nothing between us would change after ten years, and all we'd have was each other."

"I remember that," he whispers.

"Do you remember what I said to you?"

He shakes his head.

"I said, 'That sounds like the perfect life, too.'"

Graham blows out a breath, like he's been waiting a lifetime for the words I'm giving him.

"I'm sorry I lost sight of that," I whisper. "Of us. You've always been enough for me. Always."

He looks at me like he's missed my dreams as much as he's missed me. "I love you, Quinn."

"I love you, too."

He presses his lips to my forehead, then my nose. I kiss him on the chin and we lie snuggled together.

At least until the moment is ruined by the growl from my stomach.

"Does your sister have anything to eat around here?" Graham pulls me out of the bed and we quietly make our way to the kitchen. It's not even eight in the morning yet and Ava and Reid are still asleep. Graham and I scour the kitchen for all the food we need to make pancakes and eggs. He turns on the stove and I'm mixing the batter when I notice the wooden box he made me still sitting at the end of the counter.

I put down the mixer and walk over to the box. I run my hand over it, wondering if things would be different today had he not made this gift for us to close on our wedding night. I still remember writing him the love letter. I also remember slipping the nude pic inside the envelope. I wonder how different I look now than when I snapped that picture.

I open the box to pull out his letter, but when I pick it up, I notice a few scraps of paper at the bottom of the box. One of them is the yellow Post-it note I left stuck to my wall for six months. The other two are our fortunes.

I pick them up and read them. "I can't believe you kept these all this time. It's so cute."

Graham walks over to me. "Cute?" He pulls one of the fortunes out of my hands. "This isn't cute. It's proof that fate exists."

I shake my head and point to his fortune. "Your fortune says you would succeed in a business endeavor that day, but you didn't even go to work. How is that proof that we're soul mates?"

His lips curl up into a grin. "If I had been at work I never would have met you, Quinn. I'd say that's the biggest work-related success I've ever had."

I tilt my head, wondering why I never thought of his fortune from that point-of-view.

"Also . . . there's this." Graham flips his fortune over and holds it up, pointing at the number eight on the back.

I look down and also read the number on the back of mine. An eight.

Two number eights. *The date we reconnected all those years ago.*

"You lied to me," I say, looking back up at him. "You said you were kidding about these having eights on the back."

Graham takes the fortune out of my hand and carefully places both of them back in the box. "I didn't want you to fall in love with me because of fate," he says, closing the box. "I wanted you to fall in love with me simply because you couldn't help yourself."

I smile as I stare up at him with appreciation. I love that he's sentimental. I love that he believes in fate more than he believes in coincidences. I love that he believes *I'm* his fate.

I stand on the tips of my toes and kiss him. He grabs the back of my head with both hands and returns my kiss with just as much appreciation.

After several moments of kissing and a couple of failed efforts at stopping, he mutters something about the pancakes burning and forces himself away from me as he steps to the stove. I bring my fingers to my lips and smile when I realize he just kissed me and I had absolutely no desire to pull away from him. In fact, I wanted the kiss to last even longer than it did. It's a feeling I wasn't sure I would be capable of again.

I debate pulling him back to me because I really want to kiss him again. But I also really want pancakes, so I let him resume cooking. I turn toward the wooden box and reach for the letter I wrote to him. Now that I feel like we're on a path to recovery, it makes me want to read the words I wrote to him when we were first starting this journey together. I flip over the envelope to pull out the letter, but the envelope is still sealed. "Graham?" I turn back around. "You didn't read yours?"

Graham glances over his shoulder and smiles at me. "I didn't need to, Quinn. I'll read it on our twenty-fifth anniversary." He faces the stove and resumes cooking like he didn't just say something that feels more healing than anything he's ever said or done.

I look back down at the letter with a smile on my face. Even with the temptation of nude pictures, he was secure enough in his love for me that he didn't need any reassurance from reading this letter.

I suddenly want to write him another letter to go along with this one. In fact, I might even start doing what he's been doing all these years and add more letters to the box. I want to write him so many letters that when we finally reopen this box for the right reasons, he'll have enough letters to read for a week.

"Where do you think we'll be on our twenty-fifth anniversary?" I ask.

"Together," he says, matter-of-fact.

"Do you think we'll ever leave Connecticut?"

He faces me. "Do you want to?"

I shrug. "Maybe."

"I think about it sometimes," he admits. "I've already got

a few personal clients lined up. If I secured a few more, it would allow for that, but it probably wouldn't pay as much. But we could travel for a year or two. Maybe longer if we enjoy it enough."

This conversation reminds me of the night I spoke to my mother on the steps outside of her home. I don't think I give her enough credit, but she's right. I can spend my time focusing on the perfect version of the life I'll never have or I can spend my time enjoying the life I *do* have. And the life I have would provide me with so much opportunity if I would get out of my own head long enough to chase those opportunities.

"I used to want to be so many things before I became obsessed with the idea of being a mother."

Graham smiles sweetly at me. "I remember. You wanted to write a book."

It's been so long since I've talked about it, I'm surprised he remembers. "I did. I still do."

He's smiling at me when he turns to flip the rest of the pancakes. "What else do you want to do besides write a book?"

I move to stand next to him near the stove. He wraps one arm around me while he cooks with his other hand. I rest my head against his shoulder. "I want to see the world," I say quietly. "And I would really like to learn a new language."

"Maybe we should move here to Italy and piggyback off Ava's language tutor."

I laugh at his comment, but Graham sets down the spatula and faces me with an excited gleam in his eyes. He leans against the counter. "Let's do it. Let's move here. We have nothing tying us down."

I tilt my head and eye him. "Are you serious?"

"It would be fun to try something new. And it doesn't even have to be Italy. We can move anywhere you want."

My heart begins to beat faster with the anticipation of doing something that insane and spontaneous.

"I do really like it here," I say. "A lot. And I miss Ava."

Graham nods. "Yeah, I kind of miss Reid. But don't repeat that."

I push myself up onto the counter next to the stove. "Last week I went for a walk and saw a cottage a few streets over for rent. We could try it out temporarily."

Graham looks at me like he's in love with the idea. Or maybe he's looking at me like he's in love with *me*. "Let's go look at it today."

"Okay," I say, full of giddiness. I catch myself biting my cheek in an attempt to hide my smile, but I immediately stop trying to hide it. If there's one thing Graham deserves, it's for my happiness to be transparent. And this moment is the first moment in a long time I've felt this much happiness. I want him to feel it, too.

It's like this is the first time I've truly felt like I might be okay. That *we'll* be okay. It's the first time I don't look at him and feel guilty for everything I can't give him because I know how grateful he is for everything I *can* give him. "Thank you," I whisper. "For everything you said in your letters."

He stands between my legs, placing his hands on my hips. I wrap my arms around his neck, and for the first time in a long time, I kiss my husband and feel full of gratitude. I know my life as a whole hasn't been perfect, but I'm finally starting to appreciate all the perfect things within it. There are so many of them. My flexible job, my husband, my in-laws, my sister, my nieces, my nephew.

That thought makes me pause. I pull back and look up at Graham. "What did my fortune say? Do you have it memorized?"

"If you only shine light on your flaws, all your perfects will dim."

I think about it for a moment. About how fitting that fortune is for my life. I've spent way too much time putting all of my focus on my infertility. So much so, my husband and all the other things that are perfect in my life were being forced to take a backseat.

Since the moment we cracked open those fortune cookies, I've never really taken them seriously. But maybe Graham is right. Maybe those fortunes are more than a coincidence. And maybe Graham was right about the existence of fate.

If so, I think my fate is standing right in front of me.

Graham touches my mouth with the tips of his fingers and slowly traces the smile on my lips. "You have no idea what this smile means to me, Quinn. I've missed it so much."

Epilogue

"Wait, look at this one!" I pull on Graham's hand, making him stop in his tracks on the sidewalk again. But I can't help it. Almost every store on this street has the cutest children's clothes I've ever seen and Max would be adorable in the outfit displayed in the window.

Graham tries to keep moving forward, but I pull on his hand until he relents and follows me into the store. "We were almost to the car," he says. "So close."

I shove the bags of kids clothes I've already bought into Graham's hands and then find the rack with the toddler sizes. "Should I get the green pants or the yellow ones?"

I hold them up to Graham and he says, "Definitely yellow."

The green pants are cuter, but I go with Graham's choice simply because he volunteered an answer. He hates shopping for clothes, and this is only the ninth store I've forced him to follow me into. "I swear this is the last one. Then we can go home." I give Graham a quick peck on the lips before walking to the register.

Graham follows me and pulls his wallet out of his pocket. "You know I don't care, Quinn. Shop all day if you want. He only turns two once."

I hand the clothes to the cashier. In a thick Italian accent, she says, "This outfit is my absolute favorite." She looks up at us and says, "How old is your little boy?"

"He's our nephew. Tomorrow is his second birthday."

"Ah, perfect," she says. "Would you like this in a gift box?"

"No, a bag is fine."

She tells Graham the total, and as he's paying, the cashier looks at me again. "What about the two of you? Any children of your own?"

I smile at her and open my mouth, but Graham beats me to the punch. "We have six children," he lies. "But they're all grown now and out of the house."

I try not to laugh, but once we decided to start lying to strangers about our infertility, it's become a competition with who can be the most ridiculous. Graham usually wins. Last week he told a lady we had quadruplets. Now he's trying to convince someone that a couple our age could have six children already grown and out of our home.

"All girls," I add. "We kept trying for a boy, but it just wasn't in the cards."

The cashier's mouth falls open. "You have *six* daughters?"

Graham takes the bag and the receipt from her. "Yes. And two granddaughters."

He always takes it a little too far. I grab Graham's hand

and mutter a thank-you to the cashier, pulling him outside as fast as I pulled him inside. When we're on the sidewalk again, I slap him on the arm. "You are so ridiculous," I say, laughing.

He threads our fingers together as we begin to walk. "We should make up names for our imaginary daughters," he says. "In case someone probes for details."

We're passing a kitchen store when he says this, and my eyes automatically fall on a spice rack in the window. "Coriander," I tell him. "She's the oldest."

Graham pauses and looks at the spice rack with me. "Parsley is the youngest. And Paprika and Cinnamon are the oldest set of twins."

I laugh. "We have two sets of twins?"

"Juniper and Saffron."

As we're walking toward our car, I say, "Okay, let me make sure I have this right. In order of birth: Coriander, Paprika, Cinnamon, Juniper, Saffron and Parsley."

Graham smiles. "Almost. Saffron was born two minutes before Juniper."

I roll my eyes, and he squeezes my hand as we cross the street together.

It still amazes me how much has changed since we opened the box two years ago. We came so close to losing everything we had built together because of something that was out of our control. Something that should have brought us closer together but instead pulled us further apart.

Avoidance sounds like such a harmless word, but that one word can cause some severe damage to a relationship. We avoided so much in our marriage, simply out of fear. We avoided communicating. We avoided talking about the challenges we faced. We avoided all the things that made us the saddest. And after time, I began to avoid the other half of my life altogether. I avoided him physically, which led to emotional avoidance, which led to a lot of feelings that were left unsaid.

Opening that box made me realize that our marriage wasn't in need of a minor repair. It needed to be rebuilt from the ground up, with an entirely different foundation. I started out our life together with certain expectations, and when those expectations weren't met, I had no idea how to move forward.

But Graham has been the constant fighting force behind my healing. I finally stopped being as sad about our fate. I stopped focusing on what we would never have together and started focusing on all the things we did have and could have. It didn't eliminate my pain altogether, but I'm happier than I've been in a very long time.

Of course opening the box didn't miraculously solve everything. It didn't immediately take away my desire for children, although it did increase my lust for a life outside of being a mother. It didn't completely dissolve my aversion to sex, although it did open the door to slowly learning how to separate the sex from the hope from the devastation. And I occasionally still cry in the shower, but I never cry alone. I cry while Graham holds me, because he made me promise I would stop trying to hide the brunt of my heartache.

I no longer hide it. I embrace it. I'm learning how to wear my struggle as a badge and not be ashamed of it. I'm learning to not be so personally offended by other people's ignorance in relation to infertility. And part of what I've learned is that I have to have a sense of humor about it all. I never thought I would be at a point where we could turn all the painful questions into a game. Now when we're out in public, I actually look forward to when someone asks if we have kids. Because I know Graham is going to say something that will make me laugh.

I've also learned that it's okay to have a little hope.

For so long, I was so worn down and emotionally exhausted that I thought if I figured out a way to lose all hope, I would also lose all expectation and all disappointment. But it didn't work that way. The hope has been the only positive thing about being infertile.

I will never lose hope that we might actually have a child of our own. I still apply to adoption agencies and talk to lawyers. I don't know that we'll ever stop trying to make it happen. But I've learned that even though I'm still hoping to become a mother, it doesn't mean I can't live a fulfilling life while I continue to try.

For once, I'm happy. And I know that I'll be happy twenty years from now, even if it's still just me and Graham.

"Shit," Graham mutters as we reach our car. He points at the tire. "We have a flat."

I glance at the car, and the tire is definitely flat. So flat, no amount of air could salvage it. "Do we have a spare?"

We're in Graham's car, so he opens the trunk and lifts the floor portion, revealing a spare and a jack. "Thank God," he says.

I put our bags in the backseat of the car and watch as he pulls out the tire and the jack. Luckily the flat is on the passenger side, which is flush with the sidewalk rather than the road. Graham rolls the tire near the flat one and then moves the jack. He looks up at me with an embarrassed look on his face. "Quinn . . ." He kicks at a pebble on the sidewalk, breaking eye contact with me.

I laugh, because I can tell by his embarrassment that he has no idea what to do next. "Graham Wells, have you never changed a flat tire?"

He shrugs. "I'm sure I could google it. But you mentioned to me once that Ethan never let you change a flat." He motions toward the tire. "I'm giving you first dibs."

I grin. I'm loving this way too much. "Put the parking brake on."

Graham sets the parking brake while I position the jack under the car and begin to raise it.

"This is kind of hot," Graham says, leaning against a light pole as he watches me. I grab the wrench and begin removing the lug nuts from the tires.

We're on a busy sidewalk, so two people stop to ask if they can help, because they don't realize Graham is with me. Both times, Graham says, "Thank you, but my wife has got this."

I laugh when I realize what he's doing. The entire time I'm changing the tire, Graham brags about it to everyone who walks by. "Look! My wife knows how to change a tire."

When I finally finish, he puts the jack and the flat tire back in the trunk. My hands are covered in grease.

"I'm going to run inside this store and wash my hands."

Graham nods and opens the driver's side door while I rush into the nearest store. When I walk inside, I'm taken off guard as I look around. I was expecting this to be another clothing store, but it isn't. There are pet crates displayed in the window and a bird—a parakeet—perched on top of a cage near the front door.

"Ciao!" the bird says loudly.

I raise an eyebrow. "Hello."

"Ciao!" it screeches again. "Ciao! Ciao!"

"That's the only word he knows," a lady says as she approaches me. "You here to adopt or are you here for supplies?"

I hold up my greasy hands. "Neither. I'm hoping you have a sink."

The woman points me in the direction of the restroom. I make my way through the store, pausing to look at all the various animals in their cages. There are rabbits and turtles and kittens and guinea pigs. But when I make it to the back of the store, near the restroom, I pause in my tracks and suck in a breath.

I stare at him for a moment because he's staring right back at me. Two big brown eyes, looking at me like I'm the fiftieth person to walk past him today. But he still somehow has hope in those eyes—like maybe I'll be the first one to actually consider adopting him. I step closer to his cage, which is flanked by several empty cages. He's the only dog in the whole store.

"Hey, buddy," I whisper. I read the note at the bottom left corner of his cage. Beneath the Italian description is a description written in English.

German Shepherd
Male
Seven weeks old
Available for adoption

I stare at the note for a moment and then force myself to walk to the bathroom. I scrub my hands as fast as I can, because I can't stand for that puppy to think I'm just another one of the dozens of people who walked past him today and didn't want to take him home.

I've never been much of a dog person, because I've never had a dog before. I honestly thought I'd never own a dog, but I have a feeling I'm not walking out of this store without this puppy. Before I leave the bathroom, I pull my phone from my pocket and shoot Graham a text.

Come inside to the back of the store. Hurry.

I walk out of the bathroom, and when the puppy sees me again, his ears perk up. He lifts a paw and presses it against the cage as I come closer. He's sitting on his hind legs, but I can see his tail twitching, like he wants my attention but he's scared it'll just be fleeting and he'll be spending another night in this cage.

I slip my fingers between the bars of his cage, and he sniffs them, then licks me. I feel a tightening in my chest every time we make eye contact, because seeing him so full of hope but so scared of disappointment makes me sad. This puppy reminds me of me. Of how I used to feel.

I hear someone walking up behind me, so I spin around to see Graham staring at the puppy. He walks up to the cage and tilts his head. The puppy looks from me to Graham and then finally stands up, unable to stop his tail from wagging.

I don't even have to say anything. Graham just nods his head and says, "Hey, little guy. You want to come home with us?"

————

"It's been three days," Ava says. "That poor puppy needs a name."

She's clearing off the table, preparing to go home. Reid left with Max about an hour ago to put him to bed. We all try to eat dinner together a few times a week, but we usually go to their house, since Max goes to bed early. But now we're the ones with a new baby, and even though that new baby is a puppy, he naps and pees and poops as much as a human newborn.

"It's so hard coming up with a good name, though," I groan. "I want to give him a name that'll mean something, but we've tossed out every idea we've had."

"You're being too picky."

"It took you eight months to choose a name for your child. Three days isn't that long for a dog."

Ava shrugs. "Good point." She wipes down the table as I cover the leftover food and put it in the fridge.

"I thought about giving him a math-related name, since Graham loves math so much. Like maybe naming him after a number."

Ava laughs. "It's so weird that you say that. I just got my files at work today for the high school foreign exchange students I'll be tutoring when they arrive in a couple of weeks. One of them is a girl from Texas. Her birth name is Seven Marie Jacobs, but she goes by Six. I thought of Graham when I saw that."

"Why does she go by Six if her birth name is Seven?"

Ava shakes her head. "I don't know, but it's quirky. I haven't even met her yet but I already like the girl." Ava pauses and looks up at me. "What about naming it after one of the characters in your book?"

I shake my head. "Already thought of that, but those characters feel like actual people now that the book is finished. I know it's weird, but I want the dog to have his own name. I'd feel like he was being forced to share."

COLLEEN HOOVER

"Makes sense," Ava says, resting her hands on her hips. "Any news from your agent?"

"She hasn't submitted to publishers yet. It's being reviewed by an in-house editor and then they're going to try and sell it."

Ava smiles. "I hope it happens, Quinn. I'm going to freak the fuck out if I walk into a bookstore and see your book on the shelf."

"You and me both."

Graham walks inside with the puppy and Ava meets him at the door. "It's late, I gotta go," she says, talking to the puppy while scratching him on his head. "I hope when I see you tomorrow you have a name."

Graham and I tell her goodbye and he locks the door behind her. He cradles the puppy in his arms and walks over to me. "Guess who used the bathroom twice so his mommy and daddy can get a few hours of sleep?"

I pull the puppy out of Graham's arms and squeeze him. He licks my cheek and then rests his head in the crease of my elbow. "He's tired."

"I'm tired, too," Graham says, yawning.

I put the puppy into his crate and cover it with a blanket. Neither of us knows anything about dogs, so we've been reading as much as we possibly can about how to crate-train them, what they eat, how they should be disciplined, how much they should sleep.

Sleep has definitely been the most difficult thing to tackle so far. Being the owner of a new puppy comes with new hurdles, but the biggest of those hurdles is exhaustion. I wouldn't trade it for anything, though. Every time that little puppy looks at me, I melt.

Graham and I make our way to the bedroom. We leave our door open so we can hear the puppy if he starts to cry. When we crawl into bed, I roll toward Graham and rest my head on his chest.

"I can't imagine what having a newborn must be like if a puppy is this tiring," I say.

"You're forgetting about all our sleepless nights with Coriander, Paprika, Cinnamon, Saffron, Juniper, and Parsley."

I laugh. "I love you."

"I love you, too."

I curl even more into Graham, and he tightens his hold around me. I do my best to fall asleep, but my mind keeps running through potential puppy names until I'm positive I've exhausted every name in existence.

"Quinn." Graham's voice is against my ear, warm and quiet. "Quinn, wake up." I open my eyes and pull away from his chest. He points behind me and says, "Look."

I half-turn and glance over at the alarm clock, right as it changes to midnight. Graham leans in to my ear and whispers, "It's the eighth of August. Ten years later and we're happily married. *I told you so*."

I sigh. "Why am I not surprised that you remembered that?"

I don't know how I didn't expect this moment. The number eight holds so much meaning to us that the date should have been obvious to me, but I've been so preoccupied with the puppy the last few days, I didn't even realize today was the eighth of August.

"August," I whisper. "That's what we'll name the puppy."

Acknowledgements

With every book I write, there are people in the beginning who get the scraps I end up throwing away. I ruin plot twists for them. I change story lines. I make reading my words a little bit of a confusing chore. Especially with the many versions of *All Your Perfects*. A huge thank-you to Kay Miles, Vilma Gonzalez, Marion Archer, Karen Lawson, Lauren Levine, Vannoy Fite, Kim Jones, Jo Popper, Brooke Howard, and Joy Nichols for always being honest. And there.

To Tarryn Fisher. I love you and your whole stupid family.

Thank you to my agent, Jane Dystel, and her amazing team!

Thank you to the amazing Atria Books team. To my publisher, Judith Curr, for the past five years of support. To Ariele Stewart, my NPTBF. We can probably drop the first letter of our acronym now. To Melanie Iglesias Pérez, thank you for all you do! Which is a ton! And to my editor, Johanna Castillo. When I try to write how much I appreciate you, words seem dumb. I love you.

Thank you to CoHorts. A group of book-loving people who boost my ego and remind me daily of who I want to be.

Thank you to FP. The original 21. I credit all the good in this career to that first year. The love, support, and excitement we all held for one another is a thing of beauty. I will never forget it. I will always appreciate each one of you.

To my boys. My beautiful, wonderful men. Thanks to your father, my life would still be complete if I never had any of you. But I will never take for granted that I do have you. You bring joy to my life every single day. I hope you never stop asking me to tuck you in at night. You make me so proud.

And to my husband, Heath Hoover. The only times I've ever seen you come close to crying are when you're proud of your family. Nothing makes me love and appreciate you more. Almost everything good in my life is because of you.

Before *It Ends With Us*
it started with Atlas...

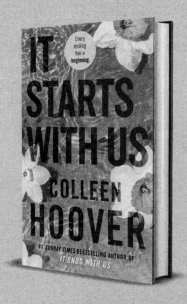

18 OCTOBER 2022

Available to pre-order now at
itstartswithusbook.com

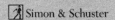